# POOR GHOST

"From its riveting opening through the wonderfully imaginative unfolding of its narrative, *Poor Ghost* is a lively hopscotch of a novel, compelling, deep and powerful."

—**T.C. Boyle, author of** *Blue Skies*

"As you read David Starkey's *Poor Ghost*, you'll be thinking deeply about how we got from *Boston* to QAnon, from Casey Kasem to Kyle Rittenhouse: what it all means to you, and what it says about us. But you won't *notice* you're thinking, because you'll be laughing too hard as Stacey the retired librarian knocks out knife-wielding Álvaro de Campos with a jug of rosé to keep him from killing you in your own backyard while other Halloween-costumed fans of the aging rock band whose plane crashed there a while back livestream the fracas. By the time you realize how involved you are in the deepening mystery, it will be too late to get out."

—**H. L. Hix, author of** *Legible Heavens* **and** *The Death of H. L. Hix*

"*Poor Ghost* opens with a bang and a fire that chars a shattered Cessna and a towering pine tree. It ends with another bang from an exploding brushfire that consumes a massive 70 acres . . . In between, this highly original novel—unlike any I've ever read—shifts among second-person revelations, text exchanges, rock magazine interviews, news articles, and government reports, exploring the ghosts of those departed and those about to be. There's an invasion of groupies, lunatic murderers, a missing dog, and the mystery of what caused the plane crash. David Starkey makes it all meaningful, bringing the dead to life and offering rich, inventive entertainment."

—**Walter Cummins, author of** *Where We Live* **and** *Seeking Authenticity*

# POOR GHOST

# POOR GHOST

## DAVID STARKEY

+ KEYLIGHT
BOOKS
AN IMPRINT
OF TURNER
PUBLISHING

KEYLIGHT BOOKS
AN IMPRINT OF TURNER PUBLISHING COMPANY
Nashville, Tennessee
www.turnerpublishing.com

*Poor Ghost*

This is a work of fiction. All the characters and events portrayed in this book are either products of the author's imagination or are used fictitiously.

Cover and book design by William Ruoto

Library of Congress Cataloging-in-Publication Data

Names: Starkey, David, 1962- author.
Title: Poor ghost : a novel / David Starkey.
Description: First. | Nashville, Tennessee : Turner Publishing Company, [2024]
Identifiers: LCCN 2022044623 (print) | LCCN 2022044624 (ebook) | ISBN 9781684429721 (hardcover) | ISBN 9781684429738 (paperback) | ISBN 9781684429745 (epub)
Subjects: LCGFT: Novels.
Classification: LCC PS3569.T335815 P66 2024  (print) | LCC PS3569.T335815 (ebook) | DDC 813/.54--dc23/eng/20220928
LC record available at https://lccn.loc.gov/2022044623
LC ebook record available at https://lccn.loc.gov/2022044624

Printed in the United States of America

For Sandy,
Always

# THE
# AFTERLIFE
# OF
# POOR GHOST

# 1

When the plane crashes in your backyard, you are sitting in the living room, flipping through the cartoons in the latest *New Yorker*.

You live just a few miles from the Santa Barbara Airport, so it's not unusual to hear low-flying planes. The sound of this one, though, is very different: much louder, and getting closer fast. You drop the magazine and hurry to the plate-glass window just as a small jet appears for a moment to your right, then the next moment is slicing into your pine tree, slamming into the earth, and bursting into flames. A huge plume of black smoke rises from the bottom of your backyard.

Strangely, the first thing that comes into your head is a lyric from an old Tom Petty song about an aeroplane falling on his block.

Then a shiver runs up your spine, and your hands begin shaking so hard that you have to clasp them together to still them.

Your daughter, Victoria, is visiting, and she begins screaming from the family room: "Jackson, oh my god, Jackson!"

For the first time ever, you are glad that Victoria is childless. Jackson is her dog.

"My God," you whisper, and you and Victoria are running outside.

Your backyard is a trapezoid that's narrower toward the house and wider—about forty yards wide—where the property ends. There's a thin strip of lawn running along the house, then a row of juniper and rosemary bushes, then the yard dips on a deep slope for another fifty yards. Lemon trees grow by the fence line on either side, and, until moments ago, a fifty-foot-tall loblolly pine grew in the center of that patch of dirt and dry grass.

The pine is now splintered about five feet from the ground, with the upper branches smashed flat beneath the plane, which looks smaller than when it appeared in your window. It's a passenger jet—or was.

The two of you make your way down the hillside into a swirl of black, acrid smoke. The jet looks as though some bad-tempered giant has torn a model airplane in half, and then torn it again for good measure.

The forward part of the fuselage has sheared off from the rest of the plane. The nose is partly buried in the loose earth near the lemon tree on the left-hand side of your yard. The right engine has detached from the rear of the plane and is leaning against the plane's door, which hangs by one hinge. Both the engine and the cockpit are on fire.

The right wing has broken off and rests precariously on the remaining branches of the pine. Some of the branches have caught fire, though, thankfully, the tree was healthy—and the early autumn afternoon is calm. The fire hasn't spread far.

The rear of the fuselage rests on the slope of the hill, near the other lemon tree, about ten feet from the front half. The left wing and engine are still attached. There's smoke, but no fire.

The right stabilizer from the tail has come off and is farther down the hill. It has ripped through the wire fence that separates your yard from the Corellis' orchard. Bent in half like a piece of aluminum foil, the stabilizer has cut into the trunk of an avocado tree.

What remains of the plane just about fills up your backyard.

For a moment, you and Victoria stand there in awe. It is silent, except for the flames feathering up from the front of the aircraft and crackling in the dry grass and pine duff and tree branches. It occurs to you that everyone on board must be dead.

The smoke from the right engine thickens. The air smells of burning rubber and what you assume must be spilled fuel.

You don't see Jackson.

Then you hear a voice.

A man about your age, with a bloody face, his right arm dangling like a broken branch, is crawling out of the back half of the plane.

"My dog?" Victoria screams. "Have you seen my *dog*?"

He shakes his head and keeps crawling toward you.

"We'll find Jackson, okay?" you tell her. "But right now people are *hurt*."

You run over and help the man to his feet, then place an arm around his back and direct him slowly away from the crash.

The ground is pocked with gopher mounds, and he trips as you move up the hill. "Ah, Jesus God!" he moans. "That hurts like fucking hell."

"Sorry, sorry," you say, "I'm just worried the plane might explode." You look down at his blood-smeared face and realize that he looks vaguely familiar. "Is anyone else alive?" you ask.

He shrugs, or seems to. "I was asleep," he murmurs. "When it happened."

Your next-door neighbor, Barton, calls your name from his backyard, on the left, then awkwardly makes his way over the low fence between your properties. He stumbles down the hillside until he is beside you and the bloodied man, who has slumped to the ground. "Are you okay?" Barton asks. "Where does it hurt?"

"Are you a doctor?" the man rasps.

"A dentist," Barton says.

"It hurts everywhere," the man mutters, then his eyes roll back into his head and he is unconscious.

You take your phone out of your pocket and dial 911, cursing yourself under your breath. You should have done that right away.

You begin to tell the operator what is happening, but Victoria is screaming again. A man climbs from the front of the plane, his shirt on fire, his face burnt ashy black. He takes a few steps toward you, then falls to the dirt, motionless.

There's a puff of smoke, and a tongue of flame shoots out of the right engine, which causes the wing suspended in the branches to flip and fall to the ground. What's left of the pine tree begins to burn in earnest.

In the distance, you hear the wail of a siren, then another, and another.

"He needs help," you say stupidly into your phone, looking at Barton and pointing to the man.

"The plane's on fire," Barton says.

"Well, Jesus, yes," you say, frustrated and frightened and buzzing with a weird energy. You end the call and shove your phone in your pocket and gently lay the man you've been cradling on the ground.

As you edge toward the forward fuselage, intense heat sears your face and hands and arms. Then a soft breeze shifts the fire in the other direction, and you pull off your shirt, rush in, and do your best to smother the flames flickering up from the prone man's clothing. Though his shirt is still smoking and his skin is hot to the touch, you grab him under his arms and pull him uphill, away from the fire.

He is unmoving, possibly dead, but you roll your shirt into something like a pillow and place it under his head. From the corner of your eye, you see Barton creeping in your direction as though the man is a monster who might suddenly spring up and grab him.

Barton reaches down and gingerly pushes a finger against the crispy flesh. He shakes his head, like someone in a movie or on a TV show, and you have a strange feeling that what is happening is something that might, indeed, be recreated by the entertainment industry.

The man's face is unrecognizable, so you don't know at the time that this is Stuart Fisher, the lead singer and main songwriter for the band Poor Ghost. If you're honest, he looks like a charred piece of meat.

# 2

Your neighbor to the right, Jimson, is spraying water at the fire with his garden hose. To the left, Barton's wife is doing the same thing. The hoses aren't long enough, and neither is doing much good, but fortunately, because the air is mostly still and the avocado orchard running along the back of your properties is well-watered, the fire is limited to the pine tree and the dead grass stubble, and the plane.

But the fire in the forward half of the plane is too intense to approach now, and what you can see of the back half looks empty, though your view is partially obscured.

You don't know what to do, though you somehow feel responsible. After all, it is your backyard.

The heat wavers, then becomes so fierce that Barton pulls the man who crawled from the back of the plane farther up the hill, while you do the same with the other man, who is surely dead. When you are far enough away from the flames and black smoke, you sit down again and stroke the man's longish tangled and singed hair, whispering, "There, there, there."

Across the canyon, people line the ridge. The late-afternoon sun flashes on what you take to be the lenses on the backs of their phones, as they send out a visual record of the disaster to their Instagram followers and Facebook friends.

In the street at the bottom of the canyon, it is the same.

Above the sound of the fire, burning with steady seriousness, you can hear the sirens getting louder and the intermittent squawking of crows.

And then, fifteen minutes after the crash at most, there are yellow-uniformed firemen swarming down the hill of your backyard. One of them carries a thick canvas hose over his shoulder, and the others hold it against their hips, as though it were a giant snake. A torrent of water douses the fire in the front of the plane, then drenches the crackling tree branches and the smoldering grass.

There is lots of steam—the brown-and-black smoke from the fires turns white. Then there's the smell of wet ash, as four paramedics rush to the two men, pushing you and Barton out of the way.

More paramedics arrive, then sheriff's deputies. Your backyard, which seemed eerily empty just minutes earlier, is now swarming with first responders, uniformed men and women who move through the world with the sort of unquestioning purpose you haven't felt for a good long while.

# 3

When the fires are out, paramedics and deputies and firemen clamber into the two halves of the plane.

There is a kind of start-and-stop motion to it all. They move toward something or someone you can't see. Then one of them freezes, and the others do too. A few moments later, the activity starts up again.

Barton has drifted toward you like a child on the first day of school sensing a possible friend, but the two of you seem to be suddenly invisible, so you sit there in the dry grass just below your juniper bushes and watch as the rescue workers bring up a body from the cockpit, and then another, and then one from the back of the plane.

It is mostly quiet near the wreck now—a susurrus of respectful whispering and one-word grunts.

Then you hear someone crying, and you look back up the hill. Above you is a line of neighbors from up and down the street who must have talked their way into your backyard. One of the neighbors, a woman in a pink dress, is holding your sobbing daughter.

You make your way up the wooden steps to the lawn and put your arms around Victoria.

"Oh, Daddy," she says, and you wonder how many years it's been since she called you anything but "Dad."

A fireman taps you hard on the shoulder.

"Who are you?" he demands. His face is soot-stained, which makes his bright blue eyes all the more intense.

"I live here," you cough—you must have inhaled more smoke than you realized.

"Is that right? Do you have some kind of identification?"

You dig your wallet from your back pocket and show him your driver's license.

He gestures at Barton, who has appeared beside you: "Who's he?"

"My neighbor."

"Go home, neighbor," the fireman says. "We've got it under control."

"Part of that plane is in my backyard too," Barton says, as if claiming his own importance in the scene.

The fireman glances toward Barton's yard. "Not much," he says. "This backyard here: this is the crash site."

He is about to chastise Barton further—clearly the fireman doesn't like him—but Victoria tugs at the fireman's coat. "Have you seen my dog?"

"Your what? Was he in the plane?"

"No, but he was down here when the plane crashed."

The fireman shakes his head. "If we see him, we'll tell you." Then he looks at you. "Did you see the crash?"

"Kind of. It happened really fast."

"People are going to want to talk to you. The NTSB. The FAA. FBI. Get ready. You're going to tell your story over and over and over again. Also," he says, staring at your bare middle-aged chest and stomach, "you might want to put on a shirt."

You wince. "I'll do that," you say, taking Victoria by the hand and walking toward the house. "Don't worry," you tell her, "we'll find Jackson." She shakes her head disconsolately, says nothing.

As you open the back door, you turn and notice that everyone with a phone—in other words, *everyone*—even a couple of sheriff's deputies, is taking pictures of the two of you. You pull back your shoulders and try to pull in your stomach. This isn't a picture you are going to be happy seeing flashed around the world.

# "HILLSDALE BOULEVARD"—THE POOR GHOST MESSAGE BOARD

## Sept. 21, 2021

**gotscoured**
What Happened???


**JimmyZ**
I can NOT believe this. I just can't.


**foolishunbearable**
People are saying "pilot error." What does that even mean?


**Arvin**
Suicide? I heard suicide.


**Tim12**
I heard terrorists. I don't believe it but that's what I heard. It's not impossible.


**janeblue**
Kerry survived. At least that's something.


**DefenestrationVolume**
Don't mean to be harsh but why is it always the bass player who survives?

**fearofthesoul**

Dude, that is SO outrageous. Like unbelievable.


**ghostkoan**

Plus Kerry is a lot more than a bass player. He's like the John Paul Jones of PG.


**sempiternalpaul**

I'm glad for Kerry and his family and everything but what about Stuart?


**Zeta**

Stuart's gone. And Gregg and Shane.


**AllMayBeWell**

This is some Buddy Holly shit. Otis Redding. Lynyrd Skynyrd. Stevie Ray Vaughan. Like only the good die young.


**linda7**

No offense, I totally LOVE them, but PG wasn't exactly young.


**alivenburbank**

linda7, fucking incredible. Where is your sensitivity?


**outre2**

PG is way more important than any of those people you mentioned, all due respect. Remember this is a band that started in what 1982? And lasted all this time. Almost forty fucking years. That's a miracle in itself.

**septembermaggie**

Where did it happen again? It looks kind of like mountains. Maybe there was fog, like Kobe's helicopter?

**basilthenaysayer**

No fog. And more like just the beginning of the foothills. It's somebody's backyard.

**hotsforholly3**

Those people must be trippin'. I mean Poor Ghost crashes in your backyard???

# TEXTS
## KS & RA

**Sun, Sep 19, 1:54 PM**

I got a really good gig! 8000 words longform article for the New Yorker (10K + expenses) on Poor Ghost.

Cool! More details?

Band's working on album 12: Old. The schtick is that the album is supposed to make old feel cool, which seems frankly impossible to me. Album drops early next year, article runs simultaneous with release.

So, like a "think piece" on PG?

Sorta. But a "think piece" on a rock band always runs the risk of looking ludicrous. You can do something for Rolling Stone, and if it's mostly about music, no big deal, because it's a music magazine. But the New Yorker wants heft, so I need multiple angles. Thoughts?

How about band conflict? The compromises necessary to stick it out for so long? Comments from poets and writers who claim Stuart F. as an influence? Maybe interview someone who's been a fan since the beginning, and how they've changed along w band?

Excellent ideas! I knew I texted you for a reason. ;-)

Didn't your dad like them?

He did. Sad.

Sorry.

No, that's okay. I just miss him sometimes.

**Tue, Sep 21, 5:26 PM**

Get online. Fast! Something about a plane crash in Santa
Barbara. Poor Ghost.

What?
Jesus!
g2g driving up there now

# POOR GHOST: AN ORAL HISTORY

## EDITOR'S NOTE

The material in *Poor Ghost: An Oral History* is, in large part, the result of interviews conducted from April through July of 2021. Band members were interviewed separately, in person, and in a variety of locations. In some cases, comments are excerpted from other sources, including anthologies, magazines, journals, and published and unpublished interviews.

## 1962–1982

**GREGG MORGAN:** It's strange how so many successful bands—I mean, the ones that stay together for a long time—start out when the band members are, like, kids, or teens, or college, or like that. Something about being young makes it feel special. You want to be successful and everything, make a lot of money, but you're striving for this higher thing. Call it art, if you want to. That's what Stuart calls it.

**STUART FISHER:** Gregg and I grew up three houses apart on Hillsdale Boulevard, in North Highlands, which is, like, a shitty suburb of Sacramento. It wasn't quite as rough as Del Paso Heights, but if you ever met somebody from another part of Sac—which wasn't very often growing up—they'd be like, "Whoa. You're from *North Highlands.*"

**GREGG MORGAN:** Walking to elementary school was not fun. We had to go through this neighborhood where bigger kids would be standing on the street corners demanding your lunch money, kicking your ass just for fun. That sort of thing. It made it a little easier if there were two of you, so Stuart and I always went back and forth to school together.

**STUART FISHER:** There were always a lot of fights in our school, even in first and second grade. Kids were not taught "conflict resolution." That concept would have been unimaginable. It was like, "I'm gonna kick your ass on the playground." *That* was conflict resolution.

**GREGG MORGAN:** I did not learn a lot at Madison Elementary School, I can tell you that. The teachers tried, God bless 'em, but for me it didn't stick.

**STUART FISHER:** My mom was a stay-at-home, and my dad worked in shipping at McClellan Air Force Base. He'd been in the Air Force, but he was a civilian now. It was not an exciting job, and the pay was not great, but it was steady work, and what he really loved to do was hunt and fish, so he was okay with it. He was always out shooting ducks or catching bass, and I went with him sometimes, but that wasn't really my scene, and he didn't force it.

**GREGG MORGAN:** My dad worked at the Base, like a lot of kids' dads in that neighborhood. He worked in the motor pool. My mom was a cashier down at 7-Eleven. Work was something you just did. You didn't talk about it.

**STUART FISHER:** Gregg and I were pretty close for most of grade school, but then in fifth grade I moved to a new school district, not great, but a little better, and I didn't really see him again until high school.

I listened to the radio a lot, Casey Kasem's Top 40, and I'd buy singles, and then I started buying albums. I listened to a lot of Elton John, and the Stones, and I memorized those Beatles albums. Put any one of them on now, and I can sing the entire record, every word.

Before long I was trying to make up my own songs. I bought my first guitar with my lawn mowing money. It was from this department store that went out of business a long time ago called Gemco. It was a Global electric guitar. A really shitty Japanese guitar with all this awful hum, but if you plugged it into your shitty little amplifier, it *would* make noise. Being able to sort of control the sounds of an electric guitar, at thirteen years old, to me that was just the pinnacle of human achievement.

**GREGG MORGAN:** Stuart and I went to the same junior high, but I was into sports for a while, and he wasn't, so, no, I don't even remember talking to him for years. I was playing football—Pop Warner at first—and music was just something happening in the background at parties or in the car.

**SHANE REED:** I went to a different elementary school than Stuart and Gregg: Woodridge. I guess it's pretty terrible now, but it wasn't so bad then. When my parents split up, my mom got the house, and I think she felt kind of bad about everything, so my last year in junior high, she bought me a drum kit. It was cheap. The hi-hat sounded like two pie tins hitting each other, but I was really into it. I practiced all the time.

**STUART FISHER:** Shane was in my math class at Foothill High, Math for Dummies—I never really got math, even though it's supposed to be so important for music—and one day we were talking and he told me he was a drummer, and I told him I'd been writing some songs. He told me to stop by sometime.

**GREGG MORGAN:** I played JV football in ninth grade for Foothill. Linebacker. And I did love hitting those other kids, but then some big offensive tackle from Rio Linda busted my ass after the whistle had blown and almost broke my ankle, and I was just, like, fuck it. Who needs football?

**STUART FISHER:** You hear how people have a spiritual conversion, and that's sort of what happened with Gregg. One day he was into football. The next day all he could talk about was rock and roll.

**GREGG MORGAN:** "Put another dime in the jukebox, baby."

**STUART FISHER:** Gregg and I weren't in the same classes. I wanted to go to college, and he thought that was bullshit. But in tenth grade, I started turning him on to some cool music.

**GREGG MORGAN:** I liked Boston. I mean, what fourteen-year-old kid in 1976 did not like Boston? If you want to learn to play guitar solos, you could do worse than listening to Tom Scholz. Stuart will deny it, but he liked that album too.

**STUART FISHER:** I hated bands like Boston and Journey. Even in my early teens, I wanted to do something different. I bought this book at Tower

Records, *Rock Critics' Choice: The Top 200 Albums*. It was a bunch of rock critics voting for their favorites, and it was all over the map—from Robert Johnson to Johnny Burnette to the Beatles to the Clash. The history of rock and roll. Once I had my guitar, I used my lawn mowing money to try and buy every album in that book. I mowed a lot of fucking lawns. That's how I got into Iggy and the Stooges, Bowie, the Velvet Underground, New York Dolls—that whole scene. It wasn't like they were playing clubs in Sacramento.

**GREGG MORGAN:** It's true that Stuart did have some influence on the music I like. He was very persistent in making me listen to it, and very persuasive about arguing why it was good.

**STUART FISHER:** After a while, Gregg and I would trade records and tape whatever new record the other guy had so we didn't have to buy it. The first Ramones album, the first Elvis Costello. *Never Mind the Bollocks, Here's the Sex Pistols*—we both bought that one.

**GREGG MORGAN:** I would say my "conversion experience" was when I spent fifteen bucks, which seemed like a fortune then, to buy the import version of the Clash. I remember how impressed Stuart was by that.

And then I started taking guitar lessons. No offense to Stuart, but I thought, "If he can do it, so can I." Music was just so much easier than football. After a few months, I just *got it*, you know? I wasn't great at making up songs, but I had a knack for soloing. I'd hear something, and my fingers just knew where to go. My parents are not musical—I don't know where it comes from.

**SHANE REED:** My house was the one place people could come over to because my mom, well, a) she felt bad about the divorce, b) she wasn't there a lot of the time, and c) when she was there, she was usually pretty drunk and sleeping it off, so the music didn't really bother her.

Pretty soon, Stuart and Gregg were coming over, and we'd do some covers to start out—"Wild Thing" and "I Wanna Be Your Dog," or whatever—but almost right away we were doing Stuart's songs. That made us different than most high school bands. We were considered more serious.

**GREGG MORGAN:** I wouldn't say kids in high school thought of Stuart as a poet. I mean, most people didn't think of him at all—he was pretty shy. But he did like to put words on paper. He had this old Smith Corona manual typewriter that his grandpa gave him, and the type was always kind of smudgy, and he had all these arrows and scratch-outs in red pencil. But, obviously, it meant something to him: writing. He wanted to play around with words.

John Lennon was probably not very good when he got his first guitar, right? And Stuart? Well, some of those first songs were pretty derivative, especially on the music end. Mostly for the verse he'd just kind of switch between two chords, like a major and its relative minor. Then he'd add a third chord, probably the dominant, for the chorus. Mozart it was not.

**STUART FISHER:** I think it's Malcolm Gladwell who says you have to do something for ten thousand hours to get really good at it. I'm not sure I spent that much time in my room writing songs—okay, I *know* I didn't—but I did put in my time. I had a poster of Jimi Hendrix at Woodstock on the wall. That headband and white fringe leather jacket? I knew I was never going to play solos like him, but I was inspired by his songwriting. "Wait Until Tomorrow," that was a good one. And "Crosstown Traffic." And, like I said, I did listen to a lot of Beatles, especially *Rubber Soul* and *Revolver*.

Being able to play with your own band as a teenager, that's a real advantage. Seeing whether or not the song in your head sounds the same when three guys are playing it in a garage. Being able to change the tempo midsong, then change it back, or have an instrument drop out for a few measures. Those were some great tricks I learned when we were first starting out.

**SHANE REED:** We changed the name of the band every few months. It was all very punk. Some of the names I remember are The Assholes, The Dicks, The Buttheads, The Sewers.

**GREGG MORGAN:** The Shit for Brains, The Spunk, The Turds, Stuart's Vomit.

**SHANE REED:** The Postal Idiots, and the Never Evers. I thought those two were pretty good.

**GREGG MORGAN:** Stuart wrote a lot of songs that summer after senior year, before he went off to UC-Davis. A couple of them ended up on our first album: "Man Gone Wrong" and "No More." I mean, some people consider those early classics. And we—well, *I*—was recording them on this TEAC cassette player I had. The mix was not good, obviously, but they didn't sound half-bad. You could tell we had something going on.

**STUART FISHER:** When I left for college, Gregg and Shane were pretty pissed. They thought we should just go for it, go out on the road, play wherever we could. But I felt I wasn't ready yet. The songs, some of them, were pretty good, but they could be better. And I felt I didn't really know much about the world. I was always a reader, so that was helpful, but I just thought college would be good for my songwriting, and Davis had this little underground scene, where they'd have two or three punk bands playing in somebody's living room on the weekends until the cops shut it down. There were a lot of frats, but they mostly left us alone, and after the bands were over, everyone would sit around listening to records, and that was a major education for me.

**GREGG MORGAN:** Stuart said he didn't ditch us, but I know he was playing with some of those bands in Davis.

**STUART FISHER:** I told the guys I wasn't playing with anyone else, but, you know, if someone needed a rhythm guitar player for a night, or some backing vocals, I didn't feel like I was betraying the guys back in Sac.

**SHANE REED:** It felt like a betrayal to us.

**STUART FISHER:** Towards the end of my freshman year, I started asking Gregg and Shane to drive over. There was a free rehearsal space on Tuesdays and Wednesdays in the back of this auto repair shop on the outskirts of Davis, and we started working up our songs again. I'd written some new material, and everything kind of went together. I mean, the songs didn't all sound the same, but, aesthetically, it was all of a piece.

**SHANE REED:** In the spring of 1981, Gregg and I would drive over to Davis and rehearse with Stuart. It sounded good, but we needed a bass player, and we asked Stuart to find somebody.

**STUART FISHER:** There was a kid in my Intro to Brit Lit class, Kerry Cruz. He had a Clash sticker on his binder, and we started talking, and it turned out he liked what I liked, and had his own equipment.

**KERRY CRUZ:** Even though I was the bass player, I guess I was considered the "musician" of the group, at first. My mom was a music teacher, and she made me take piano lessons, and then I played the sax for a while in the high school jazz band. So, I could read music, and none of the others could. Also, my dad was Mexican-American, from Durango, and I brought something different that they didn't really have, these three white guys from some working-class part of Sacramento.

**GREGG MORGAN:** Honestly, when I first met Kerry, I thought he was going to try and take over lead guitar from me. I put my guitar down during a break, and he picked it up and just started *wailing*. Like Eddie Van Halen type shit. But it just made me practice harder, and Kerry was pretty kickback. He just wanted to be part of the band. He didn't care about being the star.

**KERRY CRUZ:** I didn't hear Stuart's songs until that first year of college, when he'd been writing for a while. He definitely had something by then. He's this very sarcastic dude, as everyone knows, and that came out in the lyrics. But there was also something sweet and sentimental, and I think that combination of sweet and sour, well, that's sort of what the band is known for.

**SHANE REED:** If you listen to some of those demos Gregg taped in Larry's Auto Repair the summer of 1981, they're pretty killer. I think we all started to think we had to give it a try.

**KERRY CRUZ:** I grew up in Modesto, but I took summer school classes in Davis, and we just practiced all the time. All the other kids were gone, so we had access to that auto repair place after 8 p.m. like seven days a week.

**STUART FISHER:** The next school year, when Kerry and I were sophomores, I think we were starting to think of ourselves as musicians who were going to college rather than college kids in a band.

**SHANE REED:** Early on, I was basically the manager, and I wanted things to happen, so I started booking us gigs. First in Davis, then in Sac, then the Bay Area. I got us a gig at Mabuhay Gardens in San Francisco, and that was big. Dead Kennedys were playing there, the Avengers, the Mutants, the Offs. It was like a launching pad for that scene.

**KERRY CRUZ:** The Fab Mab was definitely a turning point. They asked us back, and I think we played four times in '81 and '82.

**STUART FISHER:** The Fab Mab was big, then we were driving down to LA. Al's Bar, Madame Wong's, The Masque. We missed a lot of class that last semester, spring '82.

**GREGG MORGAN:** We definitely kind of streamlined our sound and dressed the part for those early punk gigs. I mean, we *felt* it, but there was something more to us. Think about the Clash by that time. They'd already put out *Sandinista! Combat Rock* was in the works. We felt like that was a direction we could take, but first we had to make the scene, so we just played some kick-ass punk rock that was maybe more melodic than most people were used to.

**KERRY CRUZ:** I had a cassette of "Teenage Kicks" by the Undertones, and I started improvising those backing vocals that became part of our sound.

    After a while, I told my parents, "Look, if we don't have a hit record in one year, I'll go back to college. No regrets: I gave it a try, and it didn't work out." But if we have a hit, then that was proof we were on to something.

**GREGG MORGAN:** My parents were just happy I was leaving the house. They didn't care what the reason was.

**STUART FISHER:** I was only at UC-Davis for two years, but I learned a lot. I was an English major, so I took creative writing classes and literature classes. A whole class on Shakespeare. That was important. That's where I came up with the name "Poor Ghost," obviously. It's what Hamlet calls his father when dawn is about to break, and his father's ghost says: "My hour is almost come, / When I to sulphurous and tormenting flames / Must render myself up."

**KERRY CRUZ:** Stuart and I took this Shakespeare class together, and we both loved it when Hamlet says, "Alas, poor ghost!"

**SHANE REED:** Finally, I got us a gig at the Starwood in LA, and that was huge. That was like the Damned and the Germs and the Runaways, but also bands that really made it big like Blondie and Devo and the Go-Go's. We had that pop sound mixed in there along with the screaming guitars and heavy drumming, and at the Starwood gig we kind of punched that pop thing up, and we were really on fire.

Afterwards, Michael Kinney came up and said he wanted to represent us. Nobody else in the band knew who he was, but I did. He was big shit, especially back then. I knew he'd get us a record contract, and that's pretty much when Poor Ghost became a real-life going concern.

## Small jet carrying rock band Poor Ghost crashes near Santa Barbara; 4 fatalities reported

—AP News, September 21, 2021

A small jet crashed in the foothills approximately four miles northeast of the Santa Barbara, California, airport on Tuesday afternoon, killing at least four people, including Poor Ghost lead singer and songwriter Stuart Fisher, officials said.

The jet left Los Angeles International Airport around 3 p.m. before crashing into a suburban backyard at 3:59 p.m., Santa Barbara County Sheriff Bill Brown said.

"The weather was clear at the time of the crash," Brown said. "The cause remains under investigation."

The plane, a Cessna Citation 560X manufactured in 1998, was scheduled to land in Santa Barbara at 3:55. The pilot, whose name was not released, and three passengers were killed, Brown said. The band members listed as dead are Fisher, lead guitarist Gregg Morgan, and drummer Shane Reed. Bassist Kerry Cruz survived the crash but is in the Intensive Care Unit at Santa Barbara's Cottage Hospital.

The crash set off a brush fire, which was quickly extinguished by the Santa Barbara County Fire Department.

Poor Ghost was one of America's longest-active rock-and-roll bands. Their albums charted in the number one position in the Billboard Top 20 at least once in each of the five decades of their career, an achievement unequaled by any other pop music group.

Caleb Crane, who owns the house at the crash site, said he and his daughter, Victoria Crane, witnessed the plane's sharp descent.

"We ran straight toward it to see if we could help. We got as close as we could, but there was a fire. There was only one survivor," he told KEYT-TV.

This story is developing.

# THE
# AFTERLIFE
# OF
# POOR GHOST

# 4

Before Poor Ghost crashed in your backyard on September 21, 2021, you were simply *you*—nobody special at all.

Your little sister died when she was four, which marked you with a certain sorrow, but otherwise your childhood was unremarkable. Though none of your youthful dreams came to fruition, you married well and had a wonderful daughter.

For thirty-two years, you worked as an insurance agent for a company known for its commercials with a comic edge. Home, life, auto: you sold it all. It was a relatively prosperous gig, and, like any job, you got used to it. You were never a natural salesman, but that made you seem more authentic, and you did good business. You had a knack for talking down outraged clients, and you worked well with the underwriters and adjusters.

In short, even if your job often bored you to tears, you were doing all right.

And then you quit.

But burnout wasn't the reason you hired a brokerage firm and sold your agency. You did so because Connie, your wife of thirty years, died of Covid on May 2, 2020, almost a year and a half before the plane crash.

Her death happened fast—three weeks from beginning to end—though, of course, those three weeks seemed like forever. This occurred early in the pandemic, when nobody really knew anything, and the CDC was saying that maybe face masks weren't necessary.

You think Connie caught the virus in the local Albertson's, shopping for your dinner.

First it was a sore throat and a fever and a headache, and you both thought, *No way can it be this new disease.* But then her chest began burning, and she struggled for breath, and her doctor was able to get her tested, and it was, in fact, the new disease.

Connie was petrified. She quarantined in the bedroom, but she liked to have the hall doors open so she could lie on the bed and call out knock-knock jokes, which she had always found disproportionately funny. You made a facemask out of a T-shirt and some hair ties and sat in a chair at the far end of the hall and went along with her jokes:

*Knock knock.*

Who's there?

*Ash.*

Ash who?

*Gesundheit. You sound like you have Covid.*

She held on for five days at home after her first symptoms appeared, but as she grew weaker and more listless, you felt like the hospital was the only option.

"If I go in, I won't come out," she whispered to you as the EMTs in their HAZMAT suits lifted her onto a hydraulic stretcher and wheeled her out to the ambulance.

"Not true," you told her, though you feared in your gut she was right.

You couldn't see her in person, of course, so you had to rely on iPads held up to her by the hands of the nurses. Your own hands shook as you held your iPad. She asked if you were freezing, and you said yes, you were. You asked how she was doing, and she said it was like trying to breathe through a straw.

The nurses, suited up like astronauts in their personal protective equipment, played her favorite songs—Lauryn Hill's "To Zion" and Aimee Mann's "Lost in Space" and The Magnetic Fields' "The Things We Did and Didn't Do." They stroked her arms with their hospital gloves, and told her that researchers were desperately working on a cure, that she should just hold on and have faith.

She put on a brave front, trying to smile, though her lips were dry and cracked beneath her oxygen mask, but then she couldn't breathe on her own anymore, and the doctors intubated her, and for the last week you only saw glimpses of her on that fucking iPad, and you knew she was dying, and then, goddamn everything sacred and holy to hell, she was dead.

# 6

For two weeks after her funeral, you didn't leave the house, though, with the pandemic on, that wasn't something that most people noticed.

You stopped Zooming with policy owners, and took a leave of absence, spending a lot of time during the day sleeping, and a lot of time during the night not sleeping.

Mornings, you went on Grubhub and ordered the same breakfast bagel from the same bagel place. In the evening, you ordered the same chicken udon noodle soup from the same ramen place, and the familiarity of those dishes was so comforting that you thought you might never eat anything else.

Victoria was also devasted. Connie had nurtured her daughter through a thousand crises, and Victoria spent most of her days crying, or trying hard not to. You attempted to comfort her, and she did the same for you, but you were both inconsolable.

Nevertheless, Victoria kept driving up on the weekends from Thousand Oaks with her dog, Jackson. She mostly hid out in her old bedroom while you let Jackson sleep on your bed, where he patiently allowed you to pet him for hours.

Jackson was a rescue dog, part Saint Bernard, part Golden Retriever, and part something else big and lazy—possibly a Newfoundland. He was clumsy, but gentle and sweet, and you routinely referred to him as your "Granddog."

He loved to be scratched behind the ears, and you and Jackson spent a lot of time together, staring at each other with sad eyes.

# 7

Connie had been that rare creature, a successful cartoonist. Not quite as successful as, say, Roz Chast or Lynda Barry, but in the next tier down, and her work inhabited the same general universe of good-hearted cynicism. Reading her cartoons, you felt that even if the world was deeply imperfect, we were all in it together.

She often anthropomorphized animals—dogs were her favorite—and they would have surprisingly sophisticated conversations, about Hegelian dialectics, or the origins of the universe, or the state of the economy, but there would always be something supremely silly puncturing the gravity of their exchange. Connie hated pompous people, and she was a master at taking them down a peg or two, or three.

She'd published three successful collections with HarperCollins, and sold quite a few cartoons to the *New Yorker*. Some of her most famous ones—the Pekingese chastising the Siamese cat for her comment on Sino-American relations, the bulldog huffing at the squirrel for spilling his cup of tea, the ostrich sticking his long neck down the throat of a basset hound—are framed and hang on your walls.

Periodically, you think of taking them down, it is so painful to be reminded of her loss, but ultimately you decide that their absence would be even worse than leaving them up.

# 8

---

One of the other things that keeps you from wallowing completely in despair in the summer and fall of 2020 is the fact that your eighty-eight-year-old father is living alone in his house—your mother died three years ago. With the virus everywhere, he is emphatic that he does not want to go into assisted living, though he needs help badly. Even he will admit that sometimes.

Other than Meals on Wheels and Victoria, your father doesn't have any visitors except you. You've told yourself you have to keep your shit together for your father—and for Victoria, of course, and maybe a little bit for Jackson too.

Your father is a Trump guy, naturally. Old and white and angry at the way his body and mind are falling apart.

All day and night he watches Fox News. He falls asleep in his recliner, and no matter how long his siesta lasts, when he wakes up they are blathering the same garbage. It is all just one continuous promo for the president, and excuses for whatever foul deed he's done most recently—but what else is an old infirm man to believe?

Not surprisingly, you don't like stopping by, though you also feel guilty for not being with him. Therefore, you drive over twice a week, on Tuesdays and Sundays. You insist on turning off the TV and refuse to discuss politics, but since politics is all he hears and thinks about when you aren't there, your conversations are generally pretty brief, which neither of you seem to mind.

Your talks inevitably follow the same pattern:

"How are you, Dad?"

"I'm not well." And here he will catalog a litany of ills—from poor eyesight to arthritis to his bad lower back, which has been aching for decades, to his inability to taste food—before moving on to the state of the Union, which will fall apart without Trump's profound leadership.

You skip the politics and go straight to the care issues: "Dad, there's a lot of help available over at The Meadows"—the least expensive decent senior facility.

"I'm not going to any damned meadow. I'll leave this house when I'm good and dead."

"That's kind of an extreme statement, Dad."

"You want to try 'extreme,' boy, just try growing old. That's 'extreme.' 'Extreme' as hell."

# 9

Then Biden is elected, there's the insurrection at the Capitol, vaccines become available, and it's the one-year anniversary of Connie's death.

Time takes the edge off some things, but sharpens it on others, and when the plane carrying Poor Ghost—a band you've listened to but never really loved—crashes into your backyard on the afternoon of September 21, 2021, you are a financially solvent, more or less functioning, if often unhappy adult man in late middle age. You go grocery shopping when you are out of food. You cook your four meals—spaghetti cacio e pepe, meatloaf, vegetable stir fry, and baked potatoes with all the fixings—and you bathe regularly and once in a great while you even socialize with an old friend from the insurance company.

Yet you are mostly empty inside, and while, as an insurance salesman, you can hardly imagine the paperwork you are going to have to fill out after having a plane crash on your property, you are, strangely, ready for something to happen.

# TWITTER

## Poor Ghost Memorial
## 11,210 Tweets

**Stephen Malkmus**

Those guys were basically from the same place we were from. Their sound is the sound of trying to get the hell out of somewhere and not always succeeding. When I was writing *Slanted and Enchanted,* I was channeling Stuart Fisher.

**Rivers Cuomo**

There would be no Weezer without Poor Ghost. Everyone knows that. I am beyond heartbroken.

**Mike Campbell**

First Tom, now this.

**Jack White**

I only met him once, but Gregg Morgan taught me how to play guitar. If you were a kid and you could get the licks down from those first three albums, you could pretty much do anything.

**Iggy Pop**

These plane crashes, man. If they had planes back in Van Gogh's day, he would have been in one for sure.

**Rob Baker**

The American version of The Tragically Hip. I think that says it all.

**Jeff Tweedy**

Critics still ask me if Stuart was an unattributed co-writer on *Yankee Hotel Foxtrot.* He wasn't, but I can understand why they ask.

### Henry Rollins

Forget Shakespeare, give me Stuart Fisher any day.

### Elvis Costello

Stuart once said he learned a lot about songwriting from me. Well, same.

### Sir Paul McCartney

I would say they were the Beatles of their generation, but they went through so many generations.

### Joni Mitchell

Stuart Fisher was one of the few lyricists of the last thirty years whose work I found admirable on the page.

### Bono

September 21: the day the music died.

# POOR GHOST: AN ORAL HISTORY

## 1982–1983

### *Alas, Poor Ghost!* (1982)
### US Billboard Peak Position: 17

**MICHAEL KINNEY:** That first night I saw them at the Starwood, I knew I wanted to be their manager. I know they were the openers, only on for half an hour, but I don't remember who else was on that night. I wasn't really paying attention, because as soon as they finished their set, I went backstage to sign them.

Naturally, I started talking to the lead singer, to Stuart, but it turned out the drummer was the business guy in the band—there's always one. There has to be, or the band's not going to make it. So, yeah, Shane and I we formed a kind of connection right away. He knew who I was, and that impressed me because for most of those bands back then, it was a point of pride not to recognize the "suits" who were making things happen offstage. But Shane, although he was just this working-class kid from Sacramento, he already had something like a business plan in mind.

**SHANE REED:** It *was* a good show, I remember that. We were locked in.

**MICHAEL KINNEY:** What I liked most about Poor Ghost was the fact that while they were clearly riding the punk wave, and they obviously had that passion that I associate with punk, there were all these weird counter-currents running through the music. Like the lyrics being so literate. Stuart was kind of a nascent Joni Mitchell doing this punk sneer. And then the little harmonic touches in the bass and backing vocals that came from Kerry. Shane was already a capable drummer, and he would just keep getting better, as it turned out, and of course Gregg could really shred. His solos were short, but they weren't just the truncated scales most of the punk guitarists were doing then. You could tell he took pride in every note, and, given a little room to stretch, he might do some very interesting things.

**STUART FISHER:** That night we were all four staying in some shitty hotel on the Hollywood Strip, and Shane was just manic. He was, like, "Guys, we *have* to do this. We have to sign with Kinney. He'll make us famous."

**GREGG MORGAN:** We all wanted to be famous, so I don't remember there being any big disagreement. The next day, we went over to Kinney's office and signed a contract, and before we'd even left, he'd booked us time in Record One in Sherman Oaks. It was this really bland-looking office building on the outside, but inside, oh man, state of the art at the time. It was a quantum leap up from the auto repair shop in Davis.

**KERRY CRUZ:** It was August of 1982 when we got in the studio, and Val Garay was our producer. He'd just done that Motels album *All Four One* with "Only the Lonely" on it, so he was kind of a hot producer at the time. I'm not entirely sure if he got what we were trying to do—I mean, he was no George Martin—but he was a pretty good listener, and he seemed to respect us. He heard us out when we had an idea, even if he didn't always use it.

**VAL GARAY:** Poor Ghost was a stretch for me, this young punk band. The Motels were probably the closest group to them, musically, that I'd worked with. I was more the engineer or producer you'd go to if you were Linda Ronstadt or Kenny Rogers or Ringo Starr or Pablo Cruise. Kind of a Top 40 guy. But I think they benefited from my sense of what was commercial and what wasn't. I don't think they had to compromise. I just brought out what was already inherent in the songs, which were these insistent *hooks* that you wanted to listen to again and again.

**KERRY CRUZ:** My favorite song from our first album is "Driving a Black Mercedes at Midnight While Two People Have Sex in the Back Seat." Stuart would come up with these long titles that sounded like they were going to lead into comic folk songs, and he would have some pretty literate verses, but then the chorus would be like, "Radar guns and having fun / Speeding cars and flecks of stars"—something you could sing along to.

**GREGG MORGAN:** I think my favorite lyric was from "Touched on the Cheek by the Tip of a Vulture's Wing," that part where the guy driving almost hits a vulture, "big as a child," and "A rack of feathers exploded across my windshield from the disked earth, / So hungry for life, death itself was worth the risk." Sure, we grew up in Sacramento, and there's lots of fields around if you drive even fifteen minutes out of town, but who expects some punk kid to notice "disked earth." I thought that was really cool.

**SHANE REED:** When I talk to other drummers, they usually feel like they're not really part of the band. Onstage, sure, you're making everything happen, you're what people are dancing to, but in the studio, not so much. So, I have to hand it to Stuart. We've had our differences over the years, but he always asked for my input, and he mostly used it, though sometimes more creatively than the way I intended it. But, especially on those early albums, he made me feel like I was just as important as anyone else in Poor Ghost, just as important as he was.

**STUART FISHER:** By the time we got to that recording studio in Sherman Oaks, I think I had written two hundred songs, and I mean two hundred that I had the lyrics typed out and the chords written in pencil over the words, so that I could basically sit down and sing and play any of them on my guitar. There was a lot of material to choose from, and we only needed twelve songs, so I just talked to the guys, and we picked what we thought were our twelve best songs.

We recorded two of the songs we'd been playing since high school—"No More" and "Man Gone Wrong"—but it was mostly stuff I'd been writing in college. Still, except for "Short Order" and maybe "Instructions for Composing a Haiku," these were all songs that we'd played a lot on stage, so they came pretty easily. We recorded them in two or three takes. "Short Order" and "Haiku" took more time. Those were kind of our experimental pieces, though Val and Michael made sure neither of them was longer than four minutes. But Kerry had a chance to play keyboards on both, and then Gregg has that killer solo at the end of "Haiku," the final song on the album.

When we were listening to playback in the studio, I kept thinking, "Oh man, I hope this sounds as good to other people as it does to me."

**MICHAEL KINNEY:** I don't think I would really call *Alas, Poor Ghost!* punk or power pop or new wave, though it obviously contains elements of all of those genres, not to mention the singer-songwriter vibe that would sometimes make an appearance. The Beatles were obviously big for Stuart, but I think he took it as a point of pride that no one ever called them "the next Beatles," which was a tag going around a lot then. Think of the Knack, for instance.

There was a little Ziggy Stardust–era Bowie in the songs, and Zappa, too, but not enough to wreck the choruses. The album is considered a classic now, of course, but both Val and I had our moments when we wondered if all that brio they had in concert was going to translate to a record. Thank God, it did.

**VAL GARAY:** It took us three weeks to record the album, and it was out to market by the end of October, just when all the critics started making their best-of-the-year lists. I think it just kind of bowled people over. The early 1980s was a time when you could have a hit with something offbeat, as long as you could sing along to it on the radio. So when Warner Brothers brought out *Alas, Poor Ghost!* I had the feeling it could do well, but of course not as well as it ended up doing. I mean it was number four on the *Village Voice*'s annual *Pazz & Jop* list, right between Richard and Linda Thompson's *Shoot Out the Lights* and George Clinton's *Computer Games*. *Rolling Stone* also had it at number four, between the first Bad Brains album and The Who's *It's Hard*. That gives you a sense of how eclectic music was back then.

**JERRY DIMGARTEN:** I was writing for *Creem* in the early '80s—I took over for Lester Bangs when he left—and like a lot of critics, I took notice of *Alas, Poor Ghost!* It wasn't exactly like Wire's *Pink Flag* or Gang of Four's *Entertainment!* It didn't have that kind of coherent political or aesthetic statement, although it did have the same intense energy, like the singer was daring you to disbelieve anything he sang.

You definitely felt the influence of the Clash's *London Calling*, and, for me at least, the Beatles' *Rubber Soul*. It was like Poor Ghost had skipped right past the *With the Beatles* and *Hard Day's Night* stage, and gone straight to something more complex.

Of course, not everyone saw it that way. Dave Marsh at *Rolling Stone* was a big fan, which was one of the reasons it came in so high on their year-end list, but Robert Christgau at the *Voice* thought it was too derivative. He didn't think Stuart's influences were fully digested. Rumor was, if it hadn't been for Christgau, *Alas, Poor Ghost!* would have been number one on *Pazz & Jop*.

**STUART FISHER:** I suppose, in a way, the album cover has also become iconic. That picture of Hamlet's father, the ghost, staring at you, kind of snarling. And the punk fonts. Very cool.

**SHANE REED:** After *Alas, Poor Ghost!* our lives changed, no doubt about it. I won't say we were four hicks, but three of us grew up in Sac, and Kerry in Modesto, so we were just Central Valley kids who happened to like rock and roll. I mean, we'd played these gigs in LA and San Francisco, but we'd just go in for the gigs, and half the time we'd drive back to Davis, or just pull over in some rest area and sleep in the van until some highway patrol officer kicked us out. We didn't know much about the real world.

**GREGG MORGAN:** After the album came out, Michael had us playing *everywhere*. The whole year practically. If we had a week off, it was a big deal.

**MICHAEL KINNEY:** People loved them live, and I booked them wherever I could at the end of '82 and the start of '83. I had them opening for Bad Brains and X and Los Lobos and the Blasters and Aztec Camera, but pretty soon all those bands were opening for Poor Ghost. They opened for Talking Heads a couple of times, and The Police once—this was during their *Synchronicity* tour, so the Police were huge at the time, but Poor Ghost won over the crowd in their little thirty-minute set. I was in the audience, and you could see people looking at each other saying, "Who the fuck are *these* guys?"

**KERRY CRUZ:** 1983 is all kind of a blur to me, just one gig after another. We'd play the twelve songs from our album, and then we'd do a couple of covers—usually a punked-out version of the Supremes' "Love Child" and the Kinks' "Waterloo Sunset"—and then Stuart would try out a new song or two he was thinking about for our next album. So, we had the chance to test-drive a lot of the material on the second album live, and we were very aware of which songs people responded to, and which ones they didn't. It was a lot of fun, though I wasn't crazy about all the air travel.

**JERRY DIMGARTEN:** One of the things people love about Poor Ghost is how eclectic they are, but I caught quite a few of those '83 shows, and you could see they wanted to be *liked*. They wanted to play what they wanted to play, but they wanted the audience to enjoy listening to it. They weren't dilettantes or avant-gardists. They were a rock band.

**Tue, Sep 21, 9:32 PM**

I'm here!

What's it like??

Chaos. Took forever. Shitty traffic from LA to Ventura.
Then it got even worse.

What are you seeing?

It was dark by the time I got near the crash site. Mob
scene on the street, so I parked down by an elementary
school, put on my best Karen face and started trekking up
the hill.

You do a good Karen!

Sadly. My plan was to say, "I'm a neighbor and a good
friend, let me in."

Did it work??

Nope. Struck out with my press pass too. You would not
believe the media coverage. News vans from all the major
networks in people's driveways. Even One America News
(what the hell would their story be? Biden shot down the
plane?).

Tue, Sep 21, 10:45 PM

What's happening?

Stood as near to the house as I could and wrote down snippets of conversations.

Classic Kelsey.

Examples: "I heard someone saw a missile hit the plane." "Who?" "Not sure, but that's what I heard." "I like their early records. The later stuff, not so much." "Really, I'm the opposite. Those early records are so . . . jejune." "I can't believe you just said 'jejune' when people are dead."

Ted is coming over so I may put my phone away for a few hours. Text me tomorrow?

k

# THE
# AFTERLIFE
# OF
# POOR GHOST

# 10

The afternoon of the crash is a jumble. After you make your way inside your house, which is full of people you don't know—official and otherwise—you put on a shirt, then step onto your front porch, where a local television reporter sticks a mic in your face. You answer a few questions, then duck back inside, but, a few minutes later, men in blue windbreakers are hustling you and Victoria downtown to a federal office building you'd never really noticed before.

You sit in a large conference room and have your recollections video-taped as you answer variations on the same handful of questions—*What?* and *When?* and *Where?*—posed by members of the National Transportation Safety Board, the Federal Aviation Administration, and the Federal Bureau of Investigation.

Phrases are repeated that would seem to be better answered by a pilot or an airline representative: "intention of flight" and "hydraulic systems failure" and "zone of danger." You and Victoria are by turns bemused and annoyed and sad.

The fluorescent lights overhead buzz, and one bulb keeps flickering off and on. The chairs in the conference room are on wheels, and you push your chair slowly back and forth during the interview, at first out of nervousness and later out of boredom.

Several hours pass until they tire of the repetitiveness of your responses, and a taciturn FBI agent is assigned to drive you and Victoria home.

# 11

From Point Conception to Rincon Point, the California coast runs in a west-east direction, so that when you are looking out at the beach, you are looking south, and when you look up toward the Santa Ynez Mountains, which begin rising just a few miles from the beach, you are looking north.

Your neighborhood is called Rancho de las Pumas, although you've never seen a puma there, and your house, on a north-south ridge, is on Camino Palomino, where horses are equally scarce. The neighborhood is west of the Santa Barbara city limits, and east of Goleta, in an area locally referred to as "Noleta."

Camino Palomino starts at about one hundred feet above sea level and rises to almost five hundred feet in a third of a mile. It's the sort of hill that challenges adventurous neighborhood walkers, and results in almost inevitable wipeouts for the occasional skateboarder foolhardy enough to make a downhill run.

It's a quiet residential neighborhood that, with views of both the mountains and the ocean, is populated by lawyers and doctors and dentists, like Barton, as well as recent retirees like you, who bought in when things were more affordable. Normally there are few cars parked on the side of the road, but tonight there is not a parking spot to be had. People old and young mill about near their cars, which are all playing Poor Ghost songs: a cacophony of the group's greatest hits—familiar phrases and musical hooks mashed together into something that feels both nostalgic and spooky.

Everyone points their phone cameras at your car as you drive past.

It is twilight, and the national media has arrived. Two news vans—from ABC and CBS—are parked in the circular driveway of your neighbor across the street. The Jimsons, your neighbors to the right, have an NBC and a CNN van in their driveway, and Barton the dentist is harboring news trucks from Fox News and One America News—you wonder what conspiracy spin they plan to put on this story.

Noleta is under the county's jurisdiction, so the sheriff is in charge. Two cruisers are parked in front of the house, and, as you pull up, reporters with their cameras and lights crowd around the car. The deputies wave everyone back, and your FBI driver manages to ease the car into the driveway.

When you get out, it's a barrage of shouted questions: "What did you see? Were you scared? Who did it? What do you have to say to the fans of Poor Ghost?" This last question sounds like an accusation, as though you'd somehow lured Poor Ghost's plane into your backyard.

Your driver has rolled down his window, and, as the reporters' questions come at you, he shakes his head *No*, so you take Victoria by the elbow and go inside.

# 12

The house is dark and empty, but the backyard is a circus, and Victoria and you head outside to see what's going on.

Two sheriff's deputies are sitting in your patio chairs, looking at their phones. One has a big droopy mustache, the other doesn't. Otherwise, they could be twins. They get up when they see you, but you wave them back down and ask how it's going.

"About what you'd expect," says one. "Controlled chaos."

"In what way?"

"There's just a lot of people who want to be on your property right now."

"Any news on what might have caused the crash?"

He shakes his head, and his partner shrugs: "Could be anything. No use speculating."

You have a gas firepit in the center of the patio. You ask if they want some heat, and they do. You light the propane, and they reposition their chairs around the fire. You walk over to the edge of the lawn so you can see what is happening down the hill.

The crash scene is illuminated by halogen work lights and garlanded with yellow tape. Investigators wearing NTSB and FBI windbreakers—you count seven of them, but there may be more—poke around and peek inside the two halves of the plane. TV lights shine from your two neighbors' backyards as reporters periodically have their makeup done and give thirty-second updates from the crash site.

Overhead, a news helicopter noisily circles the scene.

The plane looks so *lonely* down there, even with all the people and the lights.

Your poor pine tree is destroyed.

You wonder to what extent your life has also been damaged, but you get a bit of a guilty thrill being there in the center of things after being alone for so many months.

Over your shoulder, you can hear Victoria asking the deputies if there's been any sign of Jackson, but they tell her they haven't seen a dog since they arrived.

# 13

With no sign of Jackson, Victoria decides to stay the night so she can conduct a thorough search for him the next day. You tell her that he has probably just run away from all the commotion, that in all likelihood he is huddled up in a neighbor's living room right now, being petted and spoiled, and that once she has a chance to look for him properly, he will jump into her arms and knock her to the floor.

Around nine, you and Victoria sit down to watch TV, a British detective show where the murder, it is suggested, has been committed by a grandmother wielding a jar of homemade raspberry preserves. The detective, a middle-aged woman in a floppy green hat and Wellington boots, is grilling the poor grandmother in the station's interrogation room, when you hear shouting in the backyard.

You put the program on pause and open the back door. The deputies are in the process of handcuffing two men in their thirties. Both are wearing Poor Ghost T-shirts. One of them is bald and clean-shaven. The other has a heavy brow and a tuft of blondish hair below his lower lip and above his chin. For a moment, your mind wanders as you attempt to recall the name of that particular style of facial hair. Whiskey button? Soul patch?

"Trespassers," the deputy with the mustache says.

"Looky-loos," the other adds. "You may get more of that until they move the plane." He turns to the two men: "Come on, you nitwits, let's go."

The man with the soul patch—you're pretty sure that's what it's called—says, "Wait." He looks directly at you, his face half blazing with the backyard floodlights, half in shadow. "What was it like?"

"The accident?"

He smiles, but says nothing.

"It was horrible," you say, as the deputy hustles him and his companion around the side yard.

You and Victoria return to the living room and restart the detective show, but ten minutes later there is more hullabaloo outside, so once again you pause the program and go outside.

The deputy with the mustache is down the hill among the accident investigators, yelling into the darkness of the avocado orchard, "Get the hell away from there! You want to get arrested? Just come on over here and I'll arrest you."

The other deputy is on his phone: "We need some help here. Now." He shakes his head at whatever is being said to him. "No, out back. Fans, or something. They're trying to get to the crash site. They're fucking up the investigation." He shakes his head even more vigorously at the person on the other end: "Tell Captain two of us can't cover the backyard. Too many people milling around. We need more Feds. This is a plane crash, for Christ's sake."

In the light from the firepit, the deputy looks like a panicked little boy.

# 14

In less than ten minutes, the agent who drove you home from the inquisition downtown is standing in your backyard. He is no longer wearing sunglasses, of course, but his eyes are expressionless—he doesn't really need the glasses.

"That was fast," the mustached deputy says. "Were you parked down the street?"

The FBI agent ignores the question. "There's been a fuck-up," he says. "A miscalculation."

"Well, no shit," says the deputy. "I mean, I love their music, but who could have predicted Poor Ghost had so many fans?"

"I should have," the agent says. "*Scoured* is the sound of a generation."

"You're a fan," you say, not a little surprised.

"Actually, I prefer *Defenestration and Decapitation*," the deputy says to the agent, his face animated, like some college kid in the dorm about to defend his favorite album.

"Eclectic choice," says the FBI agent.

"Think about the way they use twelve-string guitar with that raunchy electric lead on "The Season of High School Bands." And "Hanging Out with Bosnians," I mean, that's a game-changer."

"Remember that *Sopranos* episode?"

"*Totally*. Also, the new album's really good: *Fear of Everything*."

"I don't know," the FBI agent says. "Maybe I haven't really given that one a fair chance."

"Excuse me," you say, pointing at two figures streaking from the side yard down the wooden steps toward the crash site, "but there are people trespassing on my property. Maybe you could continue your discussion after you take care of other business?"

Victoria has joined your little group. "And find my dog," she says.

# 15

Soon, your front and backyards are once again thick with law-enforcement officers. Their presence has the desired effect on the Poor Ghost fans, but, when you finally go to bed, you find it difficult to sleep with so many strangers on your property.

With the lights out, you think about Connie. She would have been deeply touched by the deaths, of course, but she would also be coming up with some darkly humorous takes on the commotion. She would have thought the deputy with the mustache was particularly funny; you can imagine her refashioning him as a Schnauzer and the FBI agent as a Rottweiler.

But Connie's not there, and despite all the voices and lights and occasional blasts of a siren, you feel quite alone.

# TEXTS
## KS & RA

**Wed, Sep 22, 11:03 AM**

So? Are you awake? What happened last night?

More craziness. By midnight, police presence got heavier. But I followed one guy who found a path through a neighbor's yard, and we got about fifty yards from the wreck. It was all lit up, investigators everywhere. It's mostly in two big pieces and the front part is smashed to shit.

Jesus.

I know. We were getting closer but this cop spots us, starts yelling and we hightail it back to the road.

Where r u now?

I crashed at Alyssa's.

Alyssa from college?

Yeah. She has this huge house in Montecito.

What?? With that movie producer guy?

He's her husband.

God. So what's the plan?

I'm going to hang around, try and like infiltrate that house where the crash was. See what I can find out.

What about the article on PG?

I called my editor. Maybe this is the article.

# BUZZFEED

## 7 Reasons We'll Miss Poor Ghost

**1. "Spaghetti Bolognese and a Can of Coke."** Everybody loves the feel-good song of the mid-eighties.

**2. Stuart made it okay to feel sad.** When Stuart Fisher was singing about his latest heartache in that sweet, sometimes gravelly baritone of his, you knew that being down was just part of the human condition.

**3. What other band do both you *and* your grandpa like?** Seriously, it's pretty rare.

**4. They beat out U2 for a Grammy.** Again, seriously, how often does that happen?

**5. You lost your virginity to one of their songs.** If not you, then you know someone who did. Just ask around.

**6. They rocked right up to the end.** Have you heard "Sheltering in Pasadena" on *Fear of Everything*? Gregg's solo is killer.

**7. There's a new album dropping soon.** It's called *Old*, but—go ahead and say it—they will always be young in our hearts.

# POOR GHOST: AN ORAL HISTORY

## 1983–1984

### *September Pears* (1984)
### US Billboard Peak Position: 2

**STUART FISHER:** By the end of '83 we were burned out from touring, and we really wanted to record some new material. Our fans seemed to want it too. We were like: Get us off the road, we have things to say.

**MICHAEL KINNEY:** I know the band will complain that I kept them touring all through '83 when they wanted to get into the studio and record the next album, but there was a method to my madness. First off, they were still a pretty new band. Sure, they'd gigged around for a couple of years while two of them were in college, but that's hardly the 10,000 hours the Beatles put in at the Cavern Club in Hamburg. A great band is like a great sports team—they anticipate each other's moves, they cover for each other when one of them has a weakness. Putting Poor Ghost out on the road was probably the best thing I ever did for them.

**GREGG MORGAN:** Sometimes I think that year on the road was the worst thing that ever happened to us. We had so much creativity flowing, and it all just went into the same old songs, with the exception of those one or two new originals Stuart would bring out every night. Mentally and physically, I think that was the most exhausting year of my life.

**KERRY CRUZ:** That was a tough year, all the touring after *Alas, Poor Ghost!* We've always gotten along pretty well, but there was definitely some stress, some squabbles. Maybe the three of us sometimes resented Stuart getting most of the attention. I don't know. Still, it also gave us some money. When the new year came, and we sort of stuck our heads out and looked around, we were not rich, but we could afford to buy things. Like a house. I bought a two-bedroom place in Mar Vista, and I felt like a king.

**SHANE REED:** One of the reasons the band's been together so long is that Stuart is a generous guy. Right from the first album, he insisted that even though he was writing all the songs, we'd all split everything four ways, equally. He said the songs wouldn't be the same without us playing on them, and I think that's true. It wasn't in a contract or anything, it was just something he wanted to do.

**GREGG MORGAN:** That thing Stuart did, with sharing the earnings from his songwriting credits, definitely cemented us together. Whenever we recorded one of his songs, it felt like it was a song we'd all co-written.

**MICHAEL KINNEY:** I'd like to make it clear that Val Garay did a great job with their first album. Millions of people will agree. But I wanted to take Poor Ghost to the next level, so toward the end of '83, I started asking around—very subtly, mind you—who liked what the band was doing, and Steve Lillywhite's name kept coming up. And I thought, "Well, *yes*."

**KERRY CRUZ:** Steve Lillywhite was already one of the biggest producers around. Peter Gabriel, Psychedelic Furs, *Boy* and *October* and *War* by U2. And two albums with XTC—we were big fans of theirs. It felt like they never got their proper due. So, it was flattering that he wanted to work with us.

**STEVE LILLYWHITE:** I had produced *Sparkle in the Rain* by Simple Minds the previous autumn, and I was looking for a band that had more of a guitar sound, but I wanted catchy tunes and literate lyrics. I won't lie: I wanted another hit, but I wanted it with a band that was still up and coming. I liked *Alas, Poor Ghost!* and I thought I could make these guys a band that people *had* to talk about.

**GREGG MORGAN:** I'm not a huge fan of *Sparkle in the Rain*—too much echo and synthesizer—but after being on the road so long, I wanted our hard work to pay off, and who's going to say no to Steve Lillywhite?

That said, I felt like my guitar got lost in the mix on that album. Not so much muddied as *spread out*. I could hear what Steve was trying to do—get that kind of wall of sound the Edge was making on *War*, but I like a crisper vibe. One guitar, one guitarist, not a guy pretending to be an army of guitarists.

**SHANE REED:** Steve got a big drum sound for me. I liked that, of course.

**KERRY CRUZ:** Since the beginning, I've always had little ideas about how to make Stuart's really good songs just a little better, and Steve was a good listener, especially if he thought it would make something more radio-friendly. That horn chart on "A Million Reasons Not to Tell the Truth," that was my idea—and, to be fair, Stuart did give me a songwriting credit, even though I came up with the part after the song was basically complete. I also played the Farfisa organ on "The Lyon Brothers." Especially during the bridge, I think that was an important addition. And then I played piano on "September Pears."

**MICHAEL KINNEY:** Stuart always had in mind that "September Pears" would be the title track, and it would close the album. It's a beautiful, if simple, ballad in A minor that was probably the most moving piece of music he'd written up to that point. There's all the imagery about the September pears falling to the grass and "White-tipped butterflies alight, / As sweet rot bloats the fruit." I also like the line "mottled corpses scattered amid pinestraw." Kind of a *memento mori* song, which was pretty heavy for a twenty-two-year-old.

**SHANE REED:** Our first three albums, we recorded those all pretty quickly. For *September Pears*, we had ten songs that we had been playing on tour—one or two of them each night, but they felt like a *group* of songs by the time we got into the studio. We knew how all the parts went, and our first take was usually the best take, although Steve would have us rerecord, and of course he wanted the sonic palette to be a bit more complex. Not just guitars and bass and drums. But it went pretty quickly. In less than a month, Steve had mixed it, and the music was headed off to wherever they sent vinyl albums to be manufactured in those days.

**STUART FISHER:** I know from the many times they've told me, for fans of Poor Ghost, *September Pears* is an album that means a lot to them, for whatever reason. It sums up some heartache they were going through, or there's an angry snarl in there that allowed them to stand up to someone who was bullying them, or it's just a record that served as a soundtrack to their life for a while.

All that's great, and I am proud of the album, but then there's "Spaghetti Bolognese and a Can of Coke." Jesus, I wish I could take that one back.

**STEVE LILLYWHITE:** The story of "Spaghetti Bolognese" is similar to that of "Trane in Vain"—"You say you stand by your man," that song—on the Clash's *London Calling*. The album was essentially finished—both are really great statements of American art, if you ask me—and then a song appears at the very end of the recording process—a kind of accident, really—and that's the big hit.

What happened was this. Stuart was fooling around on his guitar in the studio. Everyone else was kind of shooting the shit in the control room, not paying attention. He had already come up with that famous hook that you only have to hum a few bars and everyone knows it. But he didn't have any lyrics, and he was just singing whatever came into his head. Then he started making up this little story about this white-trash couple that wants to go out to dinner on a Saturday night, but they can't afford it, so they just stay home instead, and the song implies that it's okay not to always be in the limelight. Sometimes you just take what's at hand, and it's enough to make you happy.

Suddenly, everyone in the studio—the band, the engineer, me, their manager Michael—we were just "*What* is that?" It was *so* catchy.

Michael talked Stuart into writing down the lyrics, and that afternoon they laid down the basic tracks. In post, I doubled the guitar lick with a synth, with the band's grudging approval, but I think they would have to agree it's part of what sold the song to the masses.

**MICHAEL KINNEY:** I feel like there's always a moment in popular music when people are going to be attracted to some offbeat lyric, and then suddenly everyone's singing it. So that would explain "Getting hazy, getting crazy, and it ain't no joke / Spaghetti Bolognese and a can of Coke."

**SHANE REED:** When "Spaghetti Bolognese and a Can of Coke" went to number two, I mean, that was crazy. My mom heard it on her car radio, and I think she finally thought we were doing something that might actually have legs.

**GREGG MORGAN:** We had the number two record in July and August of 1984. We would have been number one, but first it was Prince's "When Doves Cry," which I honestly didn't mind losing to. But then coming in second to that stupid *Ghostbusters* song? That was brutal. Still, we were part of what people of a certain age remember about that summer: "Getting hazy, getting crazy, and it ain't no joke / Spaghetti Bolognese and a can of Coke."

**MICHAEL KINNEY:** After "Spaghetti Bolognese," Stuart insisted on releasing "September Pears" as the second single, in September, of course—much to the consternation of Warner Brothers, which thought "The Lyon Brothers" could at least chart as a respectable follow-up. But Stuart was threatening to quit, to blow the whole thing up. He hated having a novelty song as a hit, so the execs just said, "What the fuck, we already have our hit, go ahead."

**STUART FISHER:** They had this monthly series of piano sheet music made easy, Top 40 hits mostly—it went out in a little magazine—and they featured "September Pears" in one of their issues. That's always made me happy. I picture ten-year-old kids forced to do their piano lessons memorizing that song, and then, later on in life, they sit down at the piano and trot it out from memory, and it makes them happy, in a melancholy sort of way.

**JERRY DIMGARTEN:** I reviewed *September Pears* for *Creem*, and overall I gave it a great review. I thought the wordsmithing was first-rate, Shane's drumming was just cataclysmic on "Lawnmower," and, of course, the title track can still break your heart, even after all these years. I was not a fan of "Spaghetti Bolognese," though, and I warned the band about getting so caught up looking for a hit that they ignored their own hard-won artistry. In retrospect, it was a piece of advice that they have usually taken, though not always.

**STEVE LILLYWHITE:** That was the one and only time I worked with Poor Ghost, but it was definitely a highlight of the '80s for me. My next project was the Stones' *Dirty Work*. A whole different animal, but that's a story for another day.

# NEXTDOOR

## RANCHO DE LAS PUMAS • 25 SEP

**Maria Moss**
**Deluge of Poor Ghost Fans.** Hello, neighbors. I am so distressed right now! Doesn't it feel like our neighborhood has been overrun by fans of Poor Ghost? Every night, there's someone in my backyard, climbing the fence to get down to the orchard so they can go to that crash site and do whatever it is they do. Ever since the sheriff pulled their deputies, it has been a NIGHTMARE! I have called the sheriff's department many times in the past few days to say they need full-time people here still, but they just say all they can do is increase patrols in the area. I would gladly chip in to hire a private security contractor, at least until these nutjobs go back to whatever rock they crawled out from. I am truly sorry about this tragic crash, but it is ruining my life. Help!

**Pat Lewis**
I am having the same problem. They mostly seem homeless to me. I feel sorry for them, this is the only thing they have in their lives, but stay off my lawn and stay the blank out of my backyard. I do have a registered shotgun, but of course I don't want to have to use it.

**Todd Osborne**
So you're saying you would shoot the bereaved fans of a rock band?

**Pat Lewis**
They are not "bereaved." They are a nuisance at best, criminals at worst.

### Olivia Torres

I haven't seen any of them around my house, but we're a few streets away from the crash site. Sorry for your trouble, neighbors.

### Elizabeth Hamilton

I live on Camino Palomino and they are up and down the street all night. Keep your cars parked in your driveway, all your doors locked, and keep your outside lights on all night. That seems to help a little.

### Pat Lewis

The next one I find climbing my fence is going to be "bereaved" all right.

### Nicole Meadows

During the day, they are stealing the mail. I saw one grab a handful of mail and just run down the hill. I called the sheriff, called the post office. "Can I ID the person?" No, I CAN'T ID the person. I just saw his back while he was TAMPERING WITH FEDERAL PROPERTY.

### Danielle Turner

Hope they are caught!!

### Kendra Lozano

Stay vigilant! I used to be so trusting, but these people are making me wish I'd never moved here.

### Lisa Patel

I wish we could all get along better. I actually gave some food to some young kids that were sitting on my lawn. They were playing acoustic guitar and singing "Driving a Black Mercedes at Midnight While Two People Have

Sex in the Back Seat," and it really brought me back to my early twenties, when we used to sit around the stereo and listen to that first album— remember albums!—and sing along and try and interpret the lyrics. Yes, all these people in the neighborhood right now are pests, but they are human beings and they will go away soon. I think we should try and put ourselves in their place. Someday they will be the homeowners and hopefully they'll be generous to the generation that comes after them.

**Brian Case**

I WANT to try and sympathize, but it's not like Jesus Christ's plane crashed in our neighborhood. Let's be honest, it was just a rock band whose best songs were behind them.

# THE
# AFTERLIFE
# OF
# POOR GHOST

# 16

The National Transportation Safety Board investigators are there the entire night after the plane crash, and into the next day, taking photographs, squatting over parts of the plane and having intense discussions, then gradually removing the smaller pieces of debris by hand. You watch from your patio as they stride about deliberately in their hard hats, goggles, and steel-toed boots, labeling each piece, then placing it in the back of one of the two white vans that have made their way up the narrow dirt road that circles the Corellis' avocado orchard.

That process takes a full day.

On September 23, two days after the crash, a truck carrying a crane maneuvers up the road, taking out a small avocado tree along the way.

After the crane is finally close enough to secure the rear of the plane, the truck takes several hours to back down to the street, beeping the entire way. The fuselage is loaded onto the back of a flatbed truck. Then the truck with the crane slowly wends its way back to the crash site and repeats the process for the front half of the plane. Finally, the truck makes a third trip to retrieve the detached engine, wing, and stabilizer.

You're not the only one watching this laborious process. All your neighbors are watching too. People and camera crews line the backyards on the other side of the canyon. Apparently, they have a better view. As though it were a sporting event, a cheer goes up each time a piece of the plane is picked up or put down by the crane.

Barton the dentist comes over and offers you a beer, and then Jimson, your other neighbor, whose occupation is unknown to you, joins the two of you, uninvited.

"Quite a mess," Jimson says, as though you had a hand in making it. You nod, and he continues: "It's not just your backyard that got messed up. That is, it's *mostly* your backyard, but not entirely."

You flash him a tight, fake smile. "Well, I'm sure we all have robust homeowner's policies. I wouldn't worry about it."

He looks unpacified. "I've been meaning to say I'm sorry about your wife."

"Ah. All right. Thank you. That was a while ago, though."

"Was it?"

"A year and a half." He nods skeptically, as though you're exaggerating. "Listen," you say to the two of them, "I have to go inside. I'll leave you to it."

You watch Barton and Jimson from your kitchen window as they confer quietly, occasionally glancing toward your house. After about fifteen minutes, they depart, and you head back outside, leaning against the wall of your house so neither of them can see you.

A few minutes later, one of the members of the NTSB "Go Team"—a woman in a navy-blue windbreaker who seems no older than your daughter—comes up and asks to use your restroom. When she's back outside, you ask her what they've been looking for at the crash site.

"Same as any incident," she says. "Impact angles. Power and system issues—electrical, hydraulic, pneumatic, and so forth. Human performance, maintenance, weather—anything, really."

"What were they doing so low to the ground this far away from the airport?" you ask.

"When we can answer that question, I think we'll be able to answer most of the other questions as well."

You start to ask about the pilot, but she gives you a curt smile and heads back down the hill.

# 17

Unfortunately, the absence of wreckage at the crash site does not, initially, deter the Poor Ghost fans who make a nightly pilgrimage to your backyard. They are a motley, if enthusiastic, bunch, with their tattoos and torn denim and Poor Ghost tour T-shirts—the brooding face of Hamlet, Sr., on the front of *Alas, Poor Ghost!*; the DayGlo Brillo pad on the back of *Scoured*; the guitar neck that looks like a two-lane road at night on the front of *Everything Good Is on the Highway*. In general, they do not seem to give much of a fuck about anything except mourning their favorite band.

Fortunately, sheriff's deputies hang around through the end of the month to address the onslaught, though they stay in ever-decreasing numbers—first four, then two, then just one. Their presence and their swift arrests—you have counted at least two dozen—have become well known on social media.

The whole scene is more than a little overwhelming. You call your father on Tuesdays and Sundays, but skip the actual visits. It sometimes takes you a couple of days to respond to Victoria's texts, when they've always been a highlight of your day. Even your constant memories of Connie are cutting in and out, replaced by faces from the PG menagerie.

Gradually, though, the fact that the plane is long gone, and your pine tree—which some PG fans seemed to think acquired special powers during the crash—has been chain-sawed down and hauled off to who knows where, dampens their enthusiasm for nightly visits.

Then, on the night of October first, no one shows up at all.

The next evening, the deputy on duty—the man with the droopy mustache—announces that this will be his final night. "I think that's the end of them," he says.

"I don't know."

"There's nothing left to see. No souvenirs left to carry away. Half of them are sitting in jail on first-degree trespassing charges. Judge Ponge is in a pretty foul mood when they come into his court."

"You're saying my fifteen minutes of fame are up?"

He frowns. "It was longer than that." The deputy pulls out his phone, apparently ending the exchange. But your daughter is in Thousand Oaks, and you ignored—then lost—most of your friends after Connie's death, and you're in the mood for a little conversation, so you offer him a beer, and he accepts. "Just don't tell anyone," he says, and you promise you won't.

"I remember that first night," you say, "the night of the crash, you were talking with the FBI guy about Poor Ghost. Sounds like you're a fan."

He takes a sip from his Sierra Nevada. "Okay, I'm thirty-three, so when I was sixteen, that's when *Defenestration and Decapitation* came out."

"I don't really remember that one."

"It's kind of a forgotten album, and, to tell you the truth, I only listened to it because my older brother had the CD. I didn't even know what those two words meant until I looked them up. And then I thought, Oh, that's pretty cool."

"Wait. Was that the album with 'Against the Euro' on it?"

"That's right." He sings: "'The Austrian schilling and German mark / Clinked like their coiners' tongues.'" He takes a long swallow of beer. "Actually, I didn't know what a euro was either, but I really liked the tune."

"I do remember that song. It must have been on the radio, at least for a while. It was a good one."

The deputy sighs. "So, since this is the last night and everything, I guess I can say, off the record, that I've had some sympathy for these fans."

"No one would ever have known it."

"That's good. That's my job: acting like I don't care. But you know I have a soft spot for Poor Ghost."

# 18

The first night you're on your own, things are quiet. If you have any visitors, you don't know it, and you sleep until morning.

When you wake up, you think things might be going back to normal. It is just after dawn, the birds are twittering, and there is fog in the canyon, though not so much that you don't notice the absence of your pine tree, which in some ways had been your favorite thing about the yard.

Still, when the sun hits the fog, it radiates a mellow gold, and it seems like Poor Ghost is giving the place its blessing and moving on.

Throughout the day, you look out the window, expecting company, but it's only the bees buzzing in the rosemary bushes, a dragonfly darting between the tricolored torch lilies, a California thrasher pecking through fallen leaves with its long, curved beak.

As a murder of crows circles the place where the pine tree was and flies off, squawking, down the canyon, you think about Victoria's big lovable dog, Jackson. No sign of him was ever discovered in the crash. And, despite the photocopied signs Victoria stapled to every telephone pole in the neighborhood, there has been no word from anyone.

Probably he is dead, you admit to yourself. What other explanation could there be?

# 19

Early evening of that same day, you are sitting on your porch, which faces east. The sun is behind you, so it's flashing on the picture windows of the houses across the canyon. You watch the Santa Ynez mountains fade to a golden-purple glow before going inside to make yourself a dinner omelet.

You are just sitting down, spooning a little salsa on your plate, when you hear voices in the backyard. You bolt up from the table and turn on the back floodlights, expecting whoever is there to scatter, but, instead, two men and a woman who look to be in their thirties stand on the edge of your lawn, looking down at the crash site. All three glance over their shoulders at you, and the woman gives a little wave, but they don't say anything.

"Excuse me," you call out. "This is my house. What the hell are you doing here?"

"Worshipping, man," says one of the guys. He wears a light blue T-shirt with Christ catching a wave. *Surfin' for Jesus*, it says. He rubs at the soul patch beneath his lower lip, and you remember that he is one of the first people arrested by the deputies, and that he returned on several other nights before they frightened everyone away.

"This isn't a church," you say. "It's my backyard."

"It's God's house," he says. He gestures at the night sky. "All of it."

"Well, God told me that this little corner of the grid is mine, so beat it."

The man smiles, doesn't move.

You ask: "What's your name?"

"Elineo," he replies, sounding it out: "El-ee-nee-o."

"I'd like you to leave, Elineo."

Rather than leaving, he says, "Maybe you've heard of me? I run a Christian surf school. We bring people to the Lord through the waves."

"Is that the slogan for your business?"

"It actually is." His hands move frantically as he talks. Even when he's not speaking, his long fingers are doing little dances in the air.

"Again, Elineo, I'd like you to leave. You make me uncomfortable."

You realize that the other man, who is balding and pudgy, and the woman, who is wearing a UCLA sweatshirt, have seated themselves in patio chairs and are watching your conversation with interest.

"Dude, I am just here for Jesus. And Stuart. They had a bond."

"I'm pretty sure Stuart was an atheist."

"That's what he told people. It was a test. The world is full of tests. You pass them or you fail them. Stuart was looking for the true believers." Elineo raises his hands above his head, as though he is testifying.

"I don't know what you're talking about."

"You can hear it in Stuart's lyrics. Take 'Lucky for Some,' for example. You know the chorus, 'Lucky for some, unlucky for others. / The children of men are men without mothers'?"

"So?"

"Well, don't you get it?" Elineo's hands make little itsy-bitsy spider motions, as though they are climbing up the waterspout. "'The children of men are men without mothers' is about Jesus."

"But Jesus *had* a mother: Mary. He just didn't have a father."

"God was his father. His mother," and Elineo pauses here, QED, "was a *virgin*."

"Okay, but I don't see how that's supposed to be a message for true believers."

"That's because you don't get it."

Frustrated, you say: "But you're not *explaining* it to me."

"If you have to ask, you'll never know. That's what Louis Armstrong said about jazz. Dude, maybe you should pray on that little koan tonight."

"I'm not praying on anything, Elineo. And if you don't get out of here, I'm calling the cops. On everyone."

The other man and the woman, who have until then sat silently watching you and Elineo as though you were a YouTube video, regard each other. It's hard to tell if any of them knows the others.

"Maybe we should all leave," the woman says finally. "Give this man some peace and quiet."

"He needs to pray," says Elineo.

"Dude," says the balding man. "Let's go. You can come back another time."

Elineo's hands, which seem to be choreographing a free jazz concert, suddenly go limp and drop to his sides. He nods, but says nothing, and walks toward the gate to the street.

"Thank you," you tell the man.

He frowns. "He'll be back. And he won't be alone."

# 20

The man is right. The next night is the same, only worse. Ten people this time instead of three, and you count twenty the following night. They are a more diverse crowd than the original mourners—old and young and homeless and well-heeled. There's a man who's at least in his eighties with eyebrow and lip piercings, and there's a prim schoolgirl who looks like she just left the church choir. The only thing connecting them is their love of Poor Ghost.

You call the sheriff's department, and a car does swing by several times each evening, but the deputy tells you that they just don't have the manpower to cover your house every night of the week. If someone gets violent, fine: arrests will be made. But as long as your visitors remain relatively quiet and well behaved, you're basically on your own.

"Don't worry," the deputy tells you on the third night. "After a while, they'll get bored. How long can this possibly last?"

# TEXTS
## KS & RA

**Thu, Sep 23, 10:02 AM**

What's happening up there?

Hello?

Earth to Kelsey. Rebecca here. Are you receiving me?

**Fri, Sep 24, 8:35 AM**

Kelsey, are you okay?

> Yeah, sorry. Just caught up in things. I'll text you later, okay? I'm fine.

**Sat, Sep 25, 9:15 PM**

I guess you must be really busy.

> I am, yeah. Sorry. Sorry, sorry. Just doing a lot of research and trying to fit in with the PG crowd.

What do you mean by fitting in with the crowd?

> Just, you know, getting my story. Trying to see the world from the eyes of the true-believer fans. It's this weird quasi-religious scene.

Sounds unpleasant.

> Not totally.

Well, Ted's here. He says hi.

> Hi, Ted! Sorry, Becca, but I have to run. I'll text you
> more when I know what's happening. Things are kind of
> opening up, but I'm fine. Don't worry about me.

Okay. Well, luv u.

> Same!

### Mon, Oct 4, 9:30 AM

I told myself I'd wait a whole week, and I did. But what is
going on up there?

> People were just totally converging on this guy's house
> where the crash happened. And it got so overwhelming
> that it seemed like they called in half the cops in Santa
> Barbara County.

What were you doing all that time?

> I spent a lot of time listening to PG's music. They have
> A LOT of albums. Interviewing fans. I got in touch with
> family and friends of the band. Most of them didn't
> want to talk with me, but I found out that, in conjunction
> with their new album, PG had also just finished an oral
> history.

You said the new album was called Old??

Right. So ironic. Anyway, finally, all the cops left—I was checking every night—and so last night I went over there to the guy's house, his name is Caleb Crane, and I hung out for a little while.

Did you tell him you were a reporter?

No. I mean, he didn't ask, so I didn't have to lie. There was this really weird fan there. Kind of freaked everyone out. But I'm going to go back tonight. There's a story, definitely.

Are you still staying with Alyssa?

Yeah. She's not as bad as you remember. Plus she's a huge PG fan, so she's interested in what I'm doing.

I get it. You're working. Text me when you can, okay?

I will! There's something about this band, Becca—they've been around forever—but it's like now that most of them are gone, they're more present than they ever were when they were alive.

# POOR GHOST: AN ORAL HISTORY

## 1985–1988

### *The Unbearable* (1987)
### US Billboard Peak Position: 1

**KERRY CRUZ:** It was after *September Pears* that we started getting compared to U2, though we were more like their less-successful kid brothers. They had four albums out by that time, and we only had two, but we were both popular and "political," if you want to call it that, but in a way that didn't put off a mainstream audience. Stuart didn't have the Irish charm of Bono, but he was pretty charismatic, and a lot more articulate.

**STUART FISHER:** I've never liked the U2 comparison, but what are you going to do? Two bands that last forty-plus years with the exact same personnel. That's pretty unheard of.

**GREGG MORGAN:** Even though we were both "new wave"—a totally meaningless descriptor, by the way—and had songs on the radio, our sounds were pretty different. As I've said before, and nothing against the Edge, but he makes *sounds* for his band. I play guitar.

**KERRY CRUZ:** We also had the Steve Lillywhite connection. But I think the comparison really came to the fore during Live Aid.

**MICHAEL KINNEY:** I got them on Live Aid, which at the time was probably the biggest multi-act concert since Woodstock. I was friends with Harvey Goldsmith, the promoter, and I also had some connections to the Boomtown Rats. I talked to Harvey and Bob Geldof, and neither of them really knew who Poor Ghost was. But after they listened to the two albums, they saw how PG would be a good fit.

Honestly, I've never really felt like the band was sufficiently grateful for all the work I did getting them on that stage. Let's face it: *everyone* wanted to play Live Aid.

**SHANE REED:** We had been touring again, *a lot*, in the first half of '85, still promoting those *September Pears* songs, and Michael called me on the road and told me about Live Aid. I was stoked, but the rest of the guys didn't really get it. Something like that makes you *world*-famous.

**MICHAEL KINNEY:** The concert was held on a Saturday in July 1985 in two locations: Wembley Stadium in London, and JFK in Philadelphia. Poor Ghost was at JFK.

**STUART FISHER:** We did a four-song set, between Judas Priest and Bryan Adams. We wanted to rock, so we played "Short Order," "Haiku," "Lyon Brothers," and that stupid "Spaghetti" song.

**KERRY CRUZ:** "Spaghetti Bolognese" got the biggest response, which really bummed Stuart out. Afterwards, backstage, he told me he was never going to write a song like that again, and I think he more or less kept his promise.

**STUART FISHER:** I don't know how much of that money ever made it to Ethiopia, but I have to say that I've never seen so many egos in one single place as backstage at Live Aid. I'd been worried that, as we got bigger and bigger, my ego was getting pretty outsized. But compared to Jagger or Robert Plant or Bob Dylan, or—and he was the worst—Simon Le Bon? Well, no comparison.

**JERRY DIMGARTEN:** I was working for *Rolling Stone* by then, covering the concert, and it was total chaos backstage. It was all I could do to jot down two or three sentences for each band—there were so many of them!

But I do remember Poor Ghost's set. It's been said so many times that we forget to say it—but one thing about them, they are a great live band. They generate the same energy you'd find at a Ramones concert or Judas Priest or Metallica at their peak. Just *vroom*. The set starts, and you are off, and even in the quieter songs they're not really letting up, they're just building up steam for the next explosion of rock and roll. And when it's over, you just think: "Man, what was *that*?"

It's kind of like a Springsteen show, but shorter, and without the Midwestern breadbasket vibe.

Anyway, I was in Philadelphia, and doing a lot of pre-concert interviews, so I've only seen video performances of Queen's show at Wembley, which was obviously unparalleled, whatever you think of their music. But, for my money, the best set in Philly was Poor Ghost, and then Madonna, though it was totally different in character, of course.

**SHANE REED:** After Live Aid, we went back on the road, at Michael's insistence. And we pretty much played out for the rest of '85. It is *draining* putting on a good show. At the end of the year, I was beat. My hands were just two giant blisters. I didn't even want to *look* at a drum kit.

**KERRY CRUZ:** We were exhausted again, so we insisted on four months off, until April of '86. After we rested, the plan was to play a few more shows, then head to the studio for album number three.

**SHANE REED:** It was Tax Day, I remember that, because I knew I was going to get screwed on my taxes, and we were headlining for two nights at the Showbox in Seattle before we went back to the Record Plant in LA.

We were about halfway through the gig when Stuart did a kind of Pete Townshend sort of leap and fell off the stage.

**STUART FISHER:** I was trying to be ironic, doing this kind of windmill windup to "The Lyon Brothers," and I jumped and landed awkwardly and just fell off the stage. I broke my right arm and my left leg. It hurt like holy fucking hell.

**MICHAEL KINNEY:** I was not happy, no. Stuart had a fractured ulna and a fractured tibia, so he had a cast on his arm *and* his leg. I'd already booked time in the Record Plant, and that money was not going to be refunded.

**STUART FISHER:** It took longer to heal than the doctors expected, but I was finally cast-free by the end of August of '86. In September, I got a cabin up in the Sierras, and I sat up there and read, and took short hikes, or just sat on the porch and stared. I didn't even bring my guitar, so I can't say I really wrote any songs, but *ideas* for songs were starting to form. I still had this big backlog of unrecorded material, but I wanted to do something new for the next album. All new songs that captured what we'd been through since we'd been out on the road starting in '82.

Then I went home to my parents' house in Sacramento and holed up in my old bedroom for a week with an acoustic guitar, and when I came out of my daze, I realized I had an entire album ready to go.

**GREGG MORGAN:** After Stuart left that log cabin, he spent a week in Sac, then he came down to the warehouse I was renting in Berkeley, and we started working together on the basic instrumentation of the songs. He gave me three co-songwriting credits, but that was generous. He pretty much had everything worked out in his head by then.

**KERRY CRUZ:** I think Stuart and Gregg had been in that warehouse for a week before they called me and Shane up. With another band, I could see how we might have felt like just add-ons. Like, okay, they're the singer and the guitarist and here are the songs and this is what they want the bass and drums to do.

But Stuart doesn't like to work that way. I mean, he could have gone solo at any time in the past forty years, but he likes to work with a band, he likes *input* from a band—our band—and I think he'd admit that his really good songs become something special when they get the Poor Ghost treatment.

**MICHAEL KINNEY:** I thought Trevor Horn would be ideal as a producer, but he wasn't available—or, to be truthful—and why not, at this point?— he wasn't interested.

**GREGG MORGAN:** It's weird that we ended up with Bob Clearmountain as producer for *The Unbearable*. I don't think he was really anyone's first choice. He was producing people like Bryan Adams and Hall & Oates. But, at heart, Bob was just a really good engineer—he mixed *Born in the USA* and *Tattoo You* and *Let's Dance*—and that's what we needed most: a guy who could transform the sound we heard in our heads into a record that people would want to listen to.

**BOB CLEARMOUNTAIN:** I was told by Steve Lillywhite that they worked fast and were pretty cooperative, and I happened to have a three-week hole in my schedule. So I said okay. They asked if I wanted a producer credit, and I said, "Sure, why not?" Of course, I never had any idea the record was going to become a musical touchstone for the entire decade.

**KERRY CRUZ:** It's a really good album, obviously, some would say great. A lot of people's favorite. I like all the songs on there, but my personal favorite is "All May Be Well." Shane's brushwork on that is amazing. You would not think it was the same drummer who was pounding away on "The Lyon Brothers."

**STUART FISHER:** As usual, Kerry added a lot of instrumental touches: harmonium, melodica. He actually plays the viola da gamba on "Viola da Gamba." And that melody on the virginals in "Uphill, Both Ways" is really beautiful. He's kind of the John Paul Jones of the band.

**KERRY CRUZ:** I'd never even heard of a virginals, but I'd become kind of friends with a classical pianist named Jeremy Higgs, and he told me, if you can play the harpsichord and the spinet, which I could, then you could also play the virginals.

**GREGG MORGAN:** "In Praise of Happy Endings" is my favorite, just the way it builds and builds over seven minutes—kind of like "Hey Jude" but without all the lyric repetition. I think my solo is pretty killer, if I do say so myself.

**MICHAEL KINNEY:** I had wanted a new album out by the summer of '86, but then there was the broken arm and leg. Finally, in early October, I was told by Stuart that he had a new batch of songs, so March 1987 seemed like a good target to release the albums.

**SHANE REED:** We heard U2 was also making an album that was supposed to be out at the same time. Some people would have shied away from the competition, but we just said, Fuck it.

**STUART FISHER:** I think *The Joshua Tree* was mostly being recorded in Dublin, though it was an album about America. Meanwhile, we were at the Record Plant in LA recording this album about how unbearable the world was becoming.

**GREGG MORGAN:** Up to that time, I would have said *War* was a great album, but U2 was a band that mostly hadn't lived up to their potential. I thought *The Unforgettable Fire* was pretty lame.

**MICHAEL KINNEY:** This was the heyday of music videos on MTV, so I told the guys we were going to have to make one for each single. They weren't thrilled.

**STUART FISHER:** If you look at the videos of 1987, there's a lot of bad hair and a lot of bad acting. I did not want to be part of that, but I liked how Peter Gabriel was getting around it with the videos for "Sledgehammer" and "Big Time." Claymation and stop action. He was *in* it, but he wasn't the star.

**KERRY CRUZ:** Michael got in touch with Stephen Johnson, who directed Peter Gabriel's videos, and Stephen was able to do something similar for us with "Dreadful Trade" and "Traveling by Train."

**SHANE REED:** I especially like the sequence in "Traveling by Train" when the train becomes Stuart's face and then it morphs into a rocket ship that crashes into Saturn and then Claymation figures of the band emerge and we're rocking out in space. That was cool.

**MICHAEL KINNEY:** Obviously, the videos had an enormously beneficial effect on album sales, so I wasn't totally surprised when *The Unbearable* was nominated for two Grammys. The awards were in March of 1988, a year after the album was released. But that was also the year of Michael Jackson's *Bad* and, of course, U2's *The Joshua Tree*. I did not think we had a chance.

**KERRY CRUZ:** That was brutal, going up against U2 for Album of the Year and Best Rock Performance. After they won the Rock Performance category, I thought we had no chance at all.

**GREGG MORGAN:** The Edge got up there and gave this crazy speech thanking, like MLK, Bob Dylan, Dr. Ruth, Pee Wee Herman, Walt Disney. I don't remember who else. It was like the warm-up speech for the big win for Album of the Year that he was expecting, and you knew Bono was going to be at the mic for that one.

**STUART FISHER:** We just sat there at our table, drinking ourselves into a kind of stupor. I'd never been to an awards show before, and when you lose in a category, no one wants to look at you. Like you've gone from being a famous rock band to a bunch of lepers.

**SHANE REED:** I swear, when *The Unbearable* was announced as winner of Album of the Year, bookies all over the country were just shitting their pants.

**STUART FISHER:** When I got up there behind the podium, I went totally blank. It would have been a huge moment if social media had been around.

**SHANE REED:** Stuart was pretty much speechless. So, I just kind of nudged my way in there and thanked Bob and Michael and my mom. It was a short speech.

**JERRY DIMGARTEN:** The albums came out the same month, so you can't say one influenced the other, but there are similarities: the belief that music can take the listener someplace higher, the sense of drama that you can create in a single four-minute song.

Certainly, *The Joshua Tree* outsold *The Unbearable* by a good margin, but that's not always a sign it's going to be more popular with the tastemakers, which we rock critics were back then, before social media.

The lyrics on *Joshua Tree* have a lot of power when they are being sung by Bono and backed up by the band, but when you look at them on the page, well, there's no comparison to what Stuart was writing.

**STUART FISHER:** I still get embarrassed watching that *VH1 Classic Albums* show about the making of *The Unbearable*. It makes the composition and recording process seem more . . . I don't know, *bombastic* than it actually was. All we were trying to do was get the best possible sound for each track. Sometimes that involved a lot of arguing and do-overs.

**BOB CLEARMOUNTAIN:** I'm not one to gainsay my own successes, but when you look at the "classic" albums made in 1987, VH1 did *The Unbearable* and *The Joshua Tree*, but they also did Def Leppard's *Hysteria*. That kind of puts things in perspective.

**MICHAEL KINNEY:** Under my management, Poor Ghost had made three increasingly successful albums. They'd played all over the US and Europe, including at one of the biggest concerts ever. Then they win the Grammy for Album of the Year. So when Stuart called me up the day after the award, I thought he was going to give me a bonus, or at least throw me a party.

But you know what? That son of a bitch *fired* me. He said the band didn't like the direction I was taking them in. And I just thought—well, actually I *said* this—*Fuck you.*

# INSTAGRAM

## poorghostlifer92

**23 likes**

**poorghostlifer92** Sitting by the beach in Santa Barbara. When I look out at these waves that keep rolling in endlessly I cannot help but ask myself why PG had to die? What was wrong with that plane? Was it intentional? Will we ever know? For now all we have are their songs which will live in our hearts 4 ever! #poorghostcrash #whokilledpoorghost #poorghost4ever #poorghostnme #poorghost

## Personal Conflicts May Have Played a Role in Poor Ghost Plane Crash That Killed 4

—MSN, Oct. 6, 2021

National Transportation Safety Board advisors have released a preliminary report on the September 21 crash of the Cessna Citation 560X bound from Los Angeles International Airport for Santa Barbara Municipal Airport. The crash killed pilot Jeffrey Dunne and three members of the rock band Poor Ghost. The sole survivor, bassist Kerry Cruz, was interviewed by teams from the NTSB and the Federal Aviation Administration.

While Evan Tyson of the FAA said the flight recorder, or "black box," has been recovered, he indicated that only the flight data recorder, which shows the recent history of the flight, was intact. The cockpit voice recorder, which captures the sounds in the cockpit, including pilot conversations, stopped recording before the plane made its approach to Santa Barbara. When asked if this was a frequent occurrence in plane crashes, Tyson responded, "No." However, he added, "It is possible, on this older model of aircraft, to turn off the voice recorder midflight by flipping a circuit breaker. Nevertheless, at this time we have no idea why the cockpit voice recorder was disabled, whether or not the disabling was intentional, and why the pilot deviated from his approved flight plan."

Cruz, 58, told investigators that prior to the plane's departure from LAX, lead singer Stuart Fisher and guitarist Gregg Morgan had been arguing about the future direction of the band. Cruz said he had taken a strong sedative before departure because he is afraid of flying, and he was not conscious again until the plane crashed in a suburban backyard approximately 4 miles northeast of the airport.

"I wish I could tell you what happened," Cruz told reporters outside his home in the Hancock Park neighborhood of Los Angeles, "but I was sound asleep." Cruz said he was unaware of any weather- or equipment-related issues that might have caused the crash. "Could have had something to do with that argument," he said. "I just don't know."

Poor Ghost was flying to Santa Barbara to perform a small private concert for what Cruz called "our biggest, most intense fans" to celebrate the waning of the pandemic and the imminent release of their new album, *Old*. Many of the fans gathered for the concert have remained in Santa Barbara, with some making nightly, and illegal, visits to the crash site.

"It's time for these visitors to go home," Sheriff Bill Brown said in a news conference. "We're all mourning the death of Poor Ghost, but at the same time, people need to get on with their lives."

# REDDIT

## Questions About Poor Ghost Pilot

**preghost878**

Have you ever noticed that they don't say much about the pilot? A friend of mine did some research, and the guy is a big Republican. So what's some Trump-lover doing flying PG's plane? Was he trying to bring them down for statements Stuart made in the past? I wonder.

**ghstmniac**

A lot of these "Republicans" are really just QAnon freaks trying to disguise themselves as semi-normal people. If the pilot was Q, it was definitely intentional. At the very least, it should be the lead line of investigation.

**hillsdaleblvd5447**

Usually the person you don't hear about for a long time is the person who actually did it. We never hear about the pilot. QED.

**rghtofstalinbtch**

Fuck you idiots. The pilot is ex-Air Force. A total patriot would never pull this terroristic shit. The culprit is obviously the libtards and their Deep State masters. #WWG1WGA

# THE
# AFTERLIFE
# OF
# POOR GHOST

# 21

As it turns out, the second round of Poor Ghost fans is more persistent than the first. Eventually, you get so tired of trying to chase them off that you just tell them to keep it down when you're ready to go to bed.

The average number of "visitors," as you've decided to call them, is twenty-five or so, about the size of a college class, and they do have a kind of undergraduate enthusiasm for their favorite subject, arguing or agreeing passionately, keen to share some tidbit of arcana about the band—which instrument Kerry played on the bridge of "Defenestration," or the number of the Shakespearean sonnet Stuart was alluding to in "Decapitation."

Usually, about half of your visitors are down by the crash site, while the others hang out on the patio, sharing a quiet joint and a box of cheap wine, musing about the life and times of Stuart Fisher. You've found that they are mellower when the firepit is lit, so you turn it on at dusk—your gas bill is going to be enormous—and turn it off when you wake in the night to take a pee, by which time they are usually gone.

The October nights are generally pleasant, with crickets chirping and the stars shining over the mountains and the ocean. Across the ridge, big-screen TVs flash through the windows. The murmur of earnest voices is sometimes interrupted by a car gunning down the street, or a small pack of yipping coyotes zeroing in on a rabbit or a cat.

Occasionally, when your guests seem especially mournful, you sit down and join them. Among the more memorable regulars is an adjunct philosophy professor at the university. Another is a third-grade teacher who has regular "percussion days" with his students. There's the woman who is always taking notes, and whom you suspect is a reporter, and Elineo, who you've come to detest.

A lot of discussion focuses on the meaning of Stuart's lyrics, and the way the music either emphasizes or contradicts the message of a particular song, but it doesn't take long to realize that for these lonely people, Poor

Ghost is just the mirror that shines their own complicated truths back on themselves.

# 22

You find the perpetual motion of Elineo's hands hard to bear, so you do your best to steer away from him, staying in the house when he's sitting by the firepit, trying to avoid him when he pops up in the dark.

"Do you know about Q?" Elineo asks you one night, as a nearly full moon rises above the jagged black silhouette of the Santa Ynez mountains.

"You mean the conspiracy theory thing?"

"It's not a thing. It's the truth."

"I don't know. It sounds a little . . . *off* to me."

Elineo's hands are flittering around like psychotic bats as he gets closer and closer to you. "So, here's the deal: you can't believe everything you hear in the mainstream media. It's controlled. By— Are you Jewish?"

"No."

"It's controlled by the Jews. And Satanists. And George Soros. Do you know who that is?"

"A rich guy."

"Not just any rich guy. A rich *Democrat*. He controls practically everything. Hillary Clinton, too: she's part of it. The sex-trafficking they do, you wouldn't believe it."

You back away toward the house, but he follows you. "I don't know, Elineo. It sounds pretty far-fetched."

"That's the point. It's so outrageous, most people can't believe it."

"But doesn't Q keep making predictions that don't come true?"

"He's testing the true believers, to see if we have faith. The Storm will come. Believe me."

"Is that why you're here night after night? Something to do with QAnon?"

Elineo's hands go dead for a moment. "I can't say."

"Because I find that kind of creepy. Maybe you shouldn't be here."

His hands explode in motion once more. "Why? Are you afraid of something?"

"I'm afraid of people who aren't in touch with reality."

"Then you don't need to be afraid of me, my brother. I'm *very* in touch with reality. More so than anybody, probably."

Elineo is agitated, but you are too, so you bring up a subject that's been on your mind. "Are you vaccinated?"

That catches him off-guard. "For what?"

"Covid. What else?"

He hesitates, his hands slowing down a bit, like two birds that have been winged, but not badly. "Sure," he says, unconvincingly. "Of course. I totally trust the government."

"No, you don't."

"Dude," he says, "you have no idea who I am."

# 23

Later that evening, the woman you suspect is a reporter sidles over to you by the firepit. She gestures at the moon. "You have a beautiful view here. That's probably why people keep coming back."

You're still a little rattled by your conversation with Elineo, and a little angry at the whole situation. "Or because they're crazy assholes who don't respect private property."

"Whoa. Okay, then."

For some reason you feel bad, as though you've just insulted a dinner guest. "Sorry about that. It's just, these meetings—they have a shelf life. And it may be expiring pretty soon."

"I totally get that. One thing, and forgive me for eavesdropping, but you didn't sound very impressed by the QAnon guy."

"I wasn't. Why? Are you one too?"

"Q? No, of course not."

She sits back down by the firepit, and you take the empty chair next to her. She hugs herself, though it isn't especially cold, and tips her head down so that her long black hair is partially covering her eyes.

You clear your throat. "So, and I don't mean to sound rude, but are you a reporter?"

She defiantly brushes her hair back from her green eyes. "Why would you say that?"

"You're the only person here who takes notes."

"I just want to capture the details. For my diary. I'm a big PG fan."

"Really? What's your favorite album?"

Without hesitation, she says: "*Hillsdale Boulevard*."

"That's not one I really know."

"You probably wouldn't. It's kind of for PG purists. Some people call it 'the literary album.' The instrumentation has been described as 'alt-bluegrass.'"

"Interesting," you say, thinking, *Maybe I'll give that one a pass.* "So, your diary. What have you put in it so far?"

"Just the things I see and hear. A lot of unhappy people trying to get closure on the tragic death of their favorite band."

"Does that include you?"

"Why else would I be here?"

The fire flickering on her pale face makes it difficult to tell whether she is smiling or wincing.

# 24

As you read the Poor Ghost obituaries online, you realize that three of the members of the band are your contemporaries, all of you born in 1962.

You realize, too, that while you have never been a huge fan of their music, the nightly conversations with the fans are changing that somewhat.

Granted, PG is part of American pop culture and definitely something more than sonic wallpaper, but you haven't listened to them with the intensity that you've devoted to, say, the Clash and Talking Heads, U2 and R.E.M., Nirvana and Weezer, Radiohead and the White Stripes—a rather punkish assembly, you realize, for a former insurance salesman.

Still, there is no denying that they are all musical cousins, and for those bands who started in the mid-eighties onward, Poor Ghost is an influence.

Therefore, like many Americans in the autumn of 2021, you began listening to their complete catalog of albums, to wit: *Alas, Poor Ghost!* (1982), *September Pears* (1984), *The Unbearable* (1987), *Scoured* (1991), *Between Religion and Hygiene* (1995), *Ugly Word* (2000), *Defenestration and Decapitation* (2004), *Hillsdale Boulevard* (2007), *Everything Good Is on the Highway* (2011), *A Revelation in Burbank* (2015), and *Fear of Everything* (2020). Forthcoming—and presumably, with their post-death renaissance, sooner rather than later—is their final album, *Old*.

Listening to their catalog on Spotify turns out to be a far richer experience, both lyrically and sonically, than you would have thought possible. Yes, every album has a song or two you don't like, a couple of them even have some real stinkers—what, for instance, were they thinking with "Spaghetti Bolognese and a Can of Coke" and "Outré"?—but you understand now why so many people have flocked to your backyard. Even *Hillsdale Boulevard* turns out to have its moments of poignancy and joy.

There is an entire *world* in all that music. And the idea that it has now ended forever is, for the fans coming to your backyard—in the words of their third album—*unbearable*.

Therefore, while your QAnon encounter with Elineo temporarily makes you want to close down the nightly *salons* as soon as possible, for a time in mid-to-late-October you become as outspoken as any of your guests on the meaning of the bridge lyrics in "Bearded Lady's Mystic Museum"—"Occult for sale / There's a hole in my pail / Hobnail boots / On the guardrail"—or the antiquated sound of the virginals on "Uphill, Both Ways," or Gregg's tasty blues licks in "The Lyon Brothers."

# 25

It is noon, Tuesday, October 19, and you are visiting your father in his small, ill-kept house. Sometimes you bring him lunch from the Mexican restaurant that he can no longer drive to, and he is usually somewhat grateful for the favor.

Today, though, as he is eating his cheese enchilada and refried beans, he's edgy and irritable. He wipes his mouth with his shirtsleeve, asks, "So, that rock-and-roll outfit that crashed? It was in your backyard?"

"That's right, Dad. I've told you that several times."

"And people keep coming into your backyard? Just *trespassing*?"

"Yep."

"Why don't you call the cops?"

"I did, at first, but they stopped coming out. They say they don't have the manpower to handle the situation. And besides, these people aren't violent."

"Well, they sound troublesome."

"They are that. But they're lonely, too. I get that."

"I'll bet you do."

For your father, effective parenting has always meant getting in the last word, even if it's cruel. Still, that particular comment stings, and you wonder how badly you'd feel if you never saw him again. Not too bad, you decide after a moment's reflection.

You sit for a while, staring off, not at each other, but not exactly *not* at each other. The sound on the TV is muted, but on screen two talking heads are snapping at each other. The chyron scrolling beneath them reads: "More questions about vaccines as Biden response flounders."

Your father notices you watching, and he says: "I've seen it on TV. About the fans swarming someone's house. *Your* house. Some of the experts think they might be terrorists."

"They're not terrorists, Dad."

"Well, that's not what the experts say."

"A couple of jerks have shown up, sure, but so far, no terrorists. Who are these experts anyway?"

"Terrorism experts. Very well known."

You don't respond, so the two of you spend a few more minutes sitting in the dusty room, not looking at each other. You notice spiderwebs in each of the ceiling corners, and one of the walls has a long crack snaking horizontally above your father's head.

Finally, you say, "I guess I'd better be going, Dad."

Still not looking at you, he asks, "Do you think your sister would have liked them? This rock-and-roll group?"

"Poor Ghost? How in the world would I know that?"

"Just wondering."

"Why would you even think to wonder that?"

"It's because I think about her."

"She died when she was four, Dad."

He looks at you with the pure vengeance of the unhappy old. "Don't I know that." He wipes his runny nose with his hand. "You too. You know it pretty damned well."

"Yeah," you say, "yes, I do," and you stand up and walk out the door, without asking, as you normally do, what he needs, or telling him when you will return.

# 26

Another evening with the Poor Ghost fans.

A Santa Ana wind blows hot from over the mountains. Dust, with a hint of ash from the crash, blows up from the bottom of the yard. The leaves of the lemon trees whoosh and shiver. The flames from the firepit snake out toward the small group sitting around it.

Tonight's conversation centers on the musical genius of Kerry Cruz. "The thing about Kerry," says the adjunct philosophy professor, "is that he's more than just a bass player. I mean, his lines are very melodic—a lot more than just following Gregg note-for-chord—but what's really memorable about his work is all the instrumentation he brought to the songs. Sitar, dulcimer, marimbas, mellotron, Theremin, glockenspiel? I mean, wow: *glockenspiel*."

"I liken him to Brian Jones of the Stones," says the third-grade teacher, firelight glinting off his glasses, "circa *Between the Buttons*. Or George Harrison on *Revolver* and *Sgt. Pepper's*."

"Or the fifth Beatle: George Martin," replies the philosophy professor.

"I agree," says the reporter, as you now think of her. "Kerry is maybe more of a co-producer for a lot of the albums, even if he's not credited in that role. And I would point to the great producers of rap as his counterparts: RZA, Kanye, Dr. Dre. And of course, Timbaland."

"Come on, now," says a man with a trim mustache, a cowboy hat, and a Texas twang. "Poor Ghost is *not* rap." The man holds his hand atop his cowboy hat so the wind won't blow it off. "Not that I don't admire Timbaland's work on *Fear of Everything*."

"Obviously," says the reporter. "I'm just saying that these producers think outside the box. Kerry does, too."

As the wind whips at everyone's hair and clothing, there's a respectful silence for the brilliance of Kerry Cruz.

Then a fed-up voice rasps: "He's still just the bass player." Sitting in the shadows is Elineo.

"Elineo," you say, "I sometimes wonder if you even *like* Poor Ghost."

"I may not like Poor Ghost, but Poor Ghost likes me."

The wind knocks a plastic patio chair over and carries it halfway across the lawn.

"Elineo," says the reporter. "Enigmatic, as ever."

# 27

One morning someone knocks on your front door. It can't be a Poor Ghost fan, you reason as you walk down the hall: they never bother to knock.

But it *is* a Poor Ghost fan. In fact, it is Elineo. He's wearing a backward baseball cap and a T-shirt showing Jesus doing a handstand on a longboard.

You open the door a crack. "Yes, Elineo? How can I help you?"

"I'm wondering if you want to go surfing?"

You rub your eyes. Are you awake? "Sorry. I don't surf."

"I can teach you. Surfin' for Jesus specializes in training newbies. Maybe the spirit will move you."

"I don't think so."

Elineo furrows his heavy brow. "Dude. Come on. We'll go down to Bedwetters."

You shrug in incomprehension.

"That's what they call Ledbetter's Beach. The surf is totally chill for a beginner."

"Why are you doing this, Elineo? We aren't exactly friends."

"You've opened up your home to me and lots of other people. You know what Jesus said: *Turn the other cheek*."

"I'm not sure that's what he meant."

He taps the thumb and forefinger on his left hand together in a stop-start pattern, as though he is sending someone a message via Morse code. "I just think it's important that I reach out to you on a spiritual level. Before it's too late."

"Before what's too late?"

"Your immortal soul. It's in danger."

"And surfing will save me?"

"It might."

For a minute, you actually consider accepting the invitation. You realize you have never seen Elineo in the daylight before. He looks both scragglier and more intense. You hadn't realized how blue his eyes are. "I don't know, Elineo. I don't have a wetsuit."

"I've got one just your size."

"I'm just not sure."

He pulls a Bible from a capacious pocket of his cargo shorts. "Let's pray on it, dude."

But the sight of the Bible, its leather-bound cover deeply worn, is enough to change your mind. "I'll tell you what: some other time, okay?"

"There may not be another time," he says. As he walks toward the street, he calls over his shoulder: "Remember that."

# TEXTS
## KS & RA

**Thu, Oct 7, 4:10 PM**

How's it going in Poor Ghost Land?

Too soon to tell.

What about your story?

It's weird. There's one really strange individual named Elineo. He's not like a super fan of their actual music, but he sees some kind of Jesus thing in it. He has a surf school called Surfin' for Jesus.

Jesus. I just looked it up online. Very weird. "We shall glorify His works by shredding in His name."

I know.

Be careful.

He's harmless, I'm pretty sure.

What about the guy who owns the house?

He's chill. Kind of reminds me of my dad. Like clueless, but not in a mean way.

Well, take care out there. The whole thing sounds pretty weird.

**Thu, Oct 28, 9:42 AM**

You've been gone a long time. I miss you. LA's not that
far, you know.

> I know. I just keep going back to the crash site every
> night, waiting for something to happen. I've taken a ton of
> notes.

I thought the *New Yorker* paid by the word, not by how
many weeks you worked the story.

> I'm kind of torn right now about where to go with the
> assignment. It's interesting, but maybe not as much as
> I'd thought. If nothing earthshattering happens in the
> next few days, I'll probably go back to the original story
> idea, focusing on the band, with all this fan business at
> the crash site woven into the main piece. And I'd also like
> to see Halloween in Santa Barbara. It's supposed to be
> crazy.

I went once. Remember? A lot of drunk upper-middle-
class college students getting as wild as they're ever likely
to be. Not a pleasant experience.

> Ah.

How's Alyssa?

> She's good. She says hi!
> "Hi" back?

Right. Hi.

# POOR GHOST: AN ORAL HISTORY

## 1988–1992

### *Scoured* (1991)
### US Billboard Peak Position: 1

**JERRY DIMGARTEN:** When you think of the iconic rock-and-roll couples, you think of John and Yoko, Paul and Linda, Sid and Nancy, Ozzy and Sharon, Kurt and Courtney—and definitely Stuart and Holly.

**KERRY CRUZ:** I would not quite put Holly in the category of Nancy and Courtney because, after all, Stuart is still alive, but it was pretty much touch and go there for a couple of years.

**GREGG MORGAN:** Up to that point, for a band, we were mostly focused on making music. Yes, definitely, sex and drugs were present and accounted for, but nothing had ever really put us off course. Even when Stuart broke his arm and leg, that was just a minor setback.

**KERRY CRUZ:** After all the success of *The Unbearable*, we needed some time off. Shane was starting up his own boutique label for Geffen Records. Gregg was jamming around with a lot of bands, doing guest solos on people's albums. He really loved that. I met my wife, Candace, which was great, of course—we're still together after thirty-two years. And Stuart met Holly.

**STUART FISHER:** It's hard to discuss that period in my life. It really is.

**ED WINGFIELD:** They were without a manager for a few months, just kind of drifting, I think. Shane hired me. He was always the business end of the band, from what I could see. Who knows? In a different life, he might have been a Harvard MBA.

**SHANE REED:** We hired Ed just before Stuart got together with Holly. I felt like we needed some direction, but I wasn't counting on this . . . big thing happening in our singer's life. It wasn't exactly part of the business plan.

**KERRY CRUZ:** Stuart fell in love. What can I say? It happens.

**PENNY COOK:** Irv Lichtman ran the gossip column for *Billboard* at the time, but he didn't have much taste for contemporary rock and roll, so he farmed that out to me. That's how I ended up covering Stuart and Holly, and then when it got really big, *People* became interested, so I started writing for them instead.

**TINA ROSS:** Holly was my big sister. She deserves the truth, and if I don't tell it, I don't know who will. So, I won't say she was perfect—no one would believe that anyway—but she wasn't as bad as some of those tabloids made her out to be.

We grew up in southern Illinois, in Mt. Vernon, and she was always the prettiest girl in high school. The smartest, too. Salutatorian. But she hated it there, I can tell you that. Flat farmland. It was like she'd been born into her worst nightmare.

She headed over to New York the day after she graduated, and only came back once, after she was world-famous, and only for a couple of hours. Still couldn't stand the place, so she just left.

**KERRY CRUZ:** Except when he was on stage, Stuart was a fairly shy guy, though, of course, being famous, there were plenty of women. But he was self-protective. On a deep level, it was hard to get through to him unless he really knew you.

That's why it was such a surprise when he got together with Holly. She was this famous model, super-glamorous, and said to be really self-destructive. She wasn't even a very big fan of Poor Ghost, from what I heard.

**TINA ROSS:** People talk about Holly like she was some kind of demon, but that wasn't her. She just lived on the edge. That's how she felt alive. She wasn't trying to hurt anyone, except maybe herself.

**PENNY COOK:** They met at a party in the Hollywood Hills, appropriately, and someone must have introduced them because I didn't get the feeling Stuart Fisher was a big pick-up artist, if you know what I mean. More like the awkward guy who won't look you in the eye.

**STUART FISHER:** When we first met, I just felt like I could talk to her. I think most guys just immediately started making a move on her, but we just talked that first night. And the next. About anything, everything. And she didn't judge me. And I didn't judge her. How many couples can honestly say that about each other?

**PENNY COOK:** You hear that phrase "heroin chic"—well it started with Holly Ross. Those cheekbones, gaunt and lovely. So thin and pale. Some people point to Kate Moss, but that's wrong. They're just getting the names mixed up: Moss and Ross.

**STUART FISHER:** I'd tried heroin a few times, and mostly felt scared by its potential to just consume you. But Holly made me feel like we were in control, like we could quit whenever we wanted. I know that's such a stupid cliché, but that's how it feels when you're high, like nothing can stop you, no matter what you want to do.

**GREGG MORGAN:** We were worried about him, sure. He's with this seemingly suicidal world-famous fashion model, and she's just kind of leading him around by the nose. For a month or two in late 1990, I thought the band was going to break up. He basically refused to communicate with anyone in Poor Ghost. He was in his own little world.

**SHANE REED:** He was acting like kind of a shit. I don't know how else to put it.

**STUART FISHER:** Holly preferred New York to LA, and there was a place in the Bowery, the Pizza Haus, where we used to cop. A lot of unsavory characters in that milieu. What I remember of that time, I don't like to remember.

**ED WINGFIELD:** The band hired me as their manager in August of 1988, and by the time everything went tits-up with Stuart and Holly, I'd talked to him in person twice. Once when the band hired me, and once about a year and a half later when he came to LA demanding more money than was available. He was strung out, and she was there with him. It was a real scene.

I managed to convince Lenny Waronker to advance Stuart ten grand against their next album. I don't know how long it took him to spend it. Probably a week. Or a day.

**PENNY COOK:** Somehow they ended up in Rome, and that obviously made a big impression on Stuart. He and Holly were going everywhere, just like regular tourists, although by that time Stuart was a genuine rock star and Holly was a famous model—that's back when she was on the cover of *Vogue* and *Elle* and *Cosmo.* They were *noticed*.

This was long before the death of Diana, of course, but you had this really creepy feeling that the paparazzi were becoming malicious. And paparazzi were everywhere—they loved Rome because that's basically where it all started, right? They cherished every shot they could take of Holly and Stuart looking fucked up. And there were a lot of those shots.

*People* wanted me to do a feature on this famous couple, so I followed them around Europe for a couple of weeks. It *was* pretty insane, even for the time. Parties, dope, celebrities. Madonna always seemed to be around— she was like the opposite of anything you'd associate with Poor Ghost, but there she was, her arm around Stuart's shoulder, whispering in his ear.

Let's see, who else? There was Tyra Banks and Carol Alt and Tatjana Patitz and Johnny Depp and Matt Dillon. Also, Bono was around some, and Bowie and Iman. And George Michael. I was like, Stuart Fisher is pals with George Michael? *Really?*

**STUART FISHER:** Things were getting more and more intense. Holly and I felt we were creating so much energy that we were just going to make the world explode. One part of me wanted to be writing it all down, to make it into music, but another, more forceful part of me didn't want to miss a second of being with Holly.

Then one morning we were in Berlin, in our hotel, and she told me she was going out for a walk. She just disappeared from my life. I never saw her again.

**TINA ROSS:** "Maybe she's in Paris, / Maybe she's in Rome. / Wherever baby's gotten to / She's never coming home." That about sums it up.

**PENNY COOK:** I was in Berlin when the big split happened. It was considered a real coup at the time, and I covered the drama for all I was worth, though now I mostly feel bad about it. Two people in their twenties with too much thrown at them. It was always going to go wrong.

Anyway, Holly left Berlin—this was just before Halloween in 1990—and my photographer got this one picture of Stuart looking just *devastated*. It's snowing and gray in Berlin, and here's this rock star who's totally wrecked. It's kind of an iconic image of the times.

And then, as everybody knows, Holly flew back to New York, went into a tailspin, and on the tenth of November, 1990, she's dead. OD'd. It was very sad.

**STUART FISHER:** After I heard what happened, I went cold turkey—that was my way of grieving—and when I was clean I wrote twenty songs in a week. Then we made a record: *Scoured*. I still think it's one of our best.

**GREGG MORGAN:** So, none of us really know what's going on with Stuart. We heard he was in rehab or something but that's about it, and then one day in early December, he calls me up, and says he has an album, and he's ready to record it. And he wants to do it *now*.

**ED WINGFIELD:** I told them they should self-produce, but Shane liked their name being attached to a big-name producer. It automatically generated buzz in the music press. Amazingly, Mutt Lange was available for a week in December, and everyone knew that he made hits.

**SHANE REED:** Mutt was known mostly at that time for producing metal acts, especially AC/DC and Def Leppard. It wasn't necessarily a sound I imagined for Poor Ghost, and it wasn't really one that we ended up getting, but I think Mutt knew how to make those rough edges radio-friendly. Also, he was reportedly this kind of Zen guy, and I thought he might be able to connect with Stuart, who was still pretty raw.

**KERRY CRUZ:** I think a lot of our early fans, people who loved *Alas, Poor Ghost!* thought we had drifted too far from the guitar rock we'd started out playing. We had that same sense, that—musically, at least—we had become too clever by half.

**GREGG MORGAN:** Obviously, something was in the air. Partly it was just that those songs Stuart wrote needed a gritty sound. But also bands were getting rid of keyboards and turning up the distortion on their guitars. I loved it, of course.

**KERRY CRUZ:** Gregg had been doing that thing forever that Kurt became famous for with Nirvana—playing the verse without distortion, and then slamming into it for the chorus. He does that a lot on *Scoured*.

**GREGG MORGAN:** It wasn't rocket science. You're just trying to bring some dynamic variation to the song.

**JERRY DIMGARTEN:** About half the songs on the album are set in Rome. They aren't the songs you hear on the radio, but for real Ghost fans, "Wax Monk in a Glass Box" and "Nuns in Rome" are treasures.

**KERRY CRUZ:** I love those lines in "San Callisto": "Where barbarians came to smash the marble tombs / And fragile bones in Christians' dark, dank rooms."

**JERRY DIMGARTEN:** For me, the most poetic lyrics on *Scoured* come at the end of "Circus Maximus": "Nothing now but grass and gravel and windblown trash, / A vacant lot drab and austere, / Where once, in a single day, you might delight / In the death of three or four charioteers."

**ED WINGFIELD:** I would love to know what Mutt thought of the making of *Scoured*, but he hasn't given an interview in how many years? Not for decades, I would imagine.

**TINA ROSS:** I think Holly would have loved the record, especially the title song, which is obviously about her, about how Stuart felt when she was gone, just, you know, *scoured*. Also, she's definitely the inspiration for "Painting Her Toenails Black." I still love hearing him sing those lines: "All the other girls are doing turquoise blue. / They think they're wonderful, they make me want to puke."

**KERRY CRUZ:** If I'm remembering this correctly—and you can check me on Wikipedia—Pearl Jam's *Ten* came out in late August of '91, and then Nirvana's *Nevermind* was a few weeks later. For the record, we put out *Scoured* at the end of *July*.

**GREGG MORGAN:** People say Poor Ghost invented grunge, but really Iggy and the Stooges invented it. Or Sabbath. I mean, it's just punk slowed down, or slow metal speeded up.

**SHANE REED:** We made our bones playing in our friends' garages in Sacramento in the late '70s. Me and Gregg and Shane. Back when volume was our number-one friend. That was definitely grunge before grunge was a thing.

I thought it was hilarious that some critics didn't think Poor Ghost was grunge because we weren't from Seattle. I mean, come on, Jesus—are you seriously telling me that Seattle is grungier than *Sacramento*?

**GREGG MORGAN:** We were already an established band at that time, and I think people saw us as a little more, I don't know, "mainstream artsy" was a term I heard someone use. So, when we just ripped out the guitars and slammed into those songs on *Scoured*, if you didn't know we'd made the album months before the big grunge explosion on MTV, you might think we were just copying these newer bands.

**STUART FISHER:** When the album came out and was successful, suddenly my grief was everyone's grief. That was completely weird, but also comforting in a strange way. Like I wasn't mourning Holly on my own, but with the help of millions of other people.

**ED WINGFIELD:** Honestly, in the autumn of 1990, I was ready to quit. I'd told Shane as much, and he was pretty much at the same place. I thought Poor Ghost were done. Then, suddenly in '91, they are just huge.

**GREGG MORGAN:** One of the things I remember most is the '92 MTV Video Music Awards. We really rocked that night, though it was a disappointing haul in terms of awards. Just "Best Special Effects in a Video."

**JERRY DIMGARTEN:** The artists at the MTV awards—it kind of gives you a sense that whatever bad you may have to say about those days, it wasn't all completely chopped up into algorithm-driven audience chunks. On that one show, you had Van Halen and Tori Amos, David Byrne and Arrested Development, Madonna and the Red Hot Chili Peppers, Nirvana and En Vogue. That particular grouping of artists would probably not be found on most Spotify playlists.

**ED WINGFIELD:** The Grammys that year were not kind to grunge. But sales figures were.

**TINA ROSS:** When I think about my sister now, I try not to think about all that gutter press bullshit. I just listen to *Scoured* and remember that she wasn't just one of the most beautiful women in the world, she was also the muse for one of the best rock albums ever made. It's not enough, obviously, but it's something.

# NEXTDOOR

## RANCHO DE LAS PUMAS • 29 OCT

**Maria Moss**

**Will Poor Ghost just die already?** Am I right that those PG fans were gone for a while? When the cops were here? Honestly, I liked having a police presence in the neighborhood. It made me feel safe. But now? It's been weeks and this band of misfits keeps trooping up to that house every night. They just stay and stay and stay.

**Kelly Gonzales**

Thank God there's not as many as they use to be.

**Elizabeth Hamilton**

Still! OMG they are driving me crazy! Especially the a cappella singing of those stupid songs. This is NOT campfire night!!!

**Nicole Meadows**

I keep calling sheriff dept. and they keep telling me there's nothing they can do. As long as these maniacs don't get violent and aren't too loud it's "a free country." Not free for me though. I am practically a prisoner in my house as they converge on "that man's" house every night. I'm afraid to go in my own front yard.

**Kendra Lozano**

Is he even on Nextdoor?

**Mallory Williams**

I don't think so. If he was, he would know how pi**ed we all are in the neighborhood.


**Anne Schneider**

So many ppl are complaining. Can't we do something to get him out? What about the homeowners assoc.?


**David Silver**

Membership in this neighborhood is voluntary and not legally enforceable.


**Tammy Clark**

One of them came to my door yesterday. Trying to sell me surf lessons. Like a Bible surf camp. I told him no. But at least there is one Christian over there.


**Elizabeth Hamilton**

I have seen the guy you are talking about! His name is something like A Mimeo. Very strange guy but definitely a believer. I told him to come to my church this Sunday but he said he already has one. "The church of surf." I looked online and didn't see it.


**Todd Osborne**

I think he was pulling your leg. He means when he's surfing he's with God. I get it. That's how I feel.


**Danielle Turner**

Hubby last night went up there to the "crash house" to complain. Man answers the door, very polite, invites hubby in, says if hubby can get those people to leave he will be more than happy. Hubby makes a speech, no one leaves. Hubby comes home and has a beer.

## Brian Case

I went up there, too. Same thing. The guy, his name is Caleb, tells me if I can make those PG weirdos go away, more power to me. But they don't listen to anyone. Why should they? The cops don't do anything. The guy (Caleb) doesn't do anything. They're in heaven up there, just smoking dope and having a good time.

# AVIATION ANSWERS

### *When does a flight require a copilot?*

I am not actually a pilot, but I am writing because I'm curious about the fact that there was no copilot on the flight where the band Poor Ghost crashed. Is that suspicious in any way?

### *Answer*

The airplane manual indicates the minimum crew for an aircraft. Typically, on a long flight in a Cessna Citation, the plane that was flown in the incident, there would be both a pilot and a copilot. However, on a noncommercial flight of less than 100 nautical miles, it is not unheard of for a small plane to be flown by a single pilot. Were FAA rules broken on this flight? I don't know, I would have to see the flight manifesto. Is it suspicious? I would say anytime an aircraft crashes in these circumstances, the NTSB is going to be very suspicious.

# THE
# AFTERLIFE
# OF
# POOR GHOST

# 28

By the end of October, you are ready for it to end. You make a vow that Halloween will be the last night.

You acknowledge that you are lonely, which makes you vulnerable to any type of companionship—even from these "misfits," as the Nextdoor folks call them. (You have signed on under an assumed name and are lurking their message boards.) However, you are more than ready for some time to process everything that has happened since the afternoon of September 21.

Fortunately, the number of nightly guests has dwindled to six. Every evening, you can count on the third-grade teacher, the adjunct philosophy professor, the reporter, Elineo, and a retired librarian named Stacey.

And there is one new regular and troubling visitor, Álvaro de Campos—"With an acute accent on the first 'a,'" he says when you ask him to repeat his name. Beneath a coat of grime, he appears to be a very pale man in his fifties or sixties. Álvaro de Campos, who insists on being addressed by his full name, talks often about living in the homeless camp between the Valero station on Calle Real and the freeway, and how the fires they set to keep warm at night keep getting spread by the wind. "I always tell those motherfuckers: 'If we blow that fucking gas station up, we're going with it,'" he says. "But people don't listen. That's the problem."

You've insisted that anyone who visits you remain outside and have proof of at least two doses of the Pfizer or Moderna vaccine—your lone unbreakable rule. Elineo's vaccine card looks sketchy, but, surprisingly, Álvaro de Campos's does not.

Álvaro de Campos has come to prefer your backyard to the homeless camp, and while everyone else—even Elineo—now leaves politely at around 11, Álvaro de Campos has made a little shelter between the rosemary bushes and the junipers, which he sometimes beds in for the night, though he's never there when you wake up in the morning.

Like all your visitors, Álvaro de Campos has strong opinions about not just the Poor Ghost discography, but also the nature of the crash, which is still under investigation.

The night before Halloween, a Saturday, the seven of you sit around the firepit mostly repeating statements you've made dozens of times before. It's a warm evening. Down in the canyon, crickets are chirping. The house lights on the nearby ridges shimmer pleasantly.

When Stacey, the retired librarian, has come to the end of her disquisition on the use of parallel structure in the first three songs of *A Revelation in Burbank*, you stand and loudly clear your throat. "Tomorrow," you announce, "is the end of these visitations." There's a bit of a murmur among your guests, but you continue. "While I've enjoyed your company, it's now been forty days and forty nights since the crash. If we were on Noah's ark, the rain would be stopping tonight. It would be time to start looking for land and unloading the boat."

"That's not an *exact* analogy," the adjunct philosophy professor begins, but you cut him off.

"Doesn't matter. Are you all okay with this?"

"I thought we'd become friends," says the third-grade teacher.

"We have, yes, more or less."

He looks stricken. "This is where I go ever since my wife left me. It's the only place I feel . . . valued."

"I'm sorry if my backyard has come to seem like home to you, but friends don't take advantage of one another, and right now everyone is taking advantage of me. So, are we clear? Tomorrow night is the last night."

There is a long pause, then nods of affirmation from everyone except Elineo and Álvaro de Campos.

"Elineo? What do you say?"

"I say that I don't like it."

"I get that, but I don't care. If you are here on Monday, November the first, I'm going to have you arrested and prosecuted."

"For what?"

"For anything and everything I can think of. Criminal trespassing, for one. Also, fraud, disorderly conduct, stolen property offenses—I *saw* what you took from the crash site—and being a Peeping Tom."

"*What?* That's all bullshit."

"Actually, it's not. I've talked to a lawyer." This is not, strictly speaking, true, although you have been meaning to contact one. Instead, you've simply gone online and written down everything you think might possibly stick.

"Tell me now, or I'm going to break this party up, and start filing those charges tonight."

He holds up his frantic hands. "All right, all right, all right."

"Álvaro de Campos, what about you?"

He grins. "I'm just a homeless guy. What choice do I have when the powerful speak?"

"I'm not *powerful*, obviously, or you wouldn't be here."

It takes a moment for that to sink in, even for you. "Ouch," says the reporter.

"Look," you say, exasperated now, "I feel like I've gone far beyond what any other reasonable person would be expected to do to accommodate you all and your grief. But let's face it: none of us actually *knew* the members of Poor Ghost. They're just a band."

"'For there is nothing covered, that shall not be revealed; neither hid, that shall not be known.'"

"How's that, Elineo?"

"Nothing," he says, walking toward the front gate. "I didn't say a thing."

Shortly afterward, everyone else departs, a few muttering that they won't be back tomorrow.

You stand alone in the darkness as a soft wind rustles the long stems of fountain grass. There's the sound of a small plane going overhead. You look up at the blinking lights, then notice, among the stars, several other planes high and far away. In the distance, a dog barks, but it's not Jackson, you're sure of that.

# 29

Your house is too far up the hill to attract the trick-or-treaters who congregate in the streets down by the elementary school. Still, on Halloween you have a little bowl of Tootsie Rolls at the ready, just in case any children should come along. The Poor Ghost fans, if they show up, will have to fend for themselves.

The sun sets a little after six, and still no one is there. As the lights on the nearby ridges twinkle on, you can hear kids laughing and shouting in the street at the bottom of the canyon. Occasionally someone sets off a firecracker. The big party, down in Isla Vista, is miles away, and, from what you hear on the news, has been tamped down by the police considerably in recent years, even before Covid.

So, it's mostly quiet in the darkness, and you wonder if last night's comment about your "obviously" not wanting people at your home was all you needed to say.

Then, at eight o'clock, they arrive, all six of them at the same time, and you wonder if they are coordinating via group text. Does Álvaro de Campos even have a phone?

Everyone but Álvaro de Campos is costumed, and they are all laughing as they file through the gate into your backyard. The third-grade teacher and the adjunct philosophy professor are dressed as fairy princesses. Each man carries a wand with a sparkly star at the end. Stacey the retired librarian has on a *Squid Game* hoodie with the number 001. The reporter wears plastic fangs and a vampire cape, and Elineo sports a pitchfork and devil horns. You turn on the firepit and everyone takes their favorite patio chair.

You ask: "What are you supposed to be, Álvaro de Campos?"

"A crazy homeless fuck. What else?"

"You nailed it," you say with a smile, but he doesn't smile back.

"And you, Elineo? Ironic costume? Or maybe not?"

"'Be sober, be vigilant, because your adversary the devil, as a roaring lion, walketh about, seeking whom he may devour.'"

For a while, the conversation is convivial. People promise to meet up soon in coffee shops and for dinner. The third-grade teacher and Stacey the retired librarian appear to be making a date to see *The French Dispatch*. The reporter has brought two gallon jugs of Carlo Rossi vin rosé—"Reminds me of high school," she says jovially—and everyone but Elineo is gamely drinking away.

Then suddenly the mood changes. You don't know why, until you turn around from a conversation with the adjunct philosophy professor about the harmonies on "Sacramento Luau" and see that Elineo is standing on the edge of the firepit. With his devil horns and pitchfork, he does, indeed, look Satanic.

"Brothers and sisters," he says in a voice that would not be amiss coming from a preacher, "if I could have your attention, please."

He waits until everyone, including you, takes a seat.

"I come costumed as the Prince of Darkness that you may remember the evil you must resist."

"Elineo loves paradoxes," the reporter says.

He ignores her. "And now I have a revelation for you, brothers and sisters. It's a revelation for Santa Barbara and for the entire world. If you have your phones with you, I would ask that you take them out and start live-streaming."

Everyone except you and Álvaro de Campos does as they are told.

"Brothers and sisters," he begins again, his voice a little louder and shriller, "don't let my devil costume fool you: I speak the words of the Lord."

"Amen," says the third-grade teacher, lightheartedly, but no one else laughs.

Elineo continues, his face serious and determined. His hands are strangely calm. "There are some things many of you probably do not know. These are truths that only those with their ears cleansed can hear. For instance, mass shootings are a false flag by the cabal to convince you that they are the innocent ones. Friends, they are not innocent. They are planning to take over the world. Stuart Fisher was aware of this, and he was attempting to stop the Satanic revolution led by Hillary Clinton, Barack Obama, and George Soros."

There's a sprinkling of derisive laughter, a shouted "Preach it, Elineo!" and "That's crazy."

"You don't believe me? Of course you don't, sheeple. But here's the thing. If you take the first letters of each line in all the Poor Ghost songs and arrange them using a Fibonacci sequence, going from the seventh number of the sequence, then returning to the first Fibonacci number using 'Ugly Word' as your starting point, then back again once more, stopping at 'Fear of Everything,' you'll find that Stuart not only foresees his own death, he actually names his killer."

"Elineo," says the reporter, "I don't mean to be rude, but this is stupid."

"O ye of little faith."

"O ye of little brains," she replies.

"'Verily I say unto you, If ye have faith, and doubt not, ye shall say unto this mountain, Be thou removed, and be thou cast into the sea, and it shall be done.'"

"Is that the motto of your surfing school?" the adjunct philosophy professor calls out.

"It's the Golden Ratio, people. Stuart knew all about it."

"Just get to the big reveal, Elineo," the reporter says impatiently. "Who killed Stuart Fisher?"

Elineo stares up at the sky, his hands wriggling wildly now, then he says, "Stuart's killer is here among us." He stares straight at you.

You stand up. "*Me?* Are you suggesting that I killed Stuart Fisher?"

"All signs point to Yes, Caleb."

"How in the fuck did I do that, Elineo? Did I *lure* Poor Ghost's plane to my house?"

"This is your backyard, isn't it?"

"In which you are an unwelcome guest."

"I have no doubt about that. But first, I say to thee all: Caleb Crane stands before you on trial."

"I'm not on trial, Elineo. You're not a judge. You're a nutjob. A crazy person. Get the hell out of here!"

"Let our friends be the jury after I present my case."

You look around. The people with phones still have them out, recording everything. You suspect that they are secretly hoping something memorable, even horrible, will happen. Why else have they been coming all this time?

There is a long pause as you and Elineo wait to see how the crowd will go.

Then Álvaro de Campos is running across the patio, straight at you. "Kill the bastard!" he shouts.

The others, Elineo included, stand dumbfounded, as you push back your chair and stumble onto the lawn.

When he is about five feet away, Álvaro de Campos slows down and you get up and begin awkwardly circling each other. From his coat, he pulls what looks like a steak knife. "I'm going to carve you up," he growls. "You *traitor*."

He lunges at you, and you fall to the grass, wet with dew, rolling away just as he thrusts his knife into the sod where, moments ago, was your heart.

You get to your feet. Álvaro de Campos pulls the knife out of the lawn and edges toward you. "This time," he says, "I won't miss."

But he never gets the chance. Stacey the retired librarian comes up behind him with a half-full gallon of Carlo Rossi vin rosé and wallops Álvaro de Campos on the back of the head.

It's as if everyone has been released from a spell. The others rush to your assistance. Elineo jumps down from the firepit to look after Álvaro de Campos, who has fallen into a pool of darkness by the rosemary bushes.

Phones are still out, and those not videoing the scene are calling 911.

Chaos reigns for several minutes. People talk over and against and through one another. Somewhere nearby, a string of firecrackers goes off.

Then Stacey the retired librarian shouts: "Where is he? What happened to Álvaro de Campos?"

Elineo looks supremely guilty. "I don't know. He's gone. I'll go find him."

"No way," says the reporter. "You stay right here, Elineo. You're the one who caused all this shit."

But Elineo ignores her and sprints for the front yard. No one bothers to chase him.

As you stand there in the semi-darkness of the firepit light, you realize your pants are warm. You have wet yourself. For some reason, that seems the most traumatic incident of the entire night. "I have to go inside for a minute," you say. "Everyone else stay here until the cops come."

You're in and out in three minutes, but when you return, only the reporter and Stacey the retired librarian remain.

"Don't ask," says the reporter. "Suddenly, they had something better to do. But you can bet their videos will be all over Facebook and Instagram."

"Thank you," you tell your savior. "You probably saved my life."

"I don't know about that," Stacey says, though she clearly agrees with you. "I was trying to help out."

It's Halloween night, so most of the area's law enforcement is policing college students. As you wait for someone to arrive, the three of you quietly sip the sickly-sweet wine, exhausted of conversation.

After about an hour, a lone sheriff's deputy shows up to take statements. You mention several times that Álvaro de Campos talked about living in a homeless encampment by the Valero station. The deputy tells you they'll look into it as soon as possible, and as soon as he leaves, your two guests follow him out.

"Don't worry," the retired librarian calls from the driveway. "I have a feeling no one will be coming back here for a long, long time."

# 30

The retired librarian is right, as it turns out. Emptiness reigns in your backyard.

The next day is foggy in the morning, with low clouds in the afternoon. You wander around the house and backyard feeling both relieved that something bad has finally happened, and already a tad nostalgic for the Poor Ghost gatherings.

That night, a Monday, a sheriff's cruiser parks out front until morning, but there is no one to scare away, and he tells you he won't be back on Tuesday night, which turns out to be equally uneventful.

On Wednesday, you get your Pfizer booster shot at CVS. You feel achy that evening, and anxious, but none of the PG folks show up.

The next night, nothing also.

And the next and the next and the next.

# SANTA BARBARA COUNTY SHERIFF'S OFFICE

## Latest News

### Detectives Arrest Unhoused Person for Assault with a Deadly Weapon

### Posted November 1, 2021

Santa Barbara, Calif.—At 7:29 a.m. today, sheriff's deputies arrested 56-year-old Ricardo Reis, aka Álvaro de Campos, of Goleta for assault with a deadly weapon at 1408 Camino Palomino on October 31, 2021, at approximately 8:45 p.m. Reis attacked the homeowner, Caleb Crane, with a knife before fleeing the scene.

Deputies located the man in a camp for unhoused people near the Valero gas station on Calle Real. The knife was not recovered.

Reis was booked at the Main Jail for criminal threats (felony) and assault with a deadly weapon (felony). He is being held on $50,000 bail.

Deputies are also seeking 38-year-old Elineo Amis in connection with a criminal incitement charge.

filed under: Breaking News, General

# TEXTS
## KS & RA

**Mon, Nov 1, 11:51 AM**

How was Halloween with the college kids? Was it the
party you expected?

Definitely not. Didn't you hear? Some guy attacked the
homeowner, Caleb.

Is he okay?

I think so, physically at least. But it was intense. I was
there.

No way!

I felt so bad for him. He's been so nice to everybody, then
this dude goes fucking berserk. I had this weird flash
when it was happening that the guy was trying to kill my
dad.

Fuck.

I know. They caught the guy this morning. But I don't
know if this story needs me right now. It's all so confusing.
Anyway, I'm coming back to LA today.

Yay!!! Sorry about the story, but I was going to drive up
there if you weren't coming down this week.

It will be great to see you.

u2! So, what about the story? Is it totally dead? Are you
still going to try and write something?

Something maybe. Hopefully.

# POOR GHOST: AN ORAL HISTORY

## 1993–1998

### *Between Religion and Hygiene* (1995)
### US Billboard Peak Position: 35

**SHANE REED:** In the summer of '93, we did something we hadn't done since we were starting out, which was to tour without an album to support. We were the headliners, and we only had to play an hour show. And it was a lot of money.

**KERRY CRUZ:** We were part of that ill-fated Rock Is Rock tour that went for nine performances before imploding. It was Red Hot Chili Peppers, the Cure, Megadeth, Queensrÿche, the Beastie Boys and Soundgarden. And us. Everyone was promised exorbitant amounts of money and very little work. It was always at some professional football stadium, and it would start at eleven in the morning and end twelve hours later. There was a lot of downtime between the music, and the promoters used it to sell all sorts of shit: food and booze, merch, whatever they could hawk.

**GREGG MORGAN:** The guys in Megadeth were actually quite polite and well-behaved. Everyone else was an asshole.

**STUART FISHER:** That was kind of a low point for me, that tour. It felt like we were a commodity, and we knew it, but we were just going along with it for the money. I wanted the tour to be over, although obviously no one wanted that last concert to go so wrong.

**KERRY CRUZ:** It was early evening on that last night. I remember thinking how cool the clouds looked, the way the sun hit them. All orange and purple and red. In fact, Anthony Kiedis commented on that in the middle of the Peppers' set. He yelled out something like, "Fucking rad sunset!" and the crowd went crazy.

**GREGG MORGAN:** That sunset seemed like a good omen, but it wasn't. Just as the sun went down, this fan got up on stage and grabbed Kiedis's mic and started singing "Give It Away," and a bouncer came onstage—I don't know why I was watching their show, but I was, Kerry and I were—and anyway the bouncer just slams into the dude. The bouncer was this huge, bearded, burly guy, and the dude was really scrawny, and the dude's head hit the stage, hard, and well, as everyone knows, he died.

**KERRY CRUZ:** For a moment, the crowd just went totally silent. Then they started cheering, of course, like we were in the Roman Colosseum, or something. But the Peppers stopped playing, and the medics came on, and somebody thought to dim the stage lights, and then suddenly there were two simultaneous surges: one toward the exit, and one toward the stage. People were all mixed together, falling, trampling each other.

**GREGG MORGAN:** It was pandemonium.

**KERRY CRUZ:** Five people ended up dying, plus the dude who rushed the stage.

**SHANE REED:** That was it, of course. The end of the tour.

**ED WINGFIELD:** *Rolling Stone* called it "The Altamont of the '90s." Unfair, in my opinion, and of course PG wasn't in any way involved, but we knew we were going to have to take a break. Give it some time. Do some mourning—or at least *appear* to be doing some mourning.

**STUART FISHER:** I spent most of 1994 in an A-frame cabin in South Lake Tahoe writing the songs for *Between Religion and Hygiene*.

**JERRY DIMGARTEN:** That may be one of the most unlikely titles ever for a major-label album: *Between Religion and Hygiene*. For comparison, I'm thinking of *The Kinks Are the Village Green Preservation Society* and Fishbone's *Give a Monkey a Brain and He'll Swear He's the Center of the*

*Universe*, or Limp Bizkit's *Chocolate Starfish and the Hot Dog Flavored Water*. It's like the band is daring you to buy their album.

**STUART FISHER:** The title actually comes from something Prince Albert said: "The power of art lies somewhere between religion and hygiene." I thought that was pretty profound for a prince.

**KERRY CRUZ:** "The Biggest Mistake You've Ever Made" was a song written for *Scoured*, but somehow we never got around to recording it.

**GREGG MORGAN:** We already had fourteen songs we liked for *Scoured*, and we knew we had a couple of hits, so we sort of put "Biggest Mistake" in the "Save for Later" pile. We had no idea it was going to be a hit.

**SHANE REED:** "Biggest Mistake" pretty much saved that album from total obscurity.

**STUART FISHER:** Lyrically, I would say that album represents one of my best efforts. "Biggest Mistake" notwithstanding—that one felt a little too close to "Spaghetti Bolognese."

**KERRY CRUZ:** "Hey mister, I'm not your sister, / If you kissed her, it wasn't me." For some reason those lines crack me up.

**STUART FISHER:** For most of the album, I was writing about politics with what I thought was a pretty sure hand. Those two songs about the genocide in Rwanda—"Spring Flowers" and "Kigali"—I'm still proud of them.

**GREGG MORGAN:** Musically, the album was a little too mellow for my taste. I think the fans agreed. And we self-produced for the first and only time, which was not a success. The sound was kind of muddy.

**KERRY CRUZ:** I played more keyboards on that album than any other. An old Mellotron, a tonewheel organ, a Roland D-50 my wife bought me for my birthday. It made for a pretty lush sound. I wish we'd developed that vibe on other albums. But I am not the master of the band.

**SHANE REED:** We toured for about a month in the spring of '96, but it felt like we weren't the hot shit thing anymore, so Ed canceled the last couple of dates and said we were going on hiatus.

**ED WINGFIELD:** That hiatus thing was my idea. Their concerts were not selling out, and I didn't like the idea of people seeing them as losers. I thought "a hiatus" might generate some publicity, like, "Is Poor Ghost breaking up?" It worked, sort of. It made their fans, at least, appreciate them again.

**GREGG MORGAN:** After that tour was when I did my first album outside of Poor Ghost. With Joe Satriani. *Shredder's Ball.*

**KERRY CRUZ:** A lot of solos on *Shredder's Ball.* Pretty much only solos, in fact.

**GREGG MORGAN:** It was fun just to play guitar and not worry about the image of the band, or having to stop in the middle of a good musical idea because it was time for the third verse. Joe and I just shredded, period.

**STUART FISHER:** I spent 1997 in London, and 1998 on Bowen Island, near Vancouver. In London, I hung out a lot with Richard Ashcroft from The Verve and Jarvis Cocker from Pulp. On Bowen, I didn't hang out with anyone.

**ED WINGFIELD:** Some managers, they want the band to have a new album every year or two, and for some bands that makes financial, and maybe even artistic, sense. But I always felt PG did better with those extended stays away from the charts.

For one thing, their back catalog always sold well. This was in the time of CDs, but before people were ripping copies of albums on CD-ROMs. Cassette tapes were basically dead, so if you wanted to listen to an album, you bought it, or borrowed it from somebody. One thing I always liked about CDs was how easily they scratched. And it wasn't like a vinyl record, where the needle would probably skip over the scratch and keep playing. No, if you got a scratch on your CD, it was pretty much fucked up and you'd have to buy a new one. That gave me a good laugh!

And their music benefited from time off. It wasn't just that it gave Stuart time to write new material, or for Kerry to learn a new instrument, or Gregg to come up with some new way to shred on his guitar. It also allowed them to keep existing as a band without being tied too much to a single era. And eras in pop music can be counted in increments of less than five years.

Sure, they were always going to be classified as something like alternative rock, but they started out as more of a punk band, then they were kind of new wave, then grunge, and so on, and so forth. And they all—not just Stuart—they *all* listened to a lot of music, and they could spot a trend when it was just starting. They were like the Beatles in that regard, and in the same way as the Fab Four, PG's music was so much their own that it didn't feel like they were stealing from somebody else.

Bottom line: as long as the Ghost put out a new album every four or five years, they were golden.

# SANTA BARBARA CHRONICLE

**Letters to the Sage**

**Today's Topic: Poor Ghost in Santa Barbara**

**Dear Santa Barbara Sage,** I know this may seem petty, but I feel like over the past two months, the plane crash of Poor Ghost has been dominating the news, especially here in Santa Barbara. My husband has been a big fan of the band since their first album back in the '80s, and he's been moping around the house a lot, listening to their songs on his noise-canceling headphones. He totally blocks me out. It's worse than the way our daughter acted when the rapper Mac Miller died! What do I do to get my husband to pay attention to me again—if you know what I mean??
—*Wife of MIA*

**Dear Wife of MIA:** Let me come out and say it: I, too, am a huge PG fan. They were one of the first concerts I ever attended, in LA back in 1984. So I sympathize with your Missing in Action husband. That said, I would gently confront him with two big reality checks. Number One, while it is sad to lose great artists, there are a lot bigger things to be worried about right now: the end of habitable life on our planet, a seemingly unending pandemic, the violence inherent in institutionalized racism, and the potential destruction of American democracy all come to mind! Number Two, if his attention doesn't return to you pretty soon, you may start paying attention to other people, and other people may start paying attention to you. There's a particular Sage I know who might be interested in meeting up! Kidding!! Maybe!!! ;-)

*

**Hi Sage,** My brother "Peter" (not his real name) is a professor (adjunct) here in town, and he was spending a lot of time at that house where Poor Ghost's plane crashed. As you may have heard, someone (homeless) attacked the nice man who was letting people congregate in his backyard to discuss their feelings for PG. Now "Peter" is obsessed with finding the attacker, and the person who apparently egged him on. He is acting like he's some kind of a private detective, but he's not. He's not teaching his classes and I'm worried that he's going to lose his job (no tenure). Help!

—*Worried in Goleta*

**Dear Worried in Goleta:** Who knew that the demise of Poor Ghost would bring out so many strong feelings in people? When the Beatles broke up, people were sad, but they got over it. Maybe a better example is the death of Jerry Garcia in 1995. The Grateful Dead supposedly called it quits afterwards, but their fans just couldn't move on, and today the remaining members still sell out huge concerts when playing "reunion" tours. Maybe our town is a mecca for that kind of vibe. As you probably know, at the Santa Barbara Bowl, they even have the Jerry Garcia Glen, with a giant statue of his hand—no middle finger, he lost it as a child. Possibly there will be a Poor Ghost memorial where people can go to sit with their feelings. Maybe Kerry Cruz will try to keep the band going, who knows?—he's really good at keyboard. As far as your brother's situation, I would remind him that if he loses his job, he won't be able to pay his rent or eat.

# "HILLSDALE BOULEVARD"—THE POOR GHOST MESSAGE BOARD

## Nov. 8, 2021

**sempiternalpaul**

It's been more than one and a half months and still we don't have any answers about the plane crash. Is there a government cover-up?

**alivenburbank**

Umm, if it walks like a duck, then you'd fucking better believe there is.

**Dannyndahaus**

I keep hearing mechanical malfunction. Remember that the right engine came off the plane. The #4 cylinder had a fractured exhaust valve. No one wants to talk about it because it's a structural flaw in the Cessna Citation. Enormous lawsuit potential.

**ghostkoan**

Why is no one mentioning Air Traffic Control? This plane is 4 miles off course. What if ATC sends the pilot in a big loop around the airport, knowing there are downdrafts or some other dangerous weather condition? Someone who hates PG and wants to end the band. Whoever was on duty at the Santa Barbara airport that afternoon is who they should be talking to.

**5bagsofROCK**

Somebody sabotaged something. That much is pretty clear. It's just the who and the what they need to identify.

## AllMayBeWell

A pilot friend of mine calls it the Swiss cheese factor. A bunch of holes line up, and boom, down goes the plane. Pilot error, mechanical failure, weather, whatever. It's not just one cause, it's a deadly combination.

# THE
# AFTERLIFE
# OF
# POOR GHOST

# 31

Your daughter, Victoria, has found it difficult to communicate with you since the crash. You still text each other, but you haven't felt this distant from her since she was a rebellious late teenager. She's been seeing a therapist in Thousand Oaks, and she hasn't felt comfortable returning to the site of her trauma. Knowing the place has been crawling with strangers made it even less appealing.

However, now that those strangers are gone, she's back, sitting in her car in your driveway, listening to—can it be?—Poor Ghost's *Between Religion and Hygiene*, a record, you've learned, that is mostly beloved by PG devotees and certain white suburbanites who came of age in the middle '90s.

You tap on the window, and she looks surprised to see you, as though you weren't standing in the driveway of your own house.

She turns off the music, gets out of the car, and gives you a tepid hug.

Inside, you've put Apple TV on pause. You click off the screensaver—drone footage of Dubai at night—and the screen shows a grainy black-and-white shot of people gathered for a speech.

"What are you watching, Dad?"

"*Zelig.*"

"*Seriously?* You realize Woody Allen's been canceled, right?"

"I know, I know, but this is one of my favorites. I love the way he keeps popping up during all those unlikely historical events."

"Well, I'm not going to watch Woody Allen. I can drive back home, if that's what you want."

"Of course not," you say, turning off the television. "Let's sit out back."

It's late afternoon. The air is dry and warm. Bees are buzzing in the light purple flowers of the rosemary bushes. All around the yard, the yellow, orange, and red spikes of the torch lilies are in bloom. "I forgot how weird-looking those things are," she says.

"They grow like weeds too. Really hardy. Someone told me another name for them is red hot pokers."

"Who told you that, Dad? One of those psychopath Poor Ghost fans?"

"Well, actually, I guess so."

"That was so weird of you to let them be here. What were you thinking?"

"I'm not sure. It seemed like it just happened. Like a big wave coming in—you just have to duck and wait for it to go over you."

But Victoria is only half-listening. She's made her way to the edge of the lawn and is peering down on the crash site. "No sign of Jackson?"

"I'm afraid not. I keep thinking someone's adopted him. He was, is, a very sweet dog."

She nods, unconvinced. "It's weird without the pine tree down there. Just some charred grass. You'd never know what happened."

"I suppose not. I must admit, it's already starting to feel like something from the distant past. Or like a movie you watch, where you forget big chunks of it after a few days."

Victoria nods. "It's worth forgetting, I'd say."

As afternoon fades into evening and then into night, you and Victoria reminisce about family trips and her briefly rebellious senior year in high school and Connie's cartooning and whatever else comes to mind. At some point, you decide to roast marshmallows over the firepit, but the twigs you broke off from the juniper bushes keep catching fire, or the marshmallows plop off into the flames.

"Who would have thought we'd miss wire coat hangers so badly?" you say.

"We'll be needing them even more if the Supreme Court keeps heading where it's going," she says. "And what about the non-progress on climate change? And the anti-vaxxers, not to mention all the viciousness in the world. It's just disgusting."

"I can't say I don't agree."

"And meanwhile, no offense to your friends, but some people are spending their lives moping over the death of a rock band. Unbelievable."

"Your mom would have had some good material for her cartoons."

"I don't think so. I think she'd be too depressed to draw anything."

You shrug. Frankly, you have no idea how Connie would have responded to all the months she's missed. Like everyone else on earth, you suppose—some good days, some bad.

"What do you miss most about her?" your daughter asks.

"Her sense of humor, definitely. It's true she could sink down into a deep depression, but it never lasted very long. Mostly when people behaved badly, she was just *disappointed*. She thought they were capable of doing better. I think a lot of her cartoons were about nudging us to become our better selves."

"Like the one where the rat's quoting Marie Kondo to the elephant?"

You chuckle. "I guess so. She wasn't a scold, your mom. Above all, she just wanted to make people laugh."

The two of you are quiet for a while, watching the moon rise above the Santa Ynez mountains. At first, it looks like a giant headlight just below the ridge, then there's the hint of a curve, and in a matter of minutes it's there, waxing and luminous.

Victoria says: "It's strange to think how fast the earth is revolving. You don't really notice it until you sit still."

You nod, afraid to say anything that will break the spell.

# 32

---

Victoria leaves the next morning, and you promise to stay in touch more faithfully. For a few days you feel hopeful, but then your mood takes a sudden turn. Maybe it's the crows that get you thinking about death—they seem to be flocking more frequently to the neighbor's oak tree, with the stragglers perching on your eaves.

Possibly it's the solitude that comes after being thrown together with people so different from you. Now that they're gone, you can't help thinking about the absolute hole left in your life by your wife's death. As hard as it is to believe, you long for the PG fans' chatter, their inanities and strangely contagious esprit de corps.

You don't miss Elineo, of course, or that madman Álvaro de Campos, who you've read has been set free. What sort of person, you wonder, would go his bail? In fact, with both Elineo and Álvaro de Campos in the wind, you don't feel especially safe. You lock your doors before the sun sets and make sure all the windows are closed up tight.

You go to sleep with a white noise machine you bought online that's intended for fussy babies. Sometimes that's what you feel like, and you're grateful for the sonic whitewash that helps drown out the lonely noises in your head.

Still, there are nights when flashes come back to you of your childhood. Your little sister. Her wispy blond hair. You looking over her shoulder as she reached out and stuck her finger into the darkness.

Almost as bad are the nights when you dream in what Connie called "Insuranceeze." *In case the mortgagor or owner shall fail to pay any premium due. . . . Unless the loss is due to neglect, wear and tear, nuclear hazard, war and military action. . . . For purposes of this provision, a plumbing system or household appliance does not include a sump, a sump pump, or related equipment. . . .* Why do all these phrases still stick in your head? What does this useless retention say about you?

One night, the week before Thanksgiving, you are awakened by what sounds like your wife's voice calling your name. You pull the covers up to your chin, skin prickling, equal parts eager to find her, and petrified of doing so. The white-noise machine is making its guttural *whoosh*.

You wait a minute to see if the voice will speak again. When it doesn't, you whisper, "Hello? Connie?"

Nothing. You get up, shivering, though it's not cold, open the bedroom door, and walk down the hall out into the living room. Through the picture windows, you can see fog outside, suffused with moonlight.

"Connie," you repeat, a little louder, which makes you feel a bit foolish. "I'm here, if you want to talk."

Nothing.

Then the refrigerator clicks on, which startles you, but the room is far from dark. There's the blue light from the microwave clock, and the gray light from the oven clock, and the blue and white lights blinking on the router and the modem. In fact, it feels almost peaceful.

You lie down on the couch and pull the throw blanket across your chest and immediately fall into a deep and restful sleep.

# 33

The next night, you lie in bed staring at the darkened ceiling, alternately trying to conjure up Connie's ghostly voice, and wondering if it might be possible to reinsert yourself into the insurance game. Yes, it was often deadly dull, and the increasing pressure to grow your business was no fun, and the irate clients were becoming more numerous. Still, it was a reason to get out of bed in the morning and something to do during the day.

Moreover, you were good at it. In some deep core, you didn't care whether or not you wrote the policy, and that made your customers trust you, almost as if you were one of them.

Of course, the events of the last year and a half may have deadened your sales magic. You are thinking this, sleepy, but very definitely awake, when you hear a dog barking in what sounds like the backyard. You realize you've forgotten to turn on the white-noise machine, so the barking comes clearly through your window, which tonight you've left a half-inch open.

For the second night in a row, you open your bedroom door and head down the hall to face your ghosts.

You pull open the sliding glass door and step out onto the cool concrete of the patio. The fog is thicker tonight. There's a yip down at the bottom of the yard. It's been two months since you last heard Jackson bark. Maybe it's him, maybe it's just a coyote nosing around.

"Jackson!" you call out in full voice, though it's after midnight in your quiet neighborhood. And then again: "Jackson! Come here, boy!"

You move over to the rickety wooden stairs and take a couple of steps toward the unseen animal. There's a combination growl-bark—it *does* sound like a noise Jackson used to make—and a black shape crosses in the fog, just enough for you to register that it's canine, or possibly vulpine, and then it's gone.

You go back to bed, but two ghosts in two nights is a lot, and you don't fall asleep until sometime after three.

# 34

Late the next morning, you are awakened by the doorbell's persistent ringing. Groggy, you wonder for a moment if it's a third ghost—or, worse, Elineo or Álvaro de Campos.

You go into the living room and call out, "Who is it?"

"It's me. The reporter."

You return to the bedroom and pull on a pair of pants and a T-shirt that says, "Insurance: You Don't Know You Need It Until You Do." When you open the door, she walks in and sits down on the couch without a word.

"Come in," you say, trying unsuccessfully to sound sarcastic. She smiles, but says nothing, and you sit down in a chair across from her and say, "I just realized I have no idea what your name is."

"Kelsey," she says. "Kelsey Symmons, with a 'y.' I kind of kept it a secret because I didn't want people googling me." Her long black hair is pulled back, and her green eyes are sharp, but the rest of her face, which you've rarely seen in full light, is pretty, but . . . blurry is the only word you can think of. It is as though you're seeing her through the lens of a camera that is slightly out of focus.

"So, you've been writing about this all along?"

"I'm trying, but I'd like to do it with your permission."

"I see. Where would it be published?"

"It *was* going to be for the *New Yorker*, but I'm afraid they've lost interest."

"And now?"

"Now it's kind of a freelance, on-spec sort of thing."

"So, no publisher?"

"Basically. But I still want to write it. I'm interested in the way the crash brought all those people together at your house, and then how hospitable you were, when I can imagine most people would have kicked everyone out after a night or two." She takes out her phone and swipes to the Voice Memos app. "Do you mind?"

"I guess not."

"Thank you." She taps *Record* and says "I'm here with Caleb Crane in his home on the morning of Friday, November 19, 2021. Are those details correct, Mr. Crane?"

"They are."

"I'd like to start by asking why you were so generous to the people who flooded your home? What made you want to welcome them?"

You pause for a moment, thinking of how much and how often you didn't want them there, but instead you say: "My wife died of Covid in May 2020. I was lonely. That was the main reason."

"I'm so sorry to hear that. Would you mind telling me a little about what happened?"

You do, and the two of you converse for two hours, recapping, clarifying, agreeing, and dissenting about what has happened since September 21. Finally, you tell Kelsey Symmons: "Enough, okay? That's enough for one day."

She consents, pushes Stop on her app, then says, "I went online and found out more about Álvaro de Campos. Did you look him up?"

"No. I just wanted to put all that behind me."

"Okay, so his name is actually one of the—they're called 'heteronyms'—that the Portuguese writer Fernando Pessoa gave himself. He was famous for writing in the personae of other people."

"That's weird."

"It is, but not as weird as this: The name that Álvaro de Campos was booked under at the county jail was Ricardo Reis, which is actually another one of Pessoa's heteronyms."

"So, the guy is obsessed."

"Yeah, but what's his real name? I'd like to know."

"You're a reporter. Surely you can find out."

"You'd think so, but he's disappeared. Did the sheriff's office tell you they'd let him out on bail?"

"I read it in the *Chronicle*."

"Keep an eye out for him," she says as she gathers up her things and prepares to leave. "He seemed like a total psycho to me."

# 35

Your father is snoring in his chair—his nose hairs could certainly use a trim—while you read the *New York Times* on your phone. It's all about the seventeen-year-old in Wisconsin who was acquitted of murder because he shot his three victims in self-defense, although they were carrying nothing more dangerous than a skateboard and a handful of candy. And "victims" apparently isn't the right word. The judge insisted that the dead only be referred to as "looters" and "rioters" in his courtroom.

The moment he wakes from his nap, your father snaps at you, as though he has been reading the story in his sleep: "Thank God that jury in Wisconsin did the right thing. Can you imagine locking up that poor boy just because he was trying to defend his own life?"

"No talking about crazy shit, Dad. Remember? No politics."

"Everything is politics."

"Okay, that's like a slogan from the Left. You can't just repurpose liberal sayings in the service of fascism."

"Who says?"

"All right, I'm officially changing this conversation. How have you been doing? How is Meals on Wheels?"

"They're always late. The food's cold, and it's not salty enough. And they're not friendly. I can barely understand what they're saying."

You look at your father more closely—eyebrows wild, white hair shaved too short by some well-meaning Meals on Wheels delivery person, a lower front tooth missing. When did he get so old and unpleasant? And why? Is it some genetic predisposition that will haunt you, too? Was it something you did, or failed to do?

"So, Victoria and I are going to come over for Thanksgiving. This coming Thursday."

"Who's Victoria?"

"Your granddaughter. My daughter."

"I don't remember her."

"Dad, she was up here just a couple of days ago. She said she was going to see you on her way home to Thousand Oaks."

He seems to be remembering something. "I don't know. Maybe she did."

"Well, anyway, we'll be here, and we'll have a grand old time."

Your father blows his nose on his shirtsleeve. "I seriously doubt that."

# 36

The Monday before Thanksgiving, the doorbell rings. It's two NTSB investigators you've never seen before: a smartly dressed African American woman in her forties, and a clean-cut white guy about ten years younger. They tell you they want to go over your testimony one more time, and you invite them into the living room. Outside the picture window, goldfinches dart in and out of the rosemary bushes. In the distance, Santa Cruz Island is shrouded in a light fog.

"So, we just want to hear it again," the woman says. "In your own words." Her voice is clipped and curt—she could be skeptical, or disgusted, or bored. Or all three. She takes out an old-fashioned spiral notepad.

"I don't think my words are going to change. Unless I've forgotten something. Whatever I told the investigators the night it happened is surely much more accurate than whatever I remember almost two months later."

"Be that as it may," she says, "indulge us."

"Okay, I was sitting here in the living room, right there on the couch, when I heard this loud roar, and then I saw the plane out the window over there. Just for a second."

"Was the plane on fire when you saw it out the window?"

"I don't think so. My daughter was here, and we both ran down to the bottom of the yard. And it was definitely on fire then, but not all of it. Not the rear part. It was in two pieces. Come on, I'll show you."

The three of you go out back and take the wooden steps down to the crash site, where the pine tree once was. The gopher mounds on the hillside look like pellet holes from a shotgun blast. The grass is dead and dry and yellow. From the street below comes the sound of someone wheeling a trashcan across a driveway. Small birds sing in the pepper tree in Barton's backyard.

"It happened here?" the woman asks.

"Surely you've seen the photos and videos?"

She ignores the question. "And you can confirm that our investigators canvassed the crash site."

"Slightly. They were here for a couple of days." You gesture with your arm to indicate a large circle. "They looked all through the avocado orchard, and in the neighbors' yards, and the neighbors' neighbors' yards. Is there something you're looking for that they didn't find?"

"If they didn't find it, there was probably nothing to find," says the man.

The woman glowers at him, like: *This is* my *investigation. Shut up.* He looks sheepish, and she says: "And who did you see come out first?"

"Kerry Cruz, the bass player. The guy who lived."

"And which part of the plane did he emerge from?"

"The rear, like I said that first day."

"He said he was sleeping when the plane crashed. Did he look like someone who'd been asleep?"

"He looked like someone who was stumbling out of a plane crash. He was in shock, clearly."

"What was he wearing?"

"I don't really remember. Something black, I think. Like something an old rock star might wear?"

"And what happened then?"

"He got out of the plane. He walked toward me and my neighbor, and he collapsed."

"Did you hear anything else when the plane was coming down?"

"Like what? It was so loud."

"Just . . . anything."

"I don't think so." The penny drops. "You mean, like a rocket being fired, or something? Was the plane shot out of the sky?"

"We're not saying that."

"But you're not *not* saying it?"

"We're investigating all possibilities." She looks down at her notepad. "And then, I see here that Stuart Fisher came from the forward fuselage."

"That's right. He was really badly burned." The image of the charred flesh of his face flashes across your memory. "I'm surprised he was able to move at all."

"And he didn't say anything? Or *try* to say anything?"

"No. He just kind of looked at me, took a few steps, then I suppose he died."

"Is there anything else you remember? Anything that's occurred to you in the past two months that you might have forgotten to tell the original investigation team?"

"No, there isn't. Listen: do I have to keep making the same statement over and over? I'm not a criminal, although I was *attacked* by a criminal who came to my house because of this plane crash."

"We understand, Mr. Crane. We're sorry about that."

You look over at the clearly cowed man. He nods. "Really sorry," he says.

# CONNIE CRANE, THE ART OF COMICS (2018)

## (Excerpt)

### INTERVIEWER

You seem to love drawing animals, particularly dogs and cats. Has your house always been a menagerie of pets?

### CONNIE CRANE

Actually, I don't have any pets, although that's primarily due to the fact that I'm allergic to dog and cat dander.

### INTERVIEWER

But you seem to have—and I hope this doesn't sound pretentious—a deep understanding of dogs and cats. The way their minds work, and how that tracks, or doesn't, with human cognition. Interestingly, you also get a lot of mileage out of the canonical Western philosophers.

### CRANE

Oh yeah, they're laugh riots.

### INTERVIEWER

I'm thinking right now of the comic where two cats are sitting by the side of the road, looking at their friend, who's just been run over by a car. One says: "If you want the present to be different from the past, study the past."

### CRANE

A lot of people really hated that one.

### INTERVIEWER

It's definitely dark, but the cats are drawn with such insouciance that it doesn't feel quite as brutal as it might otherwise. You have this pen-and-ink-wash technique that makes the world feel softer, even when the characters in your comics are confronting hard truths.

### CRANE

We are all of us nothing but contradictions.

### INTERVIEWER

And I love the single-panel where one Labrador retriever is quoting Kant to the other.

### CRANE

Well, Labs are fairly easy to draw, and they always seem happy, so they were the perfect visual foil for Kant. When you have two nearly identical-looking dogs, and one says to the other, "As Kant reminds us: 'You only know me as you see me, not as I actually am,'" I just think that's really funny.

### INTERVIEWER

It is! Are you a big reader of Kant, by the way?

### CRANE

I'm a big reader of compendiums like Paul Kleinman's *Philosophy 101*. I've lifted a lot of lines from Bertrand Russell's *The History of Western Philosophy*, and Will and Ariel Durant. And, of course, there's always the internet.

### INTERVIEWER

You don't feel obliged to delve into the originals?

### CRANE

I'm a cartoonist, for Pete's sake. I'm just trying to make people laugh.

### INTERVIEWER

And think, too, I would argue.

### CRANE

You can't laugh without thinking. Fortunately. Or unfortunately.

**INTERVIEWER**

Were you someone who loved drawing at an early age, or did you pick that up later?

**CRANE**

I didn't draw a lot as a child, but I *was* the nerdy, awkward girl in high-school art class. I grew up near Westwood—my dad was a sociology professor at UCLA—so I went to University High—Go Wildcats—and there were other weirdos there, too, but also the usual crowd of jocks and cheerleaders and bullies. Drawing was kind of a defense mechanism for me. I could make these people who were tormenting me look ridiculous in my cartoons, and that made me feel better.

I guess a big artistic breakthrough for me came when one of the popular girls saw my drawing of her with a bloody tampon sticking out of her mouth, and she practically pulled my hair out. After that, I started drawing people as animals because what seventeen-year-old kid is going to admit that he looks like a llama or porcupine?

**INTERVIEWER**

You attended Otis College of Art in Los Angeles. How was that experience?

**CRANE**

Hit-and-miss. There were some great teachers there, great artists—Donny Cisneros, Jack Nguyen, Cassidy Costa—and they did their best to get me on a fine arts track, but I had this rebellious streak that wouldn't let me settle into that. Much later, when I read Daniel Clowes's *Ghost World* in the late nineties, I really recognized myself in Enid Coleslaw.

**INTERVIEWER**

It wasn't long after you graduated that you began placing cartoons in the *New Yorker*.

**CRANE**

Sheer luck. Lee Lorenz, who was the editor choosing cartoons at the time, was a friend of Daisy Kavanagh, who was a friend of mine, and she happened to have a portfolio of my work at a dinner party they were both attending. Evidently, the conversation was dragging, so Daisy started passing around my cartoons to liven things up, and the next day Lee got in touch with me.

**INTERVIEWER**

You've said that your work changed significantly after you were married and had a child.

**CRANE**

I'd been doing cartoons that featured animals who were basically living the single life—the swingin' pig, the coy hippopotamus—that sort of thing, but then I was visiting a cousin in Santa Barbara, and I met my husband-to-be, and we just sort of clicked instantly. Pretty soon, along came a daughter, and I felt like I had enough material to last a lifetime.

# POOR GHOST: AN ORAL HISTORY

## 1999–2001

### *Ugly Word* (2000)
### US Billboard Peak Position: 1

**STUART FISHER:** I spent the better part of 1999 listening to the music that was out there, what was coming up, what the critics liked, what the fans liked. I didn't want to just copy the current trends—that always ends badly for bands that have been around for a long time—but I did want to feel that the music on our next album was going to feel relevant to the current times.

You have to remember this was in the lead-up to Y2K, where people were saying all the computers were going to crash, banks were going to lose your money, missiles were going to be auto-fired by robots and start a nuclear war. It was a pretty tense time.

However, there *was* a kind of music making it to the top of the charts that had a connection with us and our roots in punk. You had *The Battle of Los Angeles* by Rage Against the Machine and *The Fragile* by Nine Inch Nails, but they were using rap in the one case, and electronics in the other. I knew we'd be mocked mercilessly, and rightly so, if I tried to rap, but I'd always been interested in new sounds—we all had—and so that seemed like a path forward.

**SHANE REED:** I wasn't really that much into music around the time we started getting ready to record *Ugly Word*. In the five years since our last album, I'd been married and divorced—twice. No kids, thank God. And then Reed Records, my label for Geffen, folded. It was kind of a dark time for me, personally. I felt pretty alienated from the band.

**GREGG MORGAN:** *Between Religion and Hygiene* didn't totally bomb, but I don't think anyone would call it our greatest success. Like I've said, I think it was too mellow. I liked what Tom Morello was doing with *Rage*. I could dig that. And I wasn't opposed to electronics, as long as they didn't distract from the urgency of the music.

When we got to the studio, I tried to get Shane pumped for the drumming he'd be doing. Lots of kick-ass stuff, but he was really down in that period. Sort of a drag, really.

**SHANE REED:** Prozac helped, eventually.

**KERRY CRUZ:** We didn't go all in on electronics, like Radiohead on *Kid A*. But *Ugly Word* definitely responded to the zeitgeist. The synthesizer as electric guitar was how I thought of it.

**GREGG MORGAN:** We needed to amp things up. And we needed an actual producer.

**ED WINGFIELD:** The Matrix was just starting as a production team— Lauren, Graham, and Scott. They were stoked to be working with a big act like Poor Ghost, and they just had this way with power pop, power punk, whatever you want to call it. I knew it was a good fit. The Matrix wanted their songs on the radio and on MTV, and that's what I wanted, too.

**STUART FISHER:** It's strange how accordion-like time is. Sometimes it seems to really stretch out, then, man, it's squeezed together with a rush of air. Suddenly it's 1999, and it's been eight years since *Scoured*. That's like a million years in rock and roll. It felt like there was a lot of pressure to be successful again.

**ED WINGFIELD:** They only had two albums in the '90s. One was a huge hit, a kind of instant classic. The other was—how do I say this?—commercially disappointing and artistically uneven. I think one of the reasons it was easy to be their manager during those years is because they spent a lot of time not needing to be managed.

**SHANE REED:** On most of the album, I played electronic drums for the first time. At first, I hated it. But when I realized how many distinct sounds you could get out of striking the same pad, I dug it. You could say I drummed my way out of depression.

**GREGG MORGAN:** Once he got into it, Shane's drumming was a big part of that album. You could dance to our songs, like in an actual club. That was new.

**KERRY CRUZ:** Would you call it selling out? I hope not. It wasn't my favorite sound, those thick synths and electronic drums, but I understand that when you're in a successful band, there's an expectation that you have to adapt, even if, personally, it's not your jam. You're like a shark: if you're not swimming, you're dead.

**STUART FISHER:** When we went into the studio, I had the songs pretty much finished conceptually, as usual, but I did let the Matrix team have a lot of freedom with the sounds, which turned out to be a smart move.

**SHANE REED:** The big albums in 2000 were *No Strings Attached* by NSYNC and *The Marshall Mathers LP* by Eminem, and what? Santana? The first Britney Spears album had been hitting number one off and on for two years, and that was definitely not our audience. But somehow we had one week at number one at the end of July. Maybe there was some nostalgia for us? I don't know. We did have two singles that did really well: "Koan Americana" and "Outré." Kind of singalongs about the new millennium. And videos—we were getting pretty good at making those.

**GREGG MORGAN:** The video for "Outré" was a trip. First of all, I admit that I had never heard the word "outré" before in my life—classic Stuart, to go combing through the thesaurus or wherever he found it. But it was perfect for a really weird video like the one we made.

**SHANE REED:** I don't remember who directed the video, but I do remember he was famous for using all the latest cutting-edge technology of the time. So, there are these continuous cuts, practically every couple of seconds, and it was funny.

**KERRY CRUZ:** I think the closest visual equivalent to the "Outré" video is probably Eminem's "My Name Is." Both had this kind of anarchic energy.

People falling down, getting up, falling down again. Dumb costumes. The moose in a pink tutu. That firehose full of shaving cream.

**SHANE REED:** Videos always helped sales.

**JERRY DIMGARTEN:** Frankly, I was not much of a fan of *Ugly Word*. Granted, Poor Ghost had always had one ear to the charts. If you feel you've got something to say, you want the largest number of people to hear it, and to do that, you have to make compromises sometimes. Fair enough. But I felt they went too far.

If you listen to *Kid A* and *Ugly Word* back-to-back, it's like listening to somebody who's passionate about what they're saying versus someone who has their tongue in their cheek the entire time. That's fine, of course. Irony is Stuart's métier, but it's not as convincing in terms of the aesthetic experience.

That said, I *really* love "Live in the Living Room." This is a song that you could imagine PG writing for their first album. The premise is that the band, which by this time was one of the biggest acts in the world, could only find an audience if they played in their living room. So you have lines like "Over there is a chair, / Over there someone's underwear, / Shag carpet on the floor, / Big hole in the door . . . in the door." It's this celebration of amateurism—and by that I mean pursuing something out of pure love on an unpaid basis—that's both sincere, and, of course, incredibly sardonic.

**SHANE REED:** I was happy we had a hit. No doubt. But what I remember most about 2000 was watching the Super Bowl. There were all these dot-com ads, and I just had a bad feeling that things were going south, like everything else in my life at that time. I was heavy into tech stocks, but I got out the day after the game, about a month before the crash. No insider info, or anything. I just had a feeling. You grow up without money, like we did, things like that give you a scare.

**ED WINGFIELD:** The album came out in April and they toured for a couple of months during the summer. They were making some serious money at that point, but the buzz was that since CDs were so easy to rip on home computers and distribute online for free, album sales were going to start dropping, precipitously. Napster started in 1999, and it was just a matter of time before the business model changed. I told the band that I could envision a future where their primary income came from ticket sales for live concerts, but they all kind of laughed, except for Shane.

**GREGG MORGAN:** I've never had as much money, before or since, as I did at the beginning of 2000. I was actually thinking of buying a small island in the Bahamas, if you want to know the truth. Glad I didn't.

**STUART FISHER:** There was a change coming, but I wasn't sure what it was. I felt like I'd hit a wall creatively, and the start of the new millennium had come and gone, but nothing had really changed. I didn't want us to be an electropop band. I didn't want to be Radiohead. I had this feeling, like, *Ulllh*. A lack of inspiration.

After the tour was over, I went back to Rome. I rented a place in Testaccio, which is *not* the chic part of town. The band isn't really big in Italy, and it had been a long time since *Scoured*, so no one knew me, and for six months I just kind of wandered around, learning a little Italian, not writing or anything. At first I thought a lot about Holly, but after a while I didn't think about her at all. I was just in a kind of stasis.

**SHANE REED:** For some reason—maybe because I cared the most about making a decent living—I was made the unofficial caretaker of Stuart whenever he went walkabout. I flew over to Rome and met him in a trattoria. He had a bottle of red wine and an Italian newspaper, which, he admitted, he was unsuccessfully trying to read. We talked for a while, and he pretty quickly convinced me that he wasn't nuts or anything, he just needed some time off, so I said: Why the fuck not? He's earned it.

That night, I got on a plane and flew back to LA.

**GREGG MORGAN:** I think one of the reasons for our longevity is that we spent a lot of time apart. It's like a long marriage. Maybe a handful of couples need to be together every day, but most people need some space, some breathing room. We all wanted that, so no one felt left out when we weren't together.

**KERRY CRUZ:** Early 2001 was the twentieth anniversary of when the four of us first started playing together back at Davis. It was crazy to think that this band that you imagine is going to end at any time is not only still playing together, but has made six albums, and three of them have gone to number one. Rough patches notwithstanding, it was like some incredible dream.

## Poor Ghost Bassist Kerry Cruz in Fistfight at Aimee Mann's Largo Gig

—NME News | 22 November 2021

Singer-songwriter Aimee Mann, perhaps best known for her songs on the soundtrack of Paul Thomas Anderson's *Magnolia*, was playing in support of her new album *Queens of the Summer Hotel* at Largo at the Coronet when she encountered some unexpected turbulence.

After she and her four-piece band concluded "Suicide Is Murder," Mann was in the midst of quipping about her penchant for writing depressing lyrics, when a scuffle broke out in the first row of the normally laid-back Los Angeles folk club.

According to fans who were there, a man sitting next to Poor Ghost bassist Kerry Cruz, the lone survivor of the band's September 21 plane crash, began taunting Cruz about the fact that he was still alive.

In cellphone footage, Cruz is briefly seen shouting, "You don't know what you're talking about, you fucking asshole! So fuck you!" The two men exchanged punches, although neither appears to have been seriously hurt.

The show paused for twenty minutes while the club's bouncers attempted to break up the fight. Eventually, both men were escorted off the premises.

When the performance continued, Mann laughed nervously, saying, "I think this is the first time there's been a mosh pit at one of my concerts." The band then launched into her classic "Wise Up."

# THE
# AFTERLIFE
# OF
# POOR GHOST

# 37

The Tuesday night before Thanksgiving, you are sitting on the patio by the firepit, watching a lone, distant car turn off from Highway 154 and slowly snake down the mountain on San Marcos Road.

So caught up are you in the vehicle's progress that at first you don't notice one high yip, and then another.

Suddenly, though, the yapping and yipping increase in frequency and pitch, and you realize it's happening in your lower yard. You grab the shovel leaning against the chimney and make your way to the creaky wooden stairs.

In the moonlight, you can see the growling and circling of four animals—clearly, it's three against one.

You growl yourself, *"Haah!"* and wave the shovel, but as you do, you trip on the final step and roll down the hill. The shovel slips from your grasp, and when you stop tumbling you look up to see all four animals staring down at you, startled but not running away.

One of them, a large coyote, yips and growls. The hair on the back of his neck stands up—as clear in the moonlight as if there were a spotlight shining on him. The rest of the world seems to fade away, leaving the two of you in some primal scene from the era before dogs were domesticated.

You are feeling for the shovel, when the coyote bends down on his front legs, as though he's about to spring. But suddenly one of the other animals leaps onto the coyote with a vicious snarl.

The two creatures roll around in the dirt and dried grass, but you've found the shovel now, and you take a whack at your would-be attacker. The shovel blade only grazes his leg, but it's enough, and he and his two companions lope downhill, leap over your wire fence, and disappear into the darkness of the avocado orchard.

Your champion walks tentatively toward you, and you put out a hand for him to sniff, then lick. Even without tonight's bright moon, you'd recognize him anywhere: it's Jackson.

# 38

Your immediate thought, once you have heaved Jackson back up the steps and into the living room, is to take him to an emergency veterinarian, but when you place him gingerly on the couch, he gets up, and though he is limping slightly and bleeding a bit from a cut on his flank, he seems okay.

You find some hydrogen peroxide under the sink and clean the wound, which makes him yelp, but he doesn't run away from you. In fact, when you're done with your ministrations, he jumps up on the couch, big old dog that he is, curls up, and puts his head in your lap.

You can't remember the last time you felt so happy. Surely not since March of 2020.

You know you ought to call Victoria and tell her that her dog is safe, but you also know that she would immediately drive to Santa Barbara and take him away.

It can wait until tomorrow, you think, as you get a bowl of water from the tap, and dig out a can of the salmon-flavored dog food he's especially fond of.

"Where have you been, boy?" you say, as he buries his nose in his food and you scratch him behind the ears. "It's like you dropped off the face of the earth."

The next morning, the day before Thanksgiving, you are sleeping soundly, with Jackson curled up on the foot of your bed.

The doorbell rings, and it's Kelsey Symmons again. She's smiling and laughing as you ask her in, and though you are still rubbing sleep from your eyes, you realize that you're glad to see her. Your two-hour info dump from a few days earlier was surprisingly cathartic, and you wouldn't mind doing something like that again.

Jackson is out, sniffing.

"New dog?" she asks.

"My daughter's."

"Is this *the* dog that went missing during the crash?"

"It is."

She looks him over. "Other than a few scratches, he seems really healthy."

You nod and offer to make her a cup of coffee, which she accepts.

She plays with Jackson while the Keurig works its magic, and you bring back a cup for each of you.

"How can I help?" you ask.

"I'm just checking in, that's all."

"For your story?"

"Possibly."

"And what would you like to hear? I feel like I covered the last couple of months pretty thoroughly."

"I guess I'm interested in you, as a character. Again, this is all with your permission. No offense, but on the surface you seem like a pretty standard middle-aged white guy. You worked for an insurance company. You have a nice house and a successful grown daughter. Nothing that would set you apart from hundreds of thousands of other Americans of your class and generation.

"But then it turns out that your wife is a famous cartoonist, and then a plane carrying one of America's iconic rock bands crashes in your backyard.

And instead of kicking out all the crazies—myself included—you basically welcome them to a nightly backyard gathering. Until, of course, one of those crazies eggs on another one, who attacks you with a knife."

"Sounds about right."

"As I said the other day, I think there's a story there—an article, maybe a book—and I'd really love to get some backstory to flesh it out."

"Like, before the crash, could his life really have been as *boring* as it seems?"

"No one's life is as boring as it seems on the outside. That's one of the first things you learn when you start writing creative nonfiction." She pauses to give you time to think it over. "If you say no that's fine, I'll probably just drop the whole thing, but if you're interested in what I'm thinking of as a collaboration, then let's talk."

Jackson is sitting on the sofa next to you, and you're awake now, and why not? What could it possibly hurt to tell your life story to someone who actually wants to hear it?

This time you give her three hours. It's mostly a monologue peppered with her leading questions. She records it on her phone and takes notes and occasionally stops you to clarify a point of fact. It makes you feel oddly important to recount what you think of as the significant events of your life—your sorrow over the childhood death of your sister; your father's constant demands for perfection and your mother's inability, or unwillingness, to stand up to him; your fork in the road after college when you contemplated trying your hand in the arts—acting, writing, painting, music, you never settled on one thing—or going straight into business, as your father recommended; meeting Connie at a party thrown by her cousin; the birth of Victoria; and your long and mostly happy marriage. Have you secretly always wanted an autobiographer to get your story down and tell it right? Is there anyone who hasn't felt that way?

Sometime after you would normally be making yourself a sandwich for lunch, you conclude: "Up until Connie's death, it was a relatively successful life."

"And now?"

"I guess we'll see."

Kelsey has been an excellent listener, and you can't remember ever talking that long about yourself, so you ask politely: "And you? What's your story?"

"Thumbnail sketch? Wealthy kid from Scarsdale. Parents divorced when I was ten. Mom was an actress and singer who did a lot of touring with musicals once they left Broadway, so I lived with my dad, who was an entertainment lawyer."

"Did you get along with them?"

"Mom, not so much. But I loved my dad. He was the kindest, most generous lawyer you were ever going to meet. That sounds snarky, I know, but I don't mean it that way."

You clear your throat. "I notice you refer to him in the past tense."

"Yeah." She pauses, looks out the window at the mountains, looks back at you. "He died a year ago. Pancreatic cancer."

"I'm sorry. You must miss him."

She nods: of course. "Anyway, I always wanted to come to California, so I did my BA at UCLA, then I went back and got an MA from Columbia, and I've been kind of piecing freelance work together since I graduated. Mostly feature pieces on music and movies, but some politics."

"That's impressive."

"I don't know. One thing I learned early on as a journalist: unless you're the story, don't talk about yourself."

"Makes sense." You can tell she's had enough for one day, so you get up and, without really thinking why, ask her what she's doing for Thanksgiving tomorrow.

"No plans, really. What about you? Dinner with your father?"

You nod, and it pops out of your mouth before you can stop it: "You could join us. If you want."

"That's nice of you, but it seems more like family time."

"My daughter's driving up this evening. If she likes the idea, would you be interested?"

Kelsey shrugs as she gets up to go. "Sure, why not. As long as you let me bring the food."

# 40

You watch out the front window until Victoria arrives, then you put Jackson in the hall and shut the door. When you answer the front door, you tell her, "I have some very good news. I want you to—"

But he's barking and scratching on the hall door, and she's already moving past you. "Jackson! You found him!"

When she opens the door, they reunite like two characters in a children's movie. You half expect to hear swelling orchestral music, as he licks her face, and she kisses his nose and hugs him against her chest. "Jackson, baby, you're home!"

She wants to know, of course, when you found him, and you consider lying, but you admit that it was Tuesday night, that you couldn't bear the thought of parting with him that evening, and she seems to understand.

"It's weird," you tell her. "A week or so ago, I heard this barking in the middle of the night that I thought was him, but it was really foggy, and I wasn't sure what I saw, whether it was him or another dog or just a coyote."

"*The Hound of the Baskervilles*," she says.

"It *was* kind of spooky." You hesitate. "And something even spookier happened."

She looks at you: *Yes?*

"I thought I heard your mother calling me in the middle of the night."

"*What?* Dad, you're giving me chills."

"I'm sure it was a dream. I got up and walked around. I didn't hear anything after I was sure I was awake."

"Still. That's creepy."

You grunt an affirmative, then order pizza.

After it arrives, you ask Victoria about Kelsey joining you and your father for Thanksgiving.

"I guess that's okay, but, really, *why?* Why would she want to do that?"

"I asked her."

"Okaaay. What's going on with this journalist, Dad?"

"What do you mean?"

"Is it, like, a romance?"

"Seriously? She's not much older than you are, Victoria."

"That doesn't mean anything. Men are perverts."

"Well, I'm not a pervert."

"You're lonely, though, aren't you? You must be. Why else would you be hearing Mom's voice?"

"Of course I'm lonely. I was married to your mother for thirty-three years. But that's not why I asked Kelsey to come to Thanksgiving. First, her father recently died, and she seems lonely."

"So she wants a replacement father?"

"Maybe a little. I suspect she mostly sees me as an opportunity for a piece on Poor Ghost. I'm just the way in to the story."

"Sounds pretty self-serving."

"Could be. When I think about it, though, it was probably selfish on my part: she's one more person to help deal with Grandpa. Like an extra shield in a battle."

"You're really looking forward to Thanksgiving?"

"Of course not. Are you?"

Victoria shakes her head, no.

You text Kelsey and arrange for the three of you to meet at your father's house at eleven the next morning. It's early for Thanksgiving dinner, but your father prefers an early meal, and he will likely be hungry by then. Kelsey texts that she has the food taken care of, and though you text back that she's being too generous, you don't fight very hard. Neither you nor Victoria like to cook, and whatever Kelsey's plan for the menu is, it's better than the one you have now.

# 41

At eleven, you and Victoria pull into your father's driveway with a bottle of Pinot Noir, a bottle of Chardonnay, and a bottle of champagne.

Kelsey, waiting in her car on the street, emerges with two enormous plastic bags.

Victoria introduces herself, and says, "You shouldn't have."

"I didn't really. It was delivered to my door an hour ago."

You haven't broken the news yet to your father about the extra guest, but he takes it in stride, apparently assuming that she's a helper from Meals on Wheels who will leave as soon as she's set everything up.

You and the other two Cranes sit passively, watching Kelsey put the food on your father's not very clean kitchen table. "Let's see what we've got here," Kelsey says, reading from a printed menu. "Savory butter roasted turkey breast, brown butter mashed potatoes, home-made garlic and herb gravy, fresh cranberry sauce, roasted Brussels sprouts, and a delicious apple crumb pie. How does that sound to everybody?"

"I don't like Brussels sprouts," your father says.

"If I'm honest," says Kelsey with a wink, "I don't much like them either, Mr. Crane."

There's a long pause, then your father cracks a smile, something you haven't seen in months. "My father's Mr. Crane. My name's Albert."

"All right, then, Albert, the two of us will leave the Brussels sprouts to Caleb and Victoria."

Your father's face goes sour. "What do you mean the two of us? Are you eating Thanksgiving dinner *here*?"

Kelsey looks over at you. "You didn't tell him?"

"Not yet."

"What are you talking about 'not yet'?" your father asks. "Who is this lady, anyway?"

You're not exactly sure how to explain her presence, and you're fumbling for an answer when Victoria jumps in. "She was a friend of Mom's, Grandpa. Someone she knew from the *New Yorker*."

"You're a little young to be doing that job, aren't you?" he harrumphs.

"Still wet behind the ears, Mr. Crane." She smiles, and it almost wins him over.

"So, you're some kind of cartoonist?"

"Actually, I'm a reporter."

"And how did you know my late daughter-in-law?"

"Just . . . you know. Running in the same circles."

That response seems to satisfy your father for the moment. At any rate, he is hungry, and soon the four of you are sitting around the table, each with a small glass of red or white wine, digging into the pre-made food, which is quite good.

When he's finished, before everyone else, your father says, "Okay. That was good. I think I'm going to take a nap."

"Grandpa, *no*," says Victoria. "I did not drive all the way up here just to watch you eat for twenty minutes."

"Why *did* you drive up here, then?"

"For family."

He grimaces. "Some family." He picks up his fork and points at Kelsey. "And she's not family at all."

"She's a guest, Dad," you say. "You need to treat her with some respect."

"What is she, your girlfriend?"

You roll your eyes, and Victoria once again comes to the rescue. "Let's do 'What are you thankful for?' I'll start. I'm thankful for my dad and my grandpa, and thankful to have met Kelsey. I'm thankful that we are lucky enough to share this meal together when so many people around the world are starving."

"It's their own fault," says your father.

"Jesus, Grandpa."

"Don't you 'Jesus' me, young lady."

You say: "What are *you* thankful for, Dad?"

"I'm thankful I have some visitors for a change."

"I visit you twice a week, Dad. Other than Meals on Wheels, I'm your most constant visitor. And your granddaughter sees you whenever she's in Santa Barbara. I don't feel like you're very deprived."

"A lot you know."

Kelsey says, "What *should* people know, Mr. Crane?"

"Well, for one thing," your father says, staring at Kelsey, but pointing at Victoria, "did you know she had an aunt?"

"She wasn't actually Victoria's aunt," you interrupt, "because she died when she was four, decades before Victoria was born."

"Has your father ever told you *how* she died?"

Victoria says, "Something about a spider bite?"

"A black widow." Your father picks up his fork again, this time pointing it at you. "*He* made her touch it."

"Dad?" says Victoria.

"He's right. I was six. She was four. I wasn't sure what it was—it looked like this black bump on a piece of wood—but I didn't want to touch it myself. It was my fault. I had a bad feeling, but I told her to do it anyway."

"You should be *so* ashamed of yourself. It should have been you, not her," your father says in an Old Testament voice.

There's a long, strained silence. Your father glares. The two women have their heads bowed, as though they are saying grace. You look around the dining room, everything covered in dust, unwashed cups and glasses crowding the counter, newspapers stacked against the walls. There's a musty, moldy odor. It could be Miss Havisham's second home.

Then Kelsey says, "I think he *is* ashamed about it, Mr. Crane. He told me about it yesterday. He seemed really sad."

"He should be," your father says, with apparent satisfaction.

"But I'm thinking," Kelsey continues, "that must have been extraordinarily painful for a child of that age. Of course he didn't mean to kill his sister. He simply made a mistake. Doesn't that deserve some forgiveness after all these years?"

Your father dashes his fork to the floor and stands up, shakily, both hands resting on the table. "The Almighty will decide who is forgiven and who is damned. That is not for us to know."

"Grandpa, you are being *so* harsh," Victoria says. "You're better than this."

"I am who I am."

"Come on, Dad, please," you say, getting up and reaching a hand toward him.

But he slaps your hand away and shuffles toward his bedroom. Over his shoulder, your father mumbles, "Go to hell, Caleb Crane. Go straight to hell."

# TEXTS
## KS & RA

**Thu, Nov 25, 4:32 PM**

Where are you?

Hello?

We were supposed to have Thanksgiving today.
Remember????

Everyone was asking where you were, and I just said,
"She's on assignment."

I am so sorry!!!

What happened?? Do NOT tell me you went back up to
Santa Barbara.

Yes, but driving home right now. I'm in Calabasas.

I do NOT believe this. What even is the story? A bunch of
losers can't let go of a washed-up band? NO ONE wants
to read that. Believe me.

Sorry. I felt obliged to be around these people. They're
hurting.

So you didn't even forget?? You chose the weirdos over
your friends! Seriously????

190

There's a story here, Becca. Something worth telling. You have to let me follow it. We're still friends.

Are we, Kelsey? Because I'm starting to doubt it.

Look: How about dinner at Tar and Roses tomorrow? My treat. I'll tell you all about everything.

How do I even know you'll be there?

I will, I promise. I swear. The snapper is so good! At eight?

Okay?

Please!

Can I bring Ted?

Of course!

Okay.

## NTSB Holds News Conference on Fatal Poor Ghost Plane Crash

—AP News, November 26, 2021

Nicole Zelle of the National Transportation Safety Board held a press conference at the Santa Barbara Regional Airport on Monday to discuss the crash on September 21, 2021, of a Cessna Citation in which the pilot and three of the four members of the band Poor Ghost perished.

According to Zelle: "As previously reported, the plane's fuselage was split in two just aft of the wings. Both wings were impact-fractured, and exhibited leading edge damage consistent with tree impact. The empennage [tail assembly] was impact-fractured and severed and found approximately 25 feet from the rear half of the fuselage. The instrument panel was fragmented. The engine controls were in the full forward position."

When reporters asked if the position of the engine controls indicated that the plane had been intentionally crashed, Zelle responded, "We believe so." She added that the lack of eyewitnesses, and the fact that the cockpit voice recorder had been disabled, was hampering the investigation. The only survivor, bassist Kerry Cruz, 58, has said he was asleep at the time of the crash.

Zelle told reporters that the pilot, 36-year-old Jeffrey Dunne, had been thoroughly investigated, and there was no sign of suicidal or homicidal ideation, although she could not explain why Dunne apparently flipped a circuit breaker that turned off the voice recorder prior to the plane's approach to Santa Barbara.

Zelle said there was no evidence that Dunne had met any of the members of the band prior to the flight, or that he held any animosity toward anyone in Poor Ghost. Zelle read a statement from Dunne's wife, Allison, which said, in part: "Jeff was a huge fan of PG. He was thrilled to be their pilot, even though it was only a short flight."

When reporters asked whether Dunne's apparent innocence indicated the involvement of one or more members of Poor Ghost in the downing of the plane, Zelle replied, "No comment," and said that the investigation was on-going.

As she was leaving the meeting room, a reporter called out, "What about Kerry Cruz? He's the only one left alive." Zelle paused and said, "Mr. Cruz is actively assisting us with our inquiries," then ended the news conference.

# POOR GHOST: AN ORAL HISTORY

## 2002–2004

### *Defenestration and Decapitation* (2003)
### US Billboard Peak Position: 18

**KERRY CRUZ:** The thing about Poor Ghost is we'd get on a roll, like we had a number one album in 2000, but then we'd all sort of get burned out and have to go our separate ways to save our sanity.

And also, let's face it, we were dependent on Stuart for our material, and if he didn't have his downtime, there was always this implicit threat that he was going to leave the band, and that would be it for all of us.

It's not that we didn't write our own songs, me and Gregg, and even Shane, but the fact of the matter is that we are three great sidemen, no more and no less. We add a ton to the band—the Stuart Fisher solo project would be a lot weaker without us, as Stuart himself would be the first to admit—but we are incapable of writing songs like Stuart's. Over the years, all three of us have said how generous it is that Stuart has this special arrangement of paying us co-writer royalties, even though most of the songs only have "Fisher" as the official credit.

So, "Whither thou goest," as I believe the saying is.

**STUART FISHER:** I can't just write songs on command. I don't want to sound like some prima donna, but that's the way it is. I'm not a music factory. I have to recharge the batteries, and for me that means doing something different.

After the *Ugly Word* tour, I spent some time in Austin, which, despite what everyone says, seemed like any big Texas city to me.

Then I was in rural Wales for about six months. I rented a house outside a tiny town called Llandysul. No one knew who I was. As far as they were concerned, I was just some eccentric American who came into the Kings Arms in the afternoon for a couple of pints. Anyway, most people spoke Welsh as their first language, so conversations could be . . . limited. Fields and sheep and rain were big topics. It was a real head-clearer.

**GREGG MORGAN:** I spent a week jamming with Jeff Tweedy after *Yankee Hotel Foxtrot* came out and Jay Bennett had quit. I like Jeff, he's funny and smart, and he's written some great songs. I don't know if he was going to ask me to join Wilco to fill Jay's slot, but I pretty quickly figured out that it would just be another version of Poor Ghost, so it never came to that.

**SHANE REED:** My businesses were doing pretty well at that time, so I was never bothered when the band wasn't together. In fact, I took up golf around then. After six months, I was shooting in the mid-80s.

**STUART FISHER:** When I got back to LA at the end of 2002, the songs just started coming to me: "Anagram," "Ecce Homo," "Archaeology," "Against the Euro." Definitely guitar rock—not necessarily the most commercial form of pop music at the time, but "Euro" did get some airplay.

**ED WINGFIELD:** The biggest album of 2003 was 50 Cent's *Get Rich or Die Tryin'*: "We gonna party like it's your birthday." That wasn't really a Poor Ghost vibe. Still, they'd just had a number one album three years earlier, so I assumed there'd still be some enthusiasm for whatever they did. Naturally, I was always nudging them to make it as commercial as possible.

**KERRY CRUZ:** Shania Twain, Norah Jones, Ashanti, Kelly Clarkson, Hilary Duff. It's not that I don't respect what they were doing, but we were sailing against some pretty strong headwinds in 2003.

**GREGG MORGAN:** It's true that in some respects rock and roll was falling out of favor at the time, but you have to remember that that was also the era of what they called "the garage rock revival"—the Strokes, the White Stripes, The Dandy Warhols, all that. There's always going to be a place for guitar, bass, and drums.

**STUART FISHER:** We got Rick Rubin to produce the album, but that was a really busy year for him, and I'm not sure *Defenestration* had his full attention.

**GREGG MORGAN:** Sometimes over the years I've felt like Stuart was intentionally trying to sabotage our success. I mean, as a title, does *Defenestration and Decapitation* really reach out and say, "Buy me"? Like most people, I'm sure, I had no idea what "defenestration" was until I looked it up. "To throw somebody out of a window." Okay. Wow. But he's our resident genius, so we go along with whatever he cooks up.

I say this while at the same time acknowledging that I really like the songs on this album. It's a rocker, and I've got some good solos, if I do say so myself, especially on "The Afterbirth of Tragedy" and "The Season of High School Bands."

**STUART FISHER:** I was interested in the sounds you could get pairing a twelve-string with the sort of distortion-drenched sound favored by Gregg. And then I wanted a couple of songs that were just poignant and bittersweet.

**KERRY CRUZ:** It was mostly a guitar album, so I mostly played bass. I do have that short organ solo on the title track, right after Stuart screams "Ahhhhh!" but it was not a creative high point for me.

**SHANE REED:** I was like, okay, have we not figured out how to *consistently* make hit records after twenty-plus years? There's nothing wrong with giving people what they want.

**ED WINGFIELD:** The album was kind of flatlining until one of the songs, "Hanging Out with Bosnians," was a last-minute choice for an episode in Season 5 of *The Sopranos*. David Chase had heard an early version, and he gave it about 30 seconds worth of play in that episode where Bobby Bacala has to go out to "Rite Aids" and buy stool softener for Uncle Junior. It's this poignant song in E minor, so it was a real comic counterpart to the action on screen. The week after the episode aired on HBO, the album shot up from somewhere in the high 70s to its peak at number 18. It stayed there for a week, then dropped back into the 50s.

**STUART FISHER:** I was told David Chase liked one line in particular: "'Hey, are you alive?' / 'Not so as you could tell.'"

**GREGG MORGAN:** Thank you, Tony Soprano, for saving our ass on that album.

# INSTAGRAM

**poorghostlifer92**

**104 likes**

**poorghostlifer92** I am on the street where PG's plane crashed. It's the house past that palm tree on the left. From here you can barely see the airport down by the ocean, where their plane SHOULD have landed. Something creepy about this street, and not just because of the loss of life for everyone's fave band. #caminopalomino #poorghostcrash #whokilledpoorghost #poorghost4ever #poorghost

# THE
# AFTERLIFE
# OF
# POOR GHOST

# 42

The first Monday in December, you are sitting in the backyard petting Jackson. Probably because your father was so cruel to you on Thanksgiving, Victoria has said that you can keep her dog "for the time being," and he's been a great comfort to you, this hulking mishmash of an animal with sweet brown eyes who is so attentive to your every move.

It's late morning, and the fog that crept in an hour earlier has mostly receded now. A ruby-throated hummingbird darts from the top of a lemon tree, zooms past your head, and disappears down the hill. Crows caw further up the canyon, and somewhere in the distance a lawn mower starts up, then gutters out.

Suddenly, Jackson perks up, swiveling his head toward the side yard. With a great bark, he leaps away from you and heads around the house. You look around and grab the shovel you've lately been using to toss Jackson's turds down the hill, thinking: Elineo, or Álvaro de Campos.

However, when you turn the corner, a man in a suit coat is bent over the holly bushes by the gate to the front yard. His right hand is deep in a shrub, when he yelps, "Ouch!" pulling it from the sharp leaves and turning around to see you.

"Umm, hello," you say. It's someone you've seen only once before. The previous time, he was covered in soot and tattered clothes. Kerry Cruz is in your backyard.

"Oh, hi," he says, sheepish. He has a goatee and longish hair that's receding a bit. He turns on a big celebrity smile. "I, uh, thought you'd probably be at work right now."

"I'm retired."

He laughs uncomfortably. "Congratulations." He clears his throat. "Do you know who I am?"

"Of course. I helped rescue you from the plane crash."

"That's right, that's right. Thank you." He sticks out his hand, and you shake it. There's a tiny trail of blood on his thumb.

"How can I help?" you ask.

"Right." For a moment, he's thinking rather than answering. "I believe this is where the paramedics carried me when they were taking me to the ambulance."

"I assume so."

"Anyway," he continues unsteadily, "so I was wearing a chain that my wife gave me. And I have a kind of half-memory of the paramedics having to put me down to open up the gate, and for some reason, I grabbed the chain and threw it into the bushes. I suppose I must have been hysterical."

"You're right: that doesn't really make any sense. But I'm happy to help you look for it."

"No, no, no, that's fine. As we're standing here talking, I'm thinking that may have just been a dream. In fact, I'm pretty sure I know where it actually is—in my house, in LA."

"Okay, though I'm happy to help you keep looking."

"No need, no need. I'm just going to head on out, with apologies for barging into your yard."

"No problem. Do you want to come in, or anything?"

He's opened the gate and is now backing down the driveway. "No, no, no, I'm good, but thanks." He stops, then reaches into his back pocket, extracts his wallet, then walks back and hands you a business card. It has a phone number and email address atop a grayed-out image of *Alas, Poor Ghost!* with "Kerry Cruz, Musician" inscribed in gold letters.

As he walks down to his car, he says, "Call or email, if something comes up."

"Like what?" you ask.

"Anything that, you know, seems important." He gives you a little salute, and then he's in a black Ferrari. You notice Barton the dentist in his front yard next door. "Was that . . . you know who?" he asks in a too-loud voice.

You shake your head no, and the Ferrari makes a quick U-turn before speeding off down the street.

# 43

You surely would have spent more time ruminating on the visit by Kerry Cruz, but about an hour later Kelsey Symmons calls to ask if you have heard that Elineo has murdered his daughter.

"*What?*" you say into the phone. "Are you kidding?"

"I wish I were. It's insane."

"What happened?"

"Well, Elineo, as we know, was really into QAnon. Apparently he was hearing voices, or something, and he told his wife he was taking his daughter for a quick surfing lesson, and she was like, 'Okay, have fun.' Anyway, he drives up to this place called More Mesa. Do you know it?"

"Sure, It's an open space by Hope Ranch. Some bluffs along the beach."

"Exactly. So Elineo goes up to this cliff, and this old couple is walking by with their dog, and Elineo says to them, 'She's been infected by her mother's serpent DNA,' and they're all, 'What are you talking about, sir?' and he picks up the little girl and just throws her off the cliff."

You don't respond for a moment. Then: "Jesus." And: "The poor little girl." You are shaking so badly that you have to sit down on the sofa. You stare at the phone in your hand as though it were an evil talisman.

"Anyway, the old lady takes off for this path down to the beach, and the old man tries to grab Elineo, but Elineo just pushes him away, and disappears."

"And they're sure it's Elineo?"

"The lady took a picture of him with her phone right afterwards. It's all over the internet. Also, right before Elineo took off, he whispered to the old man, 'I did it for Stuart.'"

You can think of absolutely nothing to say.

"Maybe you should see if the cops will come over and watch your house. I would be worried."

You let out a long sigh. "I'd be more worried if I was his wife."

"I'm sure she has police protection. You should, too."

"I'll think about it. I appreciate your getting in touch."

After a moment, Kelsey says, "That's it?"

You think of telling her about Kerry Cruz's visit, but it seems so trivial in comparison to filicide. "Yeah. That's it."

You hang up, unsure if she was angling for an invitation to come over. If so, you're glad that didn't happen. At the moment, you don't want to see any human beings.

Still, you *are* nervous. Elineo seems like a real and present danger now. You bring Jackson inside, along with the shovel, then shut all the windows and lock all the doors. You take the sushi knife from its wooden block and carry it with you as you move around the house.

When it begins to get dark, around a quarter to five, you turn on all the floodlights around the house. And you do end up calling the sheriff's department, persuading them to do a drive-by during the night.

And yet even with Jackson on the bed, and the shovel and sushi knife near at hand, you don't sleep at all well.

# 44

The next morning, you're awakened by a call from the emergency room of the Goleta Hospital. The Meals on Wheels driver found your father unconscious in his living room, and he's being admitted for observation.

You feed Jackson, eat two bowls of Special K, then drive over to the hospital.

You haven't spoken with your father since the disastrous Thanksgiving. After he insulted you, then walked away from the dinner, you and Victoria and Kelsey had cleaned up. Victoria knocked on his locked bedroom door before you all left, but he didn't answer.

For the past two weeks, you've been letting him stew in whatever juices he prefers to stew in, but neither of you has called the other, and you experience something like elation each time you remember it is Tuesday or Sunday and you no longer feel obliged to pay your biweekly visit.

Of course, that was too good to last, and as you show your vaccination card to the guard at the hospital door, and wait for an attendant to wave her no-touch digital thermometer across your forehead, you realize how unhappy you are to be seeing your father again.

Whether or not he is unhappy to see you is unclear, as he doesn't seem to recognize who you are.

"How's it going, Dad?" you say, sitting down in the chair beside his hospital bed.

He replies, "If they got 'em, they didn't say so. They maybe . . . it's, you know, that thing, they have, that place."

"I don't know what you're talking about, Dad."

His eyes are looking beyond you, or through you, and the index fingers and thumbs of both hands are snapping at something invisible in the air just above his head, and for a moment you are reminded of Elineo. "When it's over, that will be the thing . . . where it's far," he mutters. "You know, the man, the man who had that place where the, the people. . . ." His voice trails off, then he turns to look at you, and something in his eyes shifts. "What are you doing here?" he says in a voice that is neither angry nor friendly.

"I came to see you. You fell down in your living room. You were passed out when the Meals on Wheels guy came to give you breakfast this morning."

"No, I wasn't," he says.

"All right." You pat his arm, with more than a touch of condescension. "Then what are you doing here in the hospital?"

He looks around, and his eyes go unfocused. "Not a hospital," he says. "A hotel. Waiting for your mother. She'll be here any time."

"I wouldn't count on that, Dad."

"You don't know. You've never known. She was a mysterious woman, my girl."

That, at least, is true. Your mother was kind and generous, but she always held back a part of herself, as though if she gave away too much, she might disappear.

But now your father is scowling. "They're coming after you," he says. "They've got guns."

A chill runs up the back of your neck. "Who are you talking about?"

"The assassins. They're here."

He points over your shoulder, and you jerk around, but of course no one is there.

"Can't you see them?" he asks. "What are you, blind?"

"There's nobody there, Dad."

He snorts. "You idiot. Still blind, so blind." He starts to smile, then ducks and covers his head beneath the blanket.

"What are you doing?"

He peeks out from under the blanket. "The razor blades! They're sending them! Everywhere!"

A passing nurse hears him shouting, and she comes into the room. "What seems to be the problem, Mr. Crane?"

"You idiot!" he yells at her. "They're all around. Always, always, always!"

She coos at him, "You're going to need to settle down, or you're going to pull out your IV." She puts a hand on his shoulder, and all his fear and anger seem to drain away. "That's right," she says, "let's just take it easy."

He hugs himself and begins gently rocking in his thin hospital gown.
The nurse looks at you and says, "Maybe you could come back later?"
You nod, give her a weak smile, and leave without saying anything.

# 45

The next morning, you take Jackson for a walk around your neighborhood. Despite his size, he is a well-behaved dog who sits when someone comes up to him and patiently allows everyone to pet his shaggy head.

It's a cold morning for Santa Barbara, in the upper fifties, and a few people have fires burning. The smoke rising from their chimneys makes you think of childhood, as does the smell of fabric softener coming from someone's dryer vent close to the sidewalk. Most of the other walkers are women, moms who have just dropped their kids off at school and are out for a quick stroll, although there are a handful of other men—retirees, you assume. You nod at one another as you pass, complicit, slightly ashamed.

It's an ordered, domesticated world you live in, a neighborhood of flagstone driveways and tasteful, drought-resistant plantings—agave and oleander, pyracantha and lantana, Brazilian pepper trees and birds of paradise. This is no place for maniacs like Elineo and Álvaro de Campos, or rock stars like Kerry Cruz, and it's hard to imagine that they've somehow inserted themselves into your life.

As you labor up Camino Palomino, your thoughts shift, and you feel guilty that you are not with your father in the hospital. Sure, he's an unpleasant old man who tore you down rather than built you up, but he never harmed you physically, and of course he was dealing with his own demons, though he never told you what they were.

You shower and drive back to the hospital. Your father is asleep when you arrive, and you sit down in a chair next to his bed, watching the orderlies and nurses and the occasional doctor go by. The steady drip-drip of the IV machine is punctuated by a series of mysterious beepings at the nurses' station. The specter of Covid haunts the place. The ICU, where Connie died, is one floor above you. Many of the beds, you've read online, are full of unvaccinated patients. Just outside the door, two nurses speak in low voices of "omicron" and "South Africa."

A dream startles your father awake. He looks over at you and coughs. "Caleb. You're here."

"Always, Dad."

He grins, knowing that's not true, then his eyes lose their focus, and he's waving at an invisible someone or something in the corner of the room. "I see you there, don't worry. I'm not about to forget."

"A friend of yours?"

"They're no friends of mine. This is just a fun thing for them, this business of opening up the bottom and letting it out. It's an interesting situation, and I don't know how much of it is true, because I realize it's some really strange stuff. But you have to tough it out. What else are you going to do?"

"So true."

"They like the corner, those bastards." He turns to you. "What am I doing in this place? Can I do it over, or will they stop it? They don't like it, so they stop it. There's nothing you can do about it."

There's a bit of drool in the corner of your father's mouth, and you turn away, feeling more annoyed than sympathetic. "Not sure if it's important, Dad, but I'm not really following your train of thought."

"You'll be happy you were on that train, believe me."

"The thing is, I'm not on the train."

"That's what you think, mister. That's what they want you to believe. But you're on the train all the way to the terminal."

# 46

It's strange how quickly the hospital seems like not just an entire world unto itself, but the *only* world. By Thursday, you feel as though you have been in Goleta Hospital for most of your adult life. Even though you are only there for a couple of hours in the morning and the afternoon, when you are not at the hospital it feels as though you're preparing to go there, or you should have already arrived.

Victoria has insisted on taking the day off from work and driving up from Thousand Oaks. The two of you are sitting in low, uncomfortable chairs, facing your father, who is propped up in his hospital bed, holding forth.

"It's not just the target they're making, it's the target left in the place. The other place. And you wait to see what they do with it, but they don't do anything with it, they just keep it there, or they move, and you can't see, so why is it even there?"

"Very philosophical, Dad."

Victoria pulls at your sleeve and gives you a chastising look. "*Dad,*" she whispers. "That's not cool. He can't help what he's saying."

"I got that, yes. But he doesn't seem to care whether or not anyone's listening, so I like to put my oar in the water every now and again just to remind him that I'm still here."

"I'm not deaf," he says, staring at you clear-eyed. "Listen to your daughter about respect."

"You know, Dad, I realize that you are actually speaking to me, your son, Caleb, right now, but I also know, based on my experience of spending the past one hundred years in your hospital room, that in less than a minute you're going to lose the thread and go back to la-la land."

"Well, I'm not there right now, so listen up. You may think it's a bowl of cherries growing old and ending up in a place like this, but you're wrong." He makes a fist and bends toward you, suddenly sincere. "You have to *grab it*, son. Grab it while you can."

You can't believe it. He's actually crying. You hold on to his fist, which feels like the nub of an amputated arm, and for a moment, the two of you are not at odds.

Victoria reaches in and squeezes his forearm. "Grandpa, I want to say something. While you can understand me."

"I'm listening," he says, and he is.

"I think you owe Dad an apology for what you said on Thanksgiving, about his sister. Your daughter, I mean. I'm sure Dad has been carrying guilt for that his entire life." You have, yes, though not as consistently as Victoria is suggesting. "That was something that could happen to any couple of kids. A brother tells his little sister to touch a spider, and almost always nothing is going to happen. This time something terrible did. It's not his fault she's dead, and I think it would mean a lot to him if you'd just say you're sorry for blaming him."

Your father stares at your daughter for long seconds, then he drops his hand to the sheet, and the light changes in his eyes. He turns to you and says, "They got to see the way you pull it, the way you carry, and then they back you in the, the . . . place where you call the spell. It's just, it's just—give me time to think."

But Victoria doesn't give him time to think. She's up and out of the room, and a few minutes later she texts to say she's sorry she brought up such a painful subject, and she's driving back home to Thousand Oaks.

Friday morning, your father isn't stirring, and you notice on the white-board that, under your name and phone number, "DNR" has been circled and underlined.

The first time a nurse enters the room, you point to the board and whisper, "Is it that bad?"

"It's hard to say for sure," she says. "Sometimes they turn around, but sometimes they don't. We need to be ready for whatever happens." She's a short middle-aged redhead, brusque, but not unfriendly.

"It's just I don't know that anyone's specifically told me we were possibly at that stage."

"They may have thought you already knew."

"I guess I did, and I didn't. If that makes sense."

"Perfect sense."

"So, DNR means 'no heroic measures'?"

"Something like that. The patient's comfort is the primary concern, which is why he's on morphine now. Your father was smart to have filed a health directive at some point. Everyone ought to have one. Do you?"

"Yes. I met with a lawyer after my wife died."

"Oh," she says. "I'm sorry."

"Me too," you say. "Me too, me too, me too."

# 48

Later that day, when you are back for your afternoon shift at the hospital, your father is awake, although he seems to be moving at half-speed. As you settle into the chair by his bed, a nurse is untangling his IV line. "He keeps bending his arms, and it sets off the alarm," she tells you. Then to him: "Don't do that anymore, okay, Grandpa?"

"I'm not your grandpa," he mutters.

After she leaves, you ask him, "How are you, Dad?"

"I'm not myself," he says. "Not remotely myself." He rubs a hand across his wrinkled forehead, then asks, "Am I dying?"

"I don't know," you say.

"You're honest, at least."

"I hope I'm more than that."

He seems to shrug, although he's suddenly so shrunken in his pale blue hospital gown that it's hard to tell.

Neither of you talks for a good long while, as nurses pass in the corridor, making and laughing at jokes, rushing from one crisis to the next. Your father bends his arm, and a nurse comes in to adjust the IV line and turn off the alarm. She looks at him, and smiles, but he doesn't smile back.

You put your hand on his, and he doesn't move it away. "I'm going to have to leave in a few minutes, Dad. Is there anything on your mind? Anything you want to say?"

He coughs and shakes his head slightly. "You do what you have to do."

You're retired, so you don't really have to be anywhere, but sitting in the hospital room is making your body feel so heavy—as though someone has placed weights on your ankles and wrists and neck—that you feel like if you don't leave soon, you're going to be dragged into the floor and disappear into the earth.

"I'll be back tomorrow," you tell him. He looks at you, then shuts his eyes.

# 49

You've ordered GrubHub three nights in a row, so that evening you decide to bake the two large Russet potatoes you have before they go soft.

While you wait for the oven to preheat, you clean the potatoes with a scrub pad under cold tap water, dry them off with a paper towel, and poke holes in each one with a fork. You smooth aluminum foil over the body of a baking pan, then bathe your potatoes in vegetable oil before grinding some pepper and shaking some garlic salt on their slick skins.

It's a half-hour on each side at four hundred twenty-five degrees, and to kill time you scroll through the news on your phone—the omicron variant is conquering Europe and Andrew Cuomo must forfeit the five million dollars he made on his book deal. You flip through the latest *New Yorker* cartoons; there are funny ones about a picky anteater and a hibernating bear that Connie would have liked. Then you stare out the window as shadows creep up the south side of the Santa Ynez mountains.

When your potatoes are baked, you slice them open and drop big chunks of butter in each one, slicing at their flesh as you work the butter in. Then it's more garlic salt and ground pepper. You uncap a bottle of IPA and dig in.

As you finish up, wiping butter from your chin, you feel as though you have just finished the loneliest dinner ever, and you leave the dishes in the sink, swallow a Benadryl, and go to bed as soon as possible.

That night you dream of your long-gone sister. She is both a child, picking dandelions in the backyard, and an adult woman, typing on a computer at an office desk. The scene darkens, the landscape goes jagged and grim, and the spectral figures of your wife and mother appear. The three ghosts circle one another, then merge into a solitary figure that begins trudging down a path into the unknowable distance.

You wake up sweating and take a long time falling back to sleep.

Early the next morning you receive a call from the hospital informing you that your father is dead.

# NEXTDOOR

## RANCHO DE LAS PUMAS • 19 DEC

**Maria Moss**

**So quiet.** Has anyone else noticed how quiet it's been in the neighborhood lately? Sometimes I feel like there's no one around at all.

# POOR GHOST: AN ORAL HISTORY

## 2005–2009

### *Hillsdale Boulevard* (2007)
### US Billboard Peak Position: 51

**STUART FISHER:** This is going to sound egotistical, but I don't mean it to be. People always talk a lot about my lyrics, how different they are from the average rock song, how "poetic" they are, and the simple fact is that I read a lot of poetry, especially contemporary poets. If you look at the bookshelf near my bed, at the books that I read over and over, you'll find Charles Wright, Elizabeth Bishop, Sylvia Plath, Robert Lowell, Robert Hayden, Charles Simic, Eavan Boland, Ciaran Carson, Jean Valentine. And then of course Auden and Frost, Yeats and Hardy. I could go on and on.

I mean, I was an English major, right? That was my trajectory before the band changed everything.

But above all, I especially love Seamus Heaney. Working-class Sacramento and rural Northern Ireland are very different in many ways, but there's also a kind of insistence on concrete objects, on the things of this world. Your bullshit detector's always on high. And a love of talk, which means appreciating the way sounds go together, especially consonants and short vowels—not that people are conscious of something like that, but they still *hear* it.

Anyway, when Heaney won the Nobel Prize in 1995, I sent him a letter of congratulations, and he actually wrote me back. One of his kids had really been into *Scoured*, so I made sure that he got a copy of *Between Religion and Hygiene*, which had just come out, and he wrote me a nice little note about that.

That was pretty much the extent of our correspondence, but he was giving a reading in Berkeley, years later, in the spring of 2006, and I went to it, and managed to get myself introduced to him. I became part of the drinks party afterward, with his wife, Marie, and Robert Haas, who was hosting, and I don't know who else. We ended up in San Francisco at the home of one of the sponsors. It was one of those Victorians on Russian Hill with a view of Coit Tower and Alcatraz sparkling out in the Bay. Kind of magical.

Maybe I flatter myself, and maybe it was just the whiskey, but I felt like he was genuinely fascinated by the problems of writing lyrics for popular music. And of course I couldn't get enough of his talk about the "glottal stop" and the "phonetic clip," not to mention his yarns about hanging out with Joseph Brodsky and Czeslaw Milosz, and so on.

Probably all poets secretly want to be rock stars, and vice versa.

Anyway, the end of the story is that Seamus Heaney told me I should write about my "home place," that it was the richest source of poetic material, the well that would never run dry.

And so I did, and that's where the songs on *Hillsdale Boulevard* come from.

**GREGG MORGAN:** I'd never heard of Seamus Heaney before he became part of the press kit for that album.

**SHANE REED:** Gregg and I, we grew up in basically the same neighborhood as Stuart, so those lyrics did touch us, I think. They didn't touch everyone, though, unfortunately. The album didn't sell well.

**ED WINGFIELD:** I did not hear a hit on that record, and I told them so. I told them every album needs at least one hit, no matter how good the individual songs are. Otherwise, it's going to be a dud. Stuart wanted to fire me, but the others liked my hands-off style of managing, and I think they figured, Better the devil you know, so I stayed on.

**KERRY CRUZ:** I'm from Modesto, not Sacramento, but it's pretty near the same thing, and I definitely appreciated what Stuart was trying to do, recapturing that feeling of hope and despair you have when you realize the world doesn't care as much about you as you do about it. It's like he sings in "Sacramento River"—"The Valley is hot, the Valley is dry / You're ready to leave it, dead or alive."

Still, I also thought Ed had a good point about there not being a single, something that would make us feel relevant in the age of Mary J. Blige and Busta Rhymes and Justin Timberlake. In popular music, there's always a tug-of-war between art and commerce, and in a successful record, the musicians nod to both. That didn't happen in this case. Art won, hands down.

**GREGG MORGAN:** I learned how to play the dobro and the Hawaiian guitar for that album, so I guess it wasn't a total loss.

**SHANE REED:** For a commercially unsuccessful album, we spent a lot of time in the studio. Stuart wanted to get it exactly how he heard it in his head, and we kept doing take after take until we at least got close.

**ED WINGFIELD:** I hate being the villain in the story about this album because I do like it, and I do understand where it came from. Stuart's mother had died the year before. He hadn't been very close with his family, but her death made an impression on him. It made him want to retrieve some of those early memories that were going to disappear if he didn't record them.

But when you manage a band, your primary objective is their success, and that ultimately means financial success. So, yes, "Do *Hillsdale Boulevard*," I basically said to Stuart, "but get it out of your system so you can move on to something that more people are going to like."

**KERRY CRUZ:** Bottom line: sometimes you have to take one for the team.

**STUART FISHER:** It was an honor to have the Chieftains play on two songs.

**ED WINGFIELD:** I remember paying the Chieftains a shit-ton of money just to play on two songs.

**STUART FISHER:** Paddy Moloney's tin whistle on "Mother's Day in Foothill Farms" is one of my favorite moments in our entire catalog. And Derek Bell's Irish harp on "Tomorrow's Suicides," well, that still gives me the chills.

**GREGG MORGAN:** I like the video we did for "Sacramento River." We're miming the song on a houseboat while people are getting wasted on the beach and doing cannonballs off a bridge. "Sacramento River delivers / Just a sliver of delight." Kind of an inside joke, but that song got at least a little airplay on college radio.

**JERRY DIMGARTEN:** It was the lowest-charting album of their career, but *Hillsdale Boulevard* was a critics' darling. I was among those fans, certainly. Even Christgau gave it a B+.

I grew up on Long Island, a long way from Sacramento, but I thought what Stuart was saying about the American underclass was pretty universal, and he did it in such a studied, yet inventive, way.

In the music, I hear echoes of early '70s Lindisfarne, and maybe the Fairley Brothers of the '80s. But the lyrics are what make the record special. There's the rhyme between "Everclear and trailer homes" and "plastic deer and garden gnomes" in "Rio Linda." And that image of "the faint bloom of iridescent scales" in "Cutting It Loose," when the speaker is easing a dying fish back into the water. Plus, all that business about the women with plumerias behind their ears listening to an 8-track of *Tiny Bubbles* in "Sacramento Luau." Not to mention the last line of the title song about "the swollen purple fruit of the unkillable olive trees." Maybe it's not up to Seamus Heaney's standards in terms of poetry, but it sure beats whatever was happening in *Hannah Montana 2*.

**SHANE REED:** I think we all felt a kind of letdown, but also relief, after the album came out. Like, shit, I'm glad that's over.

**STUART FISHER:** I made sure a copy of *Hillsdale Boulevard* was sent to Seamus Heaney, but I never heard anything from him, which I admit was very disappointing. Still, the album was number one in the *Voice*'s year-end Pazz & Jop poll. I'll take that over sales figures any day of the week.

# TEXTS
## KS & RA


**Sun, Dec 19, 5:22 AM**

Becca? You awake?

I didn't think so. You always turn off your phone at night, which is smart.

I'm just letting you know that I think I'm going to drop that Poor Ghost story. What a waste of time. I tried to write my way into it, but the whole thing is just too confusing. First the plane crash, then the guy, Caleb, gets attacked, then the guy who incited the attack kills his own daughter because of some crazy QAnon bullshit. Santa Barbara just feels like this weird locus of bad energy right now, and I want to stay away from it. Plus, I got hired to do a story down in San Diego.

Text or call me when you wake up, okay? Luv u!

# THE
# AFTERLIFE
# OF
# POOR GHOST

# 50

You arrive at the hospital a little before six in the morning. It's still dark out, and cold, with fog drifting across the splashes of bright yellow-orange light from the parking lot's sodium lamps. You show your vaccine credentials, have your temperature taken, get your day badge, then take the elevator up to the third floor.

Two nurses seated at the nurses' station recognize you and come around to offer their condolences. You thank them, and walk slowly into your father's room, half-expecting him to sit up and accuse you of something.

He doesn't, though. His skin is a pale gray, his eyes are closed, and his mouth is set in an *O* of disbelief. The redheaded nurse who'd asked you if you had a DNR puts her hand on your arm. "We assume you'll want to spend some time alone with your father."

"I guess so."

"Take all the time you need. And then what would you like to do afterwards? Was your father a religious man?"

"Not really, no."

"We have a hospital chaplain, if you'd like to speak with him."

"I don't think so."

"For those with non-traditional beliefs, we have a lavender oil ceremony. It's nondenominational, and many people find it comforting."

For a moment, you think, *No way*, but then something about the ceremony sounds both refreshingly unreligious, and a little bit of a poke at your father, who abhorred anything he considered New Age.

You take ten minutes at his bedside, but you're not feeling much. Once, you even surreptitiously check the news on your phone. Then you call for the nurse.

Three nurses come in. One takes off the hospital blanket and replaces it with a lavender sheet that covers your father from chest to ankles. As one reads a poem aloud, the other two dab his hands, forehead, and feet. "I am a thousand winds that blow," the nurse reads. "I am the diamond glints on snow."

For a moment, you hear nothing. Then everything seems to be spinning.

The poem ends:

> *Do not stand at my grave and weep.*
> *I am not there, I do not sleep.*
> *Do not stand there at my grave and cry.*
> *I am not there, I did not die.*

It's a corny poem, you realize that, so you are surprised to find yourself weeping, openly and unashamedly. You try to calm your breathing, but when you look up at the nurses, they are all softly crying too.

# 51

After the lavender oil ceremony, the nurses quickly, seamlessly return to business. "Your father will go down to the morgue now," one says. "Once you decide on a funeral home, have them get in touch with us."

You nod and begin signing the paperwork attached to a clipboard that one of the nurses has handed you. Afterward, you thank everyone, take one last look at your father, and drive home.

You've been through this process all too recently with Connie, so you call your father's attorney and schedule a meeting for the next day. You have a copy of his will, and since you've had power of attorney for the last two years, you're pretty sure it won't have been changed. Half of his total assets go to you, the other half to Victoria.

You call the same funeral home that "handled"—their words—Connie's death. They email you a to-do list. You call Social Security and have his payments stopped. You call the local paper and the cable TV company and close his accounts.

Those three calls take an hour and a half, and you decide to take a break from the phone and drive to your father's house to retrieve his bills, bank statements, and insurance policies.

Sitting in his driveway next to his old Camry, you think maybe you will donate the car to public radio. Your father would not have approved.

As you walk to the front door, realizing that you will have to do something about the house as well, you suddenly notice all its faults—the peeling paint, a cracked shutter, the bent downspout, loose shingles on the roof.

You let yourself in with the key he didn't know you'd copied, and you're greeted with the smell of mildew and old newspapers and burned meat.

This was never your home. You grew up in a larger house in Santa Barbara, but several years after you moved out, your father, who retired early from his job as a county code-enforcement officer, insisted that he and your mother move into a smaller home. She was never happy there, and time and lack of care have erased most of her presence.

In the living room, you plop yourself down on a dusty sofa with thin cushions and exhale. He's gone now, this man who was too much there in spirit and never enough in person.

Cardboard boxes are stacked nearly to the ceiling. In front of them are stacks of the local newspaper, some yellowing from age. A roll of wire and a wire cutter sit on an end table. Clustered around them are pieces of wire approximately an inch long—cut for a purpose no one will ever know.

On your way here, you'd considered moving yourself and Jackson into your father's house until Elineo and Álvaro de Campos are apprehended, but there's no way you could live here. It would suffocate you.

In fact, just being in the house is making you anxious. You retrieve the documents the funeral home said you should have—bills, bank statements, insurance policies—which you had the foresight to store in a single plastic bin. Then you look around. There's so much garbage to dig through, so much you will have to dispose of. You feel a wave of panic and hurry out of the house, almost forgetting to lock the front door.

# 52

Small though it was, you had a very moving ceremony for Connie. You and Victoria and Jackson went down to the far southern end of Goleta beach. Victoria read a gloomy poem with a line you still remember: "Here! Creep, wretch, under a comfort serves in a whirlwind." You both talked about how much she'd meant to you, and then you'd waded out into the cold waves and opened up the urn and scattered her ashes across the water.

But as far as you know, your father's friends are all dead or no longer his friends, and having a ceremony for him feels hypocritical. After your breakdown at the lavender oil ceremony in the hospital, you've mostly just felt a sense of relief that he's gone.

Consequently, the conversation at the funeral home is awkward.

The funeral director's office is well lit. A competent painting of a barn on a hill hangs on the wall behind him; the metal bookcases are full of three-ring binders. There's no trace of death here. You could be back in your own office at the insurance company, a space which you, too, kept mostly empty of personal information.

As you sit down, you tell the director that you'd like to keep expenses under control as much as possible.

"What I hear you saying is you're imagining something modest for your father's memorial service."

"Actually, I was imagining no service at all."

"Ah." He continues smiling, although possibly a shade less brightly. "And how would you prefer to dispose of the cremated remains?"

"Can you just do it?"

"We can." The smile continues to fade.

"Is that unusual? I don't want to be disrespectful to my father."

"It's not the usual thing, but it certainly does occur."

"And when can you give me a copy of his death certificate?"

"It normally takes three to four weeks to hear back from vital records. Are you in a hurry?"

"I want to sell the house and settle his affairs as quickly as possible. I just want it to be over, you know?"

"Of course." The smile is a ghost of its former self. "Well, I think we can accommodate your wishes. They are, as I said, very modest."

From then on out, he is all business, explaining his contract, showing you where to initial and where to sign in full.

It's all over in a half-hour, then you are back outside. Presumably to allow for the operation of its crematorium, the funeral home is beyond both the Goleta and Santa Barbara city limits. Behind the parking lot, protected by a barbed-wire fence, stretch long rows of avocado trees. They look dry and unhealthy. It's been a while since there was any rain.

# 53

That night, you are dreaming in Insuranceeze. *Service line occurrence as used herein . . . replacement cost items do not apply to the following personal property.* Then you are in some nightmare courtroom where a client is suing you for misrepresenting a clause that has invalidated an entire policy. You are guilty as sin, and all the onlookers know it. As he is about to rule against you, the judge raises an enormous gavel, and it is then that you hear Connie's voice.

You wake immediately and sit bolt upright in bed. It's dark, but a bit of moonlight slips through the slats of the blinds. You look around for her, but of course she's not there. She's not anywhere.

Still, the words she spoke, in what you are acknowledging now must have been a dream, are clear: *Follow him.*

In the morning, you decide to look for whatever Kerry Cruz had been seeking in your backyard. It's dry and chilly, and you put on a pair of work gloves so you can poke around in the thorny leaves of the holly bushes near the gate.

You're just about ready to give up, when you feel something solid through one of the gloves. It's partly wedged beneath a crack in the exterior wall's plaster sheathing, and it takes a while to get hold of it. Finally, gingerly, you grasp the thing between your thumb and forefinger and pull it out of the bushes.

It is a pistol, a very small one, almost like a toy. But the moment you pick it up, you can feel it has a heft to it. The grip is marked by an oval with the word "Browning" in raised letters.

The sun is shining, and you hold the gun up against the sky. The tiny barrel has a patch of rust near the muzzle.

Your first impulse is to call 911, but what about all the questions and suspicions that are sure to come raining down on you? What will Elineo think when the internet tells him he has been right all along?

Still, you try to imagine a rational conversation with the police, one in which you explain how Kerry Cruz came snooping around, and why you didn't bother telling anyone about his visit. Granted, you couldn't know that he was looking for—what? A murder weapon? Whatever you say, you're going to be embroiled in the Poor Ghost story once again, only this time you'll be an actual suspect. Maybe, the police—and everyone else—will think you *were* involved in bringing down the plane.

On the other hand, are you really going to hide what is obviously a crucial piece of evidence? If Kerry Cruz is involved in the downing of the plane, and you say nothing, you will be letting him get away with a horrendous crime.

You realize that your breathing has become fast and erratic. You're feeling lightheaded; before you pass out, you plop yourself down cross-legged on the path that leads to the gate. The concrete feels cold beneath your jeans. You bend over, resting your forehead against your clasped hands.

Then you remember that Kerry Cruz's card is still in your wallet. Poor Ghost is just a phone call away.

**Murder Suspect Still at Large**

**Tue Dec 21, 2021 | 10:00 AM**

Area law enforcement continue their search for first degree murder suspect Elineo Amis, 38, of Santa Barbara. Amis is accused of murdering his six-year-old daughter, Esther, on December 6, by throwing her from the More Mesa bluff onto the More Mesa beach, seventy feet below.

Bystanders reported that prior to the murder, Amis, owner of the Surfin' for Jesus surf school, claimed his daughter was "infected by serpent DNA." Afterward, Amis is alleged to have said that he committed the murder for Stuart Fisher, the late singer of the band Poor Ghost, whose plane crashed near Santa Barbara on September 21.

On December 7, Amis was reportedly seen in a grove of trees near the bike path at Patterson Avenue and Atascadero Creek. On December 10, he was sighted at the loading bay behind Costco in Goleta, and on December 15 several people claimed to have seen him in and around the Kentucky Fried Chicken on Calle Real.

Sheriff's spokesperson Claudia Hartmann said the department believes Amis is still somewhere in the Santa Barbara area. Anyone with information on his whereabouts is urged to call the Santa Barbara County Sheriff's Office. Amis is considered armed and dangerous and should not be approached under any circumstances.

# POOR GHOST: AN ORAL HISTORY

## 2010–2013

### *Everything Good Is on the Highway* (2011)
### US Billboard Peak Position: 1

**KERRY CRUZ:** It was three years since *Hillsdale Boulevard*, and we'd been doing our usual thing: Gregg jamming with other musicians, Shane doing his businesses—some succeeding, some not so much. Stuart was doing Stuart. After Holly, he never wanted to have a partner for very long, and he loved having the freedom to just move from one place to another on a whim. During that time, I believe he was living in Kuala Lumpur, Paris, Buenos Aires, and Sonora, California.

I was raising my family. I kept the house in Hancock Park, but my wife and I bought a kind of gentleman's ranch up in the San Gabriel mountains just south of Antelope Valley. We had a big old farmhouse with some horses, a little bass pond with a creek running through it. All these orange and yellow and purple wildflowers on the hills in the spring. And just an hour and a half from LA. Pretty sweet deal. I'm always happy to come home.

**ED WINGFIELD:** I'd already told them: Look, you did your artsy album that peaked at number 51. Now it's time to get back in the game and make a record that people actually want to *purchase*. But of course, that was the problem. By 2010, the record industry was basically in tatters. People wanted their music for free, and the internet was happy to oblige. The moment you released something, it was pirated and a million people downloaded it for free.

What happened, as we know, was that bands began making their primary earnings from tours instead of recorded music. Ticket prices shot up. At concerts, merch was hawked like crazy.

So, I got to thinking: What about a live album? Even if people steal it, they're going to want to go out and see PG play, and some of those people who see them play *will* want to buy the album, especially if it's a box set with a full-color booklet, and whatever else you can think of to put in there. That was the impetus for *Everything Good Is on the Highway*.

**GREGG MORGAN:** Like most rock bands, we started out as a live band, and we toured to support every album. We knew what we were doing, and that was definitely one of the sources of our staying power, being able to kick ass on stage. I think it's fair to put us in the company of Springsteen and U2 and Petty, when he was around. We have a loyal fan base that will always come out and listen to us play.

So, in the summer of 2010, we did this tour with Al Schmitt as our recording engineer. Al was famous in the studio—Neil Young, Elvis Presley, Michael Jackson, Madonna—all these huge records and Grammys and so forth. But he'd never recorded a live album, and we told him if he did ours, we'd also give him a producer credit.

**SHANE REED:** Stuart, of course, just wanted to do new material, like Neil Young's *Rust Never Sleeps*. But Ed and I convinced him that the best live album would be a retrospective of our career—a greatest-hits album, but with the extra energy of our live shows.

**STUART FISHER:** I was thinking of *Rust Never Sleeps*, an opportunity to bring out new material in the context of a live performance. It's a rare thing, which to my way of thinking doesn't mean it's a bad thing, but I was outvoted by the rest of the band.

**ED WINGFIELD:** I think the number of units Warner Brothers shipped prove I had the right idea.

**GREGG MORGAN:** The next argument was about whether or not to include "Spaghetti Bolognese and a Can of Coke." That was one of our signature hits, but we hadn't played it live for a long time. Shane and Ed definitely wanted it on the album, but Stuart was like, "No way. I do not want to be remembered for that song."

**STUART FISHER:** I won the "Spaghetti" debate. If I never hear that song again, it will be too soon.

**GREGG MORGAN:** Personally, I like to tour. My only marriage lasted about five days. I'm just not suited to settling down, or being told when I have to be home at night, or what I have to do. So, yeah, I like my place in Laurel Canyon, but I have a year-round caretaker, and if I get to rock and roll, I'm just as happy living out of a hotel room for six months. In fact, it's a lot easier, in a way. Everything comes to you. As long as you show up on stage when the lights go up, and you know all the licks to your songs, you've got it made.

**KERRY CRUZ:** Ed decided making a movie of the tour would be just the "synergy" we needed to put the album over the top. I thought, Why not? even though, God knows, I wasn't crazy about all the touring. I hate to fly.

**ED WINGFIELD:** Stuart wanted D. A. Pennebaker to direct the concert movie. He loved Dylan's *Don't Look Back*, of course, and *Monterey Pop*. I believe Pennebaker also did movies about Alice Cooper and David Bowie. And maybe Jerry Lee Lewis? Didn't matter, though. Pennebaker wasn't interested. He said he didn't like the band's music, and that was it.

I ended up hiring Rex Myers, the music-video director, and his movie obviously had a lot to do with the success of the album. We gave him a 20 percent cut of net, but he had to take on all the financial responsibilities of making the film. It turned out that everybody was a winner.

**STUART FISHER:** In a way, in a studio album you get to hide yourself somewhat. You really control every second of what people hear, and, with all the overdubs, you can cloak those things you don't want people to see. Obviously, plenty of "live" albums have a lot of overdubbing, but with a live concert and a movie about playing live, you're kind of out there in a way that often made me feel uncomfortable.

**SHANE REED:** In a studio album, when you're the drummer, it's easy to get lost in the mix. Sometimes, depending on the engineer, that happens literally, but what I mean is the listener's attention is focused on the singer and the lyrics and the melody. But when you're drumming live onstage, up on a riser above the rest of the band, you really stand out. People notice you, and they realize how important you are to the overall sound. A rock band without a drummer isn't a band.

**GREGG MORGAN:** When I watch *Everything Good Is on the Highway*, or even just listen to the album, I have good memories. I think about the four of us being together, and, my god, it's like how many years have we been doing this, and we're still kicking ass and sounding pretty fucking good for a bunch of old geezers.

**KERRY CRUZ:** I love that part in the middle of "A Million Reasons Not to Tell the Truth" when Gregg is wailing on his solo, and this woman gets up on stage, and in about ten seconds strips totally naked, then does a swan dive back into the crowd. Then Gregg's solo gets even more manic until he collapses on stage in a welter of feedback.

**GREGG MORGAN:** That naked lady thing was still earlyish YouTube, but talk about a viral moment. I remember Nancy O'Dell discussing it on *Entertainment Tonight*, how it had set feminism back fifty years.

**JERRY DIMGARTEN:** For me, the most intriguing footage was the backstage stuff. It reminded me of those bits in Bowie's *Ziggy Stardust* movie when he's changing costumes while Mick Ronson plays a long solo onstage. You get the sense of the band as performers, almost like Broadway actors, who are remembering their lines and their licks before they go out and give a crowd-pleasing show.

In particular, I'm thinking of that scene in the dressing room before one concert where Stuart and Kerry are trying to harmonize on "Koan Americana," and they keep getting interrupted by people. First it's Ed Wingfield, then Shane's girlfriend at the time—I don't remember her name—asks for Stuart's autograph, then the lighting designer wants to talk about a glitch in the console, then Gregg has a question about the order of the set list. It's chaotic. But instead of getting pissed at everyone, Stuart and Kerry just respond calmly, then go right back to trying to get that harmony right. You felt like they were professionals, and also that they were artists, really devoted to their craft.

**SHANE REED:** I honestly thought this would be our last number-one album, and we were lucky to have it. Even one week at the top, like we had, is a real sales booster.

**STUART FISHER:** The album's title comes from Emerson's essay "Experience." The line right before it is "The great gifts are not got by analysis," and I thought that was an accurate summation of PG's ethos. We're a band that has always sort of *felt* our way forward. Like: "Is this the right thing to do?" And you say: "Well, how does it *feel*?" Ultimately, that album, that tour, the movie—they felt right.

## Poor Ghost: Everything Good Is on the Highway
18,979,755 views • Jul 31, 2013

**Andrew Kennedy**

rewatching the movie for like the hundredth time i keep getting blown away by how good these guys were. every. single. song. rip.

**PGRulz**

I've never had such a strong connection to anything as I've had to their music. They saved me many times for sure when I was feeling so, so low.

**Edgar Eagle**

Check out Gregg's solo on "The Afterbirth of Tragedy" at 38:17. The Phrygian scale in E has never sounded more alive.

**Shred 2 Survive**

I still laugh every time that lady takes it off onstage. And Gregg just keeps right on jamming.

**Briana Wilson**

this is how you connect with an audience—write songs that people want to hear over and over and over again

**Owen the God**

Look at the audience shots. Those people are in pure bliss!

## Samantha Buchanan

Love how Stuart keeps the crowd going at the end of Wax monk in a glass box (around the 52-minute mark). He's all la la la la la laaaaaaaaaaaa!!!

## Brandi the Bulgar Slayer

Never seen so many happy people in one place before or since.

## Eric 805

am i the only one who feels like shane is the unacknowledged leader of this band? without the drums, pg is just a really good garage band. but with shane, they are transcendent.

## punkwontdie

Legends, pure and simple.

# THE
# AFTERLIFE
# OF
# POOR GHOST

# 55

You take Kerry Cruz's card from your wallet and, right there in the backyard, pull your phone from your pocket and give him a call.

He is in New York and has an important meeting that afternoon with Poor Ghost's lawyers, but he thinks he can be in Santa Barbara before midnight. You tell him the next morning is fine, and he says he'll text you his arrival information once he has it. There's something about his voice that, despite yourself, makes you want to trust him.

You feed Jackson a can of dog food, make a cup of tea, sit down with your computer, and pull up some YouTube interviews with the band, just to see how Kerry comes across. The interviewers, naturally, direct most of their questions to Stuart, but Kerry is clearly the next in charge, at least from an intellectual and aesthetic standpoint. He talks intelligently about the composition of a song or an album, and he clearly is not only concerned about the artistic direction of the band, but he has a hand in shaping it. Gregg is funny—the wild lead guitarist—while Shane comes across a bit pinched, more of a bottom-line guy. He only really lights up when the band's success is mentioned. None of them seem eager to bring on their own deaths.

You make another cup of tea, then call Kelsey Symmons.

"Hi," she says, apparently surprised to hear from you. "Anything new?"

"Yeah, actually. I think I found the gun that was used to force down Poor Ghost's plane."

She's silent for a moment. "You're shitting me, right?"

"I don't think so."

"Have you called the cops? Or the NTSB?"

"No. Kerry Cruz is coming over tomorrow morning to talk about it. He says it's not his, but I think it might be. I caught him looking for it in the bushes of my backyard."

"You *what?* Whoa. And you didn't tell anyone?"

"He was poking around in my bushes the day you called me about Eli-neo killing his daughter. Then my father was in the hospital, and I kind of forgot about it until after he died."

"Wait, what? When did your dad die?"

"A few days ago."

"I'm so sorry."

"Thank you."

There's a longer pause. Finally, she says, "I'm down in San Diego right now, doing a story on military personnel who refuse to get vaccinated, but I could come up there if you want me to. It might take a day or so."

"No, that's okay. I just wanted to tell someone. In case something happened to me."

"You think Kerry Cruz is going to *kill* you?"

"Not really. Just being cautious. But if it happens, you'll have quite a scoop."

"I mean, getting murdered by a rock star? Sounds unlikely. On the other hand, you did have an airplane crash in your backyard."

"I'm going to hear him out. I'll let you know what he says."

"I'd very much appreciate that." In the background, you hear some men laughing, then the sound of a jet engine coming to life. "Gotta go," she yells. "Call me after you talk with him."

"I will," you say, but she's already hung up.

# 56

It is Tuesday, December 21, and you haven't done a thing for Christmas. Last year was too raw, but this was Connie's favorite holiday, and the prospect of buying a Christmas tree and spending the day decorating for the holidays makes you suddenly and unaccountably happy.

Jackson, ever alert to your mood, perks up, and you have a hard time keeping him in the house as you head down to the garden center off Patterson where you and Connie would always buy your trees. You choose a seven-foot spruce with thick branches. Two men attach a stand, then tie the tree to the top of your SUV, and on the way home, stopped at a light, a little girl in the back seat of the car in front of you turns, waves, and mouths *Merry Christmas.*

Back at the house, you cut the twine and drag the tree into its traditional corner. Jackson sniffs at the branches, and you give him a finger wag and keep repeating, "No pee. No pee." You fill the stand with water, sweep up the trail of pine needles—the tree is much drier than you realized—then fetch the Christmas lights from the garage.

Outside, you use a staple gun to attach a string of white lights to the eaves on the front of your house. Then, for the rest of the morning, you decorate the tree, playing Christmas music on Spotify, which includes Poor Ghost's guitar-driven version of "O Come, All Ye Faithful." Jackson sits on the rug, watching as you go back and forth from the boxes to the tree.

At first, it feels as satisfying as you had imagined it would, but then memories of Christmases with Connie and Victoria come flooding back. You remember the morning when Victoria was six and you and Connie came out to find that your daughter had unwrapped not just her own, but every present under the tree. Also, the time you bought Connie a pair of diamond earrings and she lost the right one as she was putting it on. You never found the earring, though you looked for days afterward. And then her last Christmas, months before Connie got sick, when the pandemic was just a thing happening in China. The two of you bought each other

Rick Steves' travel guides: Portugal, Italy, Iceland, Scotland, Ireland, Switzerland—all the places you were going to go, together.

The blackness of loss sweeps through you.

You struggle to find the motivation to hang the last ornaments on the branches, nearly weeping when you reach one Victoria made in preschool. It's a photograph of her in a Santa hat glued inside a border of popsicle sticks. "Child of God," it says, in gold marker.

You loop the yarn around a branch, stagger to the bedroom, and collapse on the bed. Jackson curls up next to you, and the two of you sleep until three.

You get up and wander to the kitchen, feeling lonely and adrift from your life. This was supposed to be the year that you and Connie began taking some serious, month-long vacations to the places in the Rick Steves guidebooks. Connie had discovered a house-swapping website, and she'd even made some tentative overtures back in early 2020 with a couple in Dublin. Covid would have nixed those plans, of course, but there would still have been a future together—wide open and possibly wonderful.

Jackson is hungry, shaking his head back and forth until you get the message, and you open a can of food and plop it in his dish. He devours it greedily.

Jackson is another reason you're feeling blue. Victoria has told you that she'd like to take him back to Thousand Oaks after she visits you for Christmas, and you feel that's only fair.

As this is your last week together, you get him in the car and drive down to Haskell's Beach, where you let him off the leash and he runs into the crashing waves. Though it's late afternoon, the beach is crowded and Jackson makes friends with other dogs, big and small, generally exhibiting an unthinking joy in life that you desperately envy.

You sit down in dry sand and watch him cavort in the surf as the sun drops toward the horizon. There's a faint stench of drying kelp, and sand fleas hop up and down like kernels of popping corn.

Connie would have relished the scene, but you think instead of your father, and how little he liked the sea, though he lived within five miles of it for most of his life. He was always so *dissatisfied*, and something about him lingers in you like an unpleasant smell that won't go away, no matter how wide the windows are open or how hard the wind blows.

Out over the Pacific, a United jet coming down from San Francisco begins its final approach to the airport. You imagine it blowing apart in a ball of flames, wreckage and people scattering into the waves. *Why would you think such a thing?* you ask yourself. *What's wrong with you?*

The next morning, you're awakened by the hum of your phone. It's Kerry Cruz. He's just landed at the airport, and is wondering if it's okay to come straight to your house, ten minutes away. You tell him that's fine. You've just finished dressing and brushing your hair and your teeth, when there's a knock on the front door.

Although it's the third time you've seen him in person, it's still something of a shock to encounter a celebrity on your front porch. He's wearing sunglasses and a baseball cap. Out on the street, a black sedan is idling. You can just see the driver through the tinted windows.

Jackson waits near the doorsill, wagging his tail. He loves company.

"Who's this big guy?" Kerry Cruz asks.

"Jackson."

He reaches down and scratches Jackson behind the ears. "Good boy," he croons.

You invite him in and ask if he'd like a cup of coffee or tea. He says tea and you brew a cup for both of you as he wanders around your living room, looking at the prints of Connie's cartoons. "You really like her work," he says.

"I do. She was my wife."

"'Was'?"

"She died from Covid in May 2020."

"Wow. Jesus. Sorry." He lets out a long breath. "She was good," he continues, and you nod—of course she was.

You bring him his tea, and he gestures at your tree. "I see you have the Christmas spirit."

"Trying," you say. "Why don't we go outside?"

"Good idea, good idea." He clears his throat. "One thing, though, if you could leave your phone in here? I'd really appreciate it. I consider the conversation we're about to have to be a private one."

"All right." You put down your tea, take your phone from your pocket, and put it on the kitchen table. "And what about you?" you say. "Same thing?"

Kerry Cruz smiles and reaches for his phone. "Sure."

Then you and Jackson and the bass player for one of America's most famous bands go outside.

"What are those flowers?" he asks, pointing at the clusters of torch lilies that line the yard. Their colors are fading a bit in mid-December, but the tips of the stalks are still striking—yellow, orange, and red, pointing at the sky like just-shot flares.

You tell him the name of the plant, and point to two chairs by the fire-pit. It's cloudy and chilly, and you light the burner, and the two of you sit there together for a moment, silently. It's strange to have this man on your patio who, for so many nights, was the topic of so much discussion. Strange to see him at all. Jackson settles himself down at Kerry Cruz's feet.

"So," he finally begins, "I'm going to tell you the story of what happened on that plane, at least as far as I know it. Everything I tell you is in confidence, and I will deny it all, but I think you'll see that none of it was my fault."

"Okay."

"First," he says, "I'd like you to give me that gun."

"Actually, I'm not really comfortable doing that just yet. Why don't you tell me your story, and then we'll see."

He sighs. "Fair enough." Then he begins.

According to Kerry Cruz, even after all these years of touring, he'd never felt comfortable flying. Therefore, he swallowed, as was his habit, two one-milligram tablets of Klonopin about an hour before boarding the private plane. He was already sleepy when he buckled into his seat at the rear of the aircraft, which he'd always heard was the safest place to be in a crash. While he did notice Stuart Fisher and Gregg Morgan arguing about something, bickering between the two was nothing out of the ordinary. Shane Reed, who had already boarded, was staring out the window. He grunted a "Hello" but not much else. Kerry assumed Shane was having girlfriend problems, which were endemic for him.

Kerry remembers the pilot being youngish and apparently excited about flying one of his favorite bands on the short trip from Los Angeles to Santa Barbara. Nothing about him indicated that he was going to crash the plane. In fact, nothing at all seemed out of the ordinary, and Kerry fell asleep before the wheels went up.

"The next thing I remember," he tells you, as the wind increases and the fire flickers, "was this incredibly loud sound, but before I'd even opened my eyes, my head was slamming into the seatback in front of me, and my right arm twisted, and I felt a *crack*.

"Then my part of the plane stopped moving, but the front of the plane tore off and kept going forward. There was smoke and fire, but it wasn't thick yet, and I could see the others up front, and they all looked, well, *dead*.

"I was taking that fact in, when I looked down at my feet and saw a gun. A tiny one, like a toy. My right arm wasn't working, but I reached down with my left hand and put the gun in my pocket. This was right before you and a young woman showed up. I just had this feeling: they're going to blame it on me, they're going to say I was the one with the gun." He pauses and takes a long sip of his tea.

"I don't mean to be rude," you say, "but why would you do that? Why would you assume they were going to blame it on you, if the gun wasn't yours? And what was it doing at your feet?"

"See," he says. "Exactly. You're asking me why I had the gun, just like they would have."

"So, what do you think happened? Did anyone in the band own a gun?"

He takes another sip of tea and shakes his head. "Not that I know of."

"Then why don't we just give it to the police?"

"Because the very fact that I hid the gun will almost certainly lead them to believe it was mine in the first place. But I swear to you on all that's sacred, it was not mine, and I had nothing to do with the plane crash."

Jackson gives a whimper and licks Kerry Cruz's fingers. He's clearly a believer, but you wonder how far you can trust a dog's judgment.

"I guess that's about it," he says. "What do you think?"

"It's a plausible story. But I'm not sure about the gun. What if I just call the NTSB and I tell them I have it?"

"You can certainly do that. As I already told you, I will deny the story. All you'll have is a gun, with no evidentiary connection at all to the crash."

"It sounds like you've been talking to a lawyer."

"Of course I have."

"What if the gun can be traced back to you? Presumably it has your fingerprints on it."

"I'll say you called me here with some wild story and put the gun in my hand. The phone records will verify that."

"But I have your business card."

"I gave that to you just this moment, when you asked for it. And you got my phone number from some lunatic fan. In fact, *you'll* be the one with the gun. You'll have plenty of explaining to do yourself."

"I have to say that all this pre-strategizing on your part doesn't inspire a lot of confidence. You sound guilty."

"Like a lot of people who are wrongfully convicted. Look, Caleb," your name sounds oddly familiar coming from his mouth, "I understand that Poor Ghost has changed your life, and mostly for the worse. But I feel like everything I've worked for since I was a teenager is at stake. I'm already suspicious enough in the minds of most people—the bass player who survived the plane crash. I've heard the jokes. I've seen the memes. Something like this coming out, even if I were shown to be totally innocent, would be horrible not just for me, but for the very idea of Poor Ghost as a band."

Out over the canyon, a red-tailed hawk circles in a wide, casual loop.

"Let me think about it."

Kerry Cruz gives Jackson one final scratch behind the ears, then stands up. "I don't know what else I can do." He walks back into the house, and you follow him inside. He places his empty cup on the kitchen table and picks up his phone. "Thanks for the tea," he says. "Call me when you know what you're going to do. I'll be waiting."

Then Kerry Cruz opens the front door and exits your world once again.

# 58

After he departs, you sit on the couch for a long time, looking out at the far side of the canyon. You can remember a time when it would rain in December, but now it's all dry grass and parched trees, and, outside of your hastily decorated living room, it looks nothing like Christmas.

Victoria calls and confirms that she will be there on Christmas Eve, and that she will be taking Jackson home with her. You ask her what she's doing for New Year's Eve, and she says she doesn't know, but with the omicron variant sweeping into California, probably nothing.

Then it's Kelsey Symmons' turn to call. She wants to know all about your conversation with Kerry Cruz, but, for some reason, that feels private at the moment, so you simply tell her that he says he's innocent and you're weighing the facts.

"'Weighing the facts'? What are you even talking about? What did he actually *say*?"

"I'll check in with you later," you say. "Victoria's on the other line. I've gotta go."

"Well, call me back when you can. I'm interested. This is kind of *my* story, too, you know."

"Sure," you say, but it doesn't feel like her story. It feels like *yours*.

After a long afternoon of doing nothing much at all, you bake two potatoes for dinner and feed most of the second one to Jackson. Then you swallow a couple of Benadryl and retreat to the safety of your bed. As Jackson snores at your feet, you drift into a dream in which you are both the number-one fan of Poor Ghost and also all the members of the band. You swap places with each other and argue about taxes and song lists and instrumentation and social media promotion—your interests are all intertwined and yet somehow at odds—and it takes a long time for your brain to abandon this fantasy and gradually seep into the blackness of pure sleep.

# 59

You wake early on the morning of the twenty-third and know exactly what you need to do. You feed Jackson and make yourself a slice of buttered toast, then head out in the car.

The morning is overcast as you park at Goleta Beach by the restaurant that went out of business during the pandemic. It's surrounded by fencing backed by green mesh, as though it were a construction site rather than a place slowly falling into ruin.

Just before you step onto the pier, the wind shifts, and you get a face full of cold sea air. As you walk toward the end of the pier, which juts a quarter mile out into the ocean, you watch the rock doves whirl and slice through the morning.

There are only a few people about. A father headed back to land tries to corral his young son. A couple of teenaged fishermen, with backpacks and buckets of bait, jig their rods over the side of the pier. To the north, a propeller plane takes off from the airport, ascending into the gray. An old man sits smoking on a bench under a No Smoking sign.

At the pier's end, a young couple is hugging and kissing and joking. You stand just far enough away not to be deliberately rude, but close enough to make them feel uncomfortable. After about five minutes, they realize you aren't going away, and, with twin looks of disdain, they depart.

To the south, the clouds have burned off. You can see the low jagged outline of Santa Cruz Island and, further off and to the right, Santa Rosa Island. You take the tiny pistol from your jacket pocket and cup it in your hand as you turn around to make sure no one is watching.

Then you reach over the side of the pier and let it go. Twenty feet down, it makes a small, satisfying *plop* and disappears into the gray-green water.

# "HILLSDALE BOULEVARD"—THE POOR GHOST MESSAGE BOARD

## DEC. 23, 2021

**ghostkoan**

People are not posting the way they used to. It's sad. Only three months since the plane crashed and where has everybody gone?

**sempiternalpaul**

Today's society can only focus on something for like thirty seconds.

**5bagsofROCK**

I blame the media. Still no resolution on what caused the crash, but nobody talks about it anymore.

**alivenburbank**

I have to admit, I was listening to their music every day all day for a while. But now not so much. Has anyone heard the new War on Drugs album? It sounds a little like PG.

**AllMayBeWell**

Go on the WOD message board if you want to talk about them. Please! Not appropriate for this forum.

**linda7**

All I know is I wouldn't trust Kerry Cruz to catsit for the weekend.

# POOR GHOST: AN ORAL HISTORY

## 2014–2016

### *A Revelation in Burbank* (2015)
### US Billboard Peak Position: 23

**SHANE REED:** By the middle of the decade, social media was definitely a thing. It wasn't like it is today, but people were making their opinions known, and you would ride a wave, or that same wave would just crash into you. So we hired a "social media maven," Jenny Khong, to bring us into the digital age.

**JENNY KHONG:** I'm not going to lie to you: before they hired me, I had no idea who Poor Ghost was. When I started listening to their stuff, they felt like a band my parents might have liked, but didn't. That might sound like I was a poor fit for them, but, in fact, I was perfect for the job. They wanted to reach young people like me, and I could see very clearly all the things they *weren't* doing to achieve that goal. Right away, I did a SWOT analysis: strengths, weakness—there were plenty of them!—opportunities, and threats.

They did have some core competencies. Their brand was well-established, but I mean, come on, they were ancient. Like they had their first hit back when dinosaurs roamed the earth. And then they were always being outmaneuvered by U2. Those guys are *forward*-looking. But I did see a chance to increase their market share among bands of their era and genre if they would *focus* on a particular sound and theme. Something you could sum up in a tweet. And I told them that, and I think they listened.

**KERRY CRUZ:** For better or worse, we've always been an "album band." We've had some successful singles, fortunately, but I think most of our real fans think of the album as the quintessential PG unit. Consequently, a lot of the work we do is arranging the songs in a way that makes sense, that tells a kind of story, with highs and lows.

**JENNY KHONG:** I had a meeting with the band, and I was just like, I get that you guys think I'm really young, but I went to Stanford and you're paying me a lot of money, so maybe listen up? I kept asking them, what's on your mind, and Stuart kept going, "Burbank," and at first I thought, *Are you fucking kidding me?* but then I remembered you have to play the cards you're dealt, so I told him, "If you want to do Burbank, then go *all in.*"

**STUART FISHER:** The thing is, I never actually lived in Burbank, but my aunt and uncle moved down there, and I'd go visit sometimes. Usually, somebody recognizes me when I'm out walking around, but for some reason, in Burbank, nobody knew who I was, or nobody cared. So, I spent a lot of time just walking the streets, taking notes in my notebook. And then when my aunt and uncle were at work, I'd sit in their living room and make up songs. I was trying to channel Gene Clark, Gram Parsons, Roger McGuinn, that kind of vibe. But the songs were about this really suburban part of LA that people mock. Remember Johnny Carson? "Greetings from beautiful downtown Burbank." That kind of scene.

**GREGG MORGAN:** My dad, actually, turned me on to The New Lost City Ramblers, and I was really getting into that song "No Depression in Heaven."

**SHANE REED:** The drummer tries to do what the album wants him to do. I'd done everything from punk drumming on *Alas, Poor Ghost!* to electronic drums on *Ugly World* to hand percussion on *Hillsdale Boulevard*, so I listened to a lot of Michael Clarke, the drummer for the Byrds and the Flying Burrito Brothers, and used him as my guidepost. I can mimic just about any style when I put my mind to it.

**GREGG MORGAN:** Of all the instruments I've learned to play, pedal steel was definitely the hardest. All that coordination with the foot pedals and the volume pedals and the knee levers. Jesus. We talked about hiring Tommy White, but then I made a sort of breakthrough one night after practicing for, like, ten straight hours. Then I really got into it. I'm not the greatest, by any means, but I think my playing contributes a lot to that album, especially on "Bearded Lady's Mystic Museum" and "Back Lot," when Stuart is singing about Gene Autry.

**SHANE REED:** "Burbank Boulevard" is kind of a rocker. That's probably my favorite. Also "Burbank on Fire."

**KERRY CRUZ:** Lots of harmony vocals for me, which was nice. And then I picked up the Shehnai, which is this Indian double-reed horn. It's got a really limited range, almost like a kazoo, but it's a very distinctive sound. I don't know why I thought it would work with all that country-western instrumentation, but it did.

**STUART FISHER:** The David Bowie albums of the early seventies are sort of my ideal of theme and variation: coherent instrumentation and some lyric continuity, but he's not afraid to go out on a limb when he has a good idea. One critic called *A Revelation in Burbank* the country rock version of *Ziggy Stardust and the Spiders from Mars*. I think I still have that review somewhere. Or I guess you could find it online.

**ED WINGFIELD:** I thought of what a dud *Muswell Hillbillies* was for the Kinks back in the day—this country folk thing right after they'd had a big hit with "Lola." But I didn't have the same bad feeling I had about *Hillsdale Boulevard*, and fortunately *Revelation* clicked with the alt-country crowd. The video for "Golden State Freeway" was even a minor hit on CMT.

**JERRY DIMGARTEN:** I think with *A Revelation in Burbank* Poor Ghost finally made a full-on concept album. You have the song about the oboist for the "Burbank Phil," and summer nights on the Ventura freeway, and then the "Turquoise chrysalis spinning / In a landscape of plum and amethyst" in that backyard on Verdugo Avenue. And there's the "Bearded Lady's Mystic Museum" and "Wildwood Canyon Park" and "Bob Hope Airport." It's a real portrait of a city.

**JENNY KHONG:** They had never even heard of NPR's Tiny Desk Concert, but I knew it would be a great vehicle for their stuff. It's pretty fascinating watching bands do their thing in the confines of somebody's office, especially bands like PG that are used to an arena. But I had this feeling it would work, especially with the material on that album.

**JERRY DIMGARTEN:** With the Tiny Desk Concert, you're wondering, how will a band sound without all the trappings they're used to? It's like the old *MTV Unplugged* series, only more so. And I think they pulled it off. Gregg's mandolin playing on "Wildwood Canyon Park" is memorable. The harmonies between Stuart and Kerry are pure.

**JENNY KHONG:** Last I checked, their Tiny Desk show had been watched fifteen million times.

# QUORA

## ANDY DUGAN
### Financial analyst and amateur musician

If you have a suspicion that someone on board Poor Ghost's plane caused the crash, who is your chief suspect?

## MARY HURT
### Speech Therapist

I think it's obvious that Kerry is the bad actor in this tragedy. The only survivor. Buckled into the back of the plane, the very safest place. Claims he was "asleep" so he can't answer any questions about what happened. Way too many coincidences.

## EMERSON WRIGHT
### Business Owner

I am going with Gregg. I have seen quite a few videos on YouTube where he and Stuart are getting into it about something. Maybe after all these years it just built up and BOOM!

## WILBUR EISLEY
### Animator

Ugh, I hate to say it, but I'm thinking Shane. Of all of them, he always seemed the most jealous of Stuart to me.

## JERRY MCNEIL
### Content Consultant

It's pretty obvious that the culprit is Stuart himself. The band has been around for a million years, they have a surprise number one hit during the pandemic, and who doesn't want to go out on top? The news reports are that the throttle was in full forward and the cockpit recorder was turned off. Obviously, you first suspect the pilot, but he seemed like a total stand-up guy. It had to be Stuart in the cockpit, somehow sweet-talking the guy into making these horrific moves. Or maybe Stuart just killed the pilot.

## PERRY SCOTT
### *Retired Teacher*
Y'all need to get over yourselves. Poor Ghost was a super popular band. No reason in the world ANY of them would do this. Same with the pilot. Has to be some mechanical error that hasn't been discovered yet.

## GRAY GARDNER
### *Marriage and Divorce Counselor*
My vote is for Kerry. If you read about that incident at the Aimee Mann concert, he sounded like a guy with a totally guilty conscience.

## EDNA TUCKER
### *Former Advertising Director*
Shane was always getting his heart broken, from what I read. Maybe one of these honeytraps took it too far and he said Forget it, I can't take it anymore.

## BETH ANNE MITCHELL
### *Mail Carrier at US Postal Service*
Gregg. The lead guitarist is almost always the biggest a\*\*hole in the band.

# TEXTS
## KS & RA

**Fri, Dec 24, 7:24 AM**

I got up early. Christmas Eve and everything. Are you still
in San Diego?

How are you doing? The holidays can be hard.

I'm driving.

Sorry. We can talk later.

It's okay. I can voice type. I'm actually on the one oh one
headed to Santa Barbara.

What? r u insane?

The Poor Ghost story is about to break. I can feel it.

Does this have something to do with your dad?

Now I'm asking if you are insane.

Your obsession reminds me of all those stories you told
me about how when you were growing up and your dad
had a big, complicated case, he'd talk it through with
you, and how much you loved knowing all the details and
getting everything just right. You wanted to "figure it out."

That is a stretch.

Is it? I don't know, Kelsey. I really don't.

# THE
# AFTERLIFE
# OF
# POOR GHOST

On the morning of Christmas Eve, the doorbell rings, and you answer it, thinking that it's awfully early for Victoria to be arriving. But it's not her. It's Kelsey Symmons, who pushes her way into your living room and settles herself down on the couch.

"Sorry if that was rude," she says.

"It was, yes."

"I just—I've been involved with this whole story from the beginning, and I need to know what's going on. I need to make a record of it." She pauses dramatically. "In case anything happens to you."

You are puzzled. "Like what, exactly?"

"Like maybe Kerry Cruz caused that plane crash, and you know too much, and he hires someone to kill you."

You shake your head. "You said yourself on the phone that he doesn't seem like a killer."

"But it's not entirely out of the realm of possibility."

"I suppose not."

"So you have to tell me everything, from the beginning, from that first moment you looked out your window and saw the plane crash into your backyard until now."

"I've already told you a lot of it, and most of it is pretty boring."

"I don't care. I want to hear it. Again." She puts her phone on the coffee table and hits the red button on the Voice Memos app, then takes a spiral notebook and pen from her coat pocket. "Let's do this," she says.

And you do.

You talk longer, and in more detail, than you remember ever talking in your entire life. Longer than your two conversations with Kelsey back in November. Even longer than those first days after you met Connie, when the two of you wanted to tell each other everything that had ever happened in your entire lives.

You begin by talking about the gun, trying to explain why you tossed it into the ocean—a mixture of fear, anger, faith, and irritation, and maybe a little guilt, though you're not sure for what. Then you go back to that moment when you were reading the *New Yorker* and a plane flashed past your window and crashed into your yard. You attempt to recollect every moment since, though you realize many days have now blurred into noth-ingness, and what you do recall may not be the precise truth. Memory is such a blunt-edged tool. But you work hard to tell it the way you remember it happening, from one day to the next. That feels important now.

Sometime in the early afternoon, you realize you are hungry. You are winding down, retelling her how you walked out to the end of the Goleta Pier and dropped the gun in the ocean, when the front door opens.

It's Victoria. Jackson leaps up and almost knocks her over.

"Hey, boy! How's my Jackson boy!" Victoria says, nuzzling the top of Jackson's head. She looks at Kelsey. "Well, hi there."

"We've been talking about Poor Ghost," you say.

"All right, then."

"I'm just leaving," Kelsey says, stopping the recording on her phone, slipping her notebook and pen back into her coat pocket, and putting on her coat. "Thanks, Caleb," she says, and then to Victoria, "Sorry to inter-rupt your Christmas Eve."

"You're welcome to stay," Victoria says, but Kelsey, who is already at the front door, shakes her head, and, with a quick wave, is gone.

"That was kind of weird," Victoria says, settling herself on the couch.

"It was," you agree. "Now that I think about it, it really was."

# 61

Christmas morning, you and Victoria sit on the couch, with Jackson asleep at her feet. She refused to ask for any gifts, so you've given her ten $100 Amazon gift certificates, each in its own separate box. She's given you a new pair of pajama pants, and a Dodgers baseball cap, though you've only ever been a modest fan.

"You didn't really tell me what you wanted," she says, as you place the cap on your head. "I had to improvise."

"Ditto," you say.

Your most successful gift was a bag of dental bones for Jackson. You unwrap one, and he lopes off with it to the corner behind the Christmas tree, as though you or Victoria might take it away from him.

You open a bottle of champagne, top two flutes off with orange juice, and hand one to Victoria. "To mimosas," you say, "and absent friends."

She clinks her glass to yours. "Absent friends."

You are sipping on your mimosa, when you say, "I think I may sell the house."

"Really? Are you sure?"

You nod, although the thought is, in fact, just occurring to you. "Too many memories. When your mom first died, I loved having all those memories around. It was comforting to feel she was still here in a way. But now, with the plane crash, and Elineo and Álvaro de Campos, and Grandpa dying—it's just too much. I need to start over."

"I guess I can understand that. Are you going to stay in Santa Barbara?"

"I don't know, honestly. Would you be upset if I went somewhere far away, just for a while?"

"You mean like, where? Paraguay, or something?"

"Well, not there, necessarily. But someplace like that. Distant and very different. Just to clear my head."

"I'd miss you. Jackson would miss you." Hearing his name, he looks over at the two of you. "But I get it, Dad. I do."

"Anyway, it's just a thought for now."

You chat for a while longer, but Victoria is obviously keen to get back to Thousand Oaks, to visit "someone I just met," so you encourage her to go on her way.

"Goodbye, Jackson," you say, giving him a big teary hug.

After Victoria leaves, you decide—on impulse again—to take down the tree. Jackson seems to have drunk all the water from the bowl, and the branches shed needles at your slightest touch. As you unhook the ornaments from the branches and lay them gently in the tissue paper lining the bottoms of two boxes, you can't help but think of how thoroughly Connie's sense of humor was integrated into the decorating of your Christmas trees. There's a glass pickle, a robot with a Santa cap, a snowman puffing on a doobie, a Santa clinging to the back of a giraffe. Whimsy, you remember, was her go-to emotion. It was how she battled melancholy.

When all the ornaments and lights are off, you drag the tree down to the curb, sweep up the trail of dead needles, then sit on the sofa and stare out the window at the mountains. In the afternoon sun they look sharp and dry, almost brittle.

# 62

The next day, possibly inspired by the thought that you may soon be going away, you wake with a burst of energy—and another unbidden idea. You decide you will have a New Year's Eve party for all the Poor Ghost fans. You have a few email addresses, and you can probably locate some of them on Facebook. Why not, you ask yourself, put an emphatic bookend on what has probably been the three strangest months of your life?

You start by searching online for a DJ. Connie always said no party was complete without one. They are hard to find for New Year's Eve—or NYE, as it seems to be universally referred to—but you eventually locate a man in Lompoc who is willing to do it for $500, and "as much as I can drink, and I drink a lot." It's not ideal, but it's better than nothing, so you hire him.

Then you go looking for security. This seems like the sort of event that would lure Elineo and Álvaro de Campos, and you don't want to encounter them without some backup. You end up settling on a two-person team who seem to be moonlighting from campus security at the community college. When you talk to one of them on the phone, she says they've worked lots of parties in Isla Vista and know how to handle a rowdy crowd.

Next, you go online to BevMo! and put in a robust order for vodka, whiskey, beer, wine, and champagne. Then it's online to Los Canyones, where you order the NYE Special for 50—almost a thousand dollars, but what the hell.

Now that you have the party set up, all you need are guests.

You start by emailing Stacey, the retired librarian who saved your life that fateful Halloween evening, and it turns out that she is part of a Facebook group that includes not just the regulars from late October, but many of those who came and went in the weeks right after the crash.

You tell her to invite everyone, and ask them to bring either food or booze or both. You tell her masks are required, both inside and out, no exceptions, and she promises to pass that information along.

You text Kelsey Symmons, who texts right back that she will be there. Finally, you call Victoria, and ask her to bring Jackson.

"Are you sure?" she asks, hesitant. "It sounds like the sort of thing where stuff could go wrong for him. I mean, with so many people."

"We'll put him on a leash. Maybe give him one of those doggie tranquilizers? I just feel the party won't be complete without him."

Victoria sighs. "All right, Dad. One last hurrah."

You allow yourself to sleep in on NYE, but once you're up, you're a bundle of cleaning energy. Connie would be proud of you, as you vacuum, then mop, then wipe the counters down with marble cleaner and dust the bookcases with lemon-scented Pledge.

You hose down the back patio, and arrange the chairs in a wide circle around the firepit. The weather is warm and windy. Dry leaves skitter across the dry lawn. It doesn't feel quite like a Santa Ana, but that doesn't seem impossible either.

By two, you're exhausted, and you take an hour nap. It's another half-hour before you're fully awake, by which time the booze has been delivered in cardboard boxes.

The party officially starts at seven, but the DJ arrives at five, just as the sun is setting. He hauls in four very large speakers, then a rack of electronic equipment. It takes him a while to hook everything up, but when he's done, around six, he tells you he could use a drink, and by that he means his own bottle of vodka, a plastic cup, and a bucket of ice.

As you are poking through the cupboards, realizing that you have no plastic cups, the food arrives, along with Victoria and Jackson. Your daughter takes Jackson to her bedroom and shuts him in, then goes out to her car and returns with two large grocery bags full of paper plates and napkins and plastic knives and forks and stacks of red Solo cups. "I figured you'd forget about that," she says, and you nod, grateful.

The two security guards—a bulky twenty-something man, and a petite but heavily tattooed woman—arrive at quarter to seven. They are dressed in matching red windbreakers and wear red baseball caps that simply say "SECURITY."

Not long afterward, the first guest arrives: the philosophy professor from the community college, with his date—both masked—whom he introduces as "the woman who turned my life around." You welcome them in, and then it's the third-grade teacher, also masked, and then the retired librarian, unmasked, whose name you have momentarily, but obviously, forgotten. "Stacey," she tells you, as you stand there, tongue-tied. "Remember? I saved your life?"

Before long it's a steady stream of guests. Your mask mandate has been largely ignored, but at least most of the crowd is headed straight to the backyard, where the wind whips at their clothes and hair. Many of their faces are familiar, but many are not, and it quickly becomes apparent that the real hang-out area is going to be down the hill at the crash site, rather than up at the firepit. "Be careful!" you keep calling down into the backyard. "No smoking!"

Overall, though, it's a convivial crowd, and someone—not you—must have told the DJ about who these people are, so he's ditched his early mix of Rick James and Michael Jackson and "I Like Big Butts" for a steady dose of Poor Ghost. It's "Short Order" and "In Praise of Happy Endings" and "Traveling by Train" and "The Lyon Brothers" and "Painting Her Toenails Black" and "The Biggest Mistake (You've Ever Made)" and "Outré" and "The Season of High School Bands" and "Koan Americana" and "Burbank Boulevard" and "Is Harry Potter Real?" All the songs that are familiar to people, even if they couldn't tell you the titles or even sing any of the lyrics.

Whenever the DJ circles back to "Spaghetti Bolognese and a Can of Coke," a group of people are sure to start dancing, crowing out the chorus with ironic glee.

The wind continues to pick up, infusing the guests with a wild, almost apocalyptic energy. Plastic plates and Solo cups go cartwheeling across the lawn.

At some point after eight, you realize that you've forgotten to tell the security people to be specifically on the lookout for Elineo and Álvaro de Campos.

When they ask you what they look like you say, "One of them is a definitely homeless-looking guy, and the other one is the guy who threw his daughter off the More Mesa cliffs."

"Whoa," says the stocky guy, taking out his phone, finding a photo of Elineo and showing it to his partner. "This guy is seriously evil," he says. "Why isn't he in jail?"

"The cops are looking for him."

"And you think he might show up at your party?"

"It's a possibility."

"I've got a cop friend I can get to swing by if we see him. But it's a pretty busy night for them."

"I would imagine so. Hopefully, nothing will happen. But just in case."

"What's his beef with you?" the tattooed partner wants to know.

"He's crazy. I think he thinks I had something to do with Poor Ghost's plane crashing in my yard."

"Did you?" she asks.

You give her a weak smile. "Just keep an eye out for these two guys, okay?"

# 64

By eleven, the party is tipping toward a chaotic, inebriated intensity. The crash-site groupies have become bored standing in the dirt, and now they are crowding around the DJ, insisting that he take a deep dive into the PG catalog, with a focus on the less danceable songs. They want to hear "Basil the Bulgar Slayer" from *September Pears* and "All May Be Well" from *The Unbearable* and "The Garbagemen of Rome" from *Scoured* and "Rio Linda" from *Hillsdale Boulevard* and "Wildwood Canyon" from *A Revelation in Burbank* and "Five Bags of Rice" from *Fear of Everything*. They know all the words, and they sing along loudly, attracting more and more of the guests. The wind lashes at their clothes, and the manic energy around the DJ seems practically combustible.

You are standing on the patio, outside the circle of singers, when your next-door neighbor, Barton the dentist, taps you on the shoulder. "Hello, Caleb," he yells in your ear. "It was kind of loud, so I took the liberty of inviting myself over."

"That's totally fine, Barton," you yell back. "I meant to ask you, but I just got so busy."

"Big party."

"Yep. It's the end of an awful year."

"The Santa Anas are really blowing tonight."

There can be no doubt now that's what this fierce wind is. You nod. "I'm thinking of moving."

"*Really?*" he says. "You know, my sister-in-law is a realtor. A good one. You should talk to her first."

You nod and pat him on the shoulder, and turn around to see Kelsey Symmons walking through the front door.

She gives you a little wave and walks over. "Sorry I'm late. There was a wreck on the 101."

"No worries. Things are just getting started." Barton is hanging close, so you introduce him. "This is my neighbor, Barton. He's a dentist."

Kelsey gives him a knuckle-bump and shouts, "Cool!"

She's asking you where Victoria is when suddenly her attention shifts past you and up into the mountains.

"What's that?" she yells, as the crowd is singing "Is it too late to disavow / The vow I made last night?"

You turn around and see flames on the hillside, less than a quarter of a mile away.

In a moment, everyone else notices the fire, and the crowd quickly separates into two groups: those who are desperate to get away, and those who are transfixed by the sight of the flames.

The DJ is in the former camp, and he immediately turns off his system and begins pleading with the frenzied guests to help him take his gear out to his car.

No one listens to him, so he begins manhandling his speakers himself.

The security guards do their best to keep the crowd calm and orderly, but it's not working. There's shouting, and even as they are fleeing, people turn to point their cellphones at the blaze.

The Santa Ana winds are blowing south, down from the mountains directly toward you.

Despite all the wine you've been drinking, you're suddenly clearheaded. You look around at the fire-gazers, at least twenty of them. They should be gone, not drinking your booze and taking videos with their phones. You yell: "Get out, everyone! It's not safe here! Leave right now!"

Perhaps you are speaking with unusual authority, or maybe it's a new urgency from the two security guards, or possibly it's just that everyone is suddenly having the same thought: the fire is coming straight toward your house. Whatever the reason, the rest of your guests begin to vanish, a few of them now helping the panicked DJ to carry the last of his equipment outside. Sirens wail in the distance.

Kelsey Symmons and three people you've never seen before continue to loiter, undecided about how long they are willing to trade the thrill of close proximity to a wildfire against their personal safety.

You are about to give these malingerers another shouting-at, when, from the side yard, Elineo and Álvaro de Campos appear.

Elineo is wearing a black shirt with a large red, white, and blue "Q" in the center. Its logo reads, "WHERE WE GO ONE WE GO ALL." Álvaro de Campos is covered in a near-floor-length coat that makes him look like a discount store Neo from *The Matrix*. He wears a baseball cap that says "Sheep No More."

"So," Elineo says in a deep, theatrical voice, "Caleb Crane. It looks like you brought the fire down this time." His hands, as always, are making nervous, erratic gestures in the air. "Or, more accurately, we have brought it down on you."

Álvaro de Campos sniggers. "We're going to kill you, dude."

"Why?" you mutter because you can think of nothing else to say.

Elineo says, "Because you refuse to swallow the red pill, my man. And because I'm in constant communication with Stuart Fisher, and I do what he tells me."

"He told you to start this fire?"

"That, and a lot more."

You glance around for the security guards. The burly guy is gone, but the tattooed girl slips out of the shadows and stands by your side.

Elineo turns to Álvaro de Campos. "I'm thinking she is not going to be enough to stop us."

Álvaro de Campos nods. "I'm thinking the same thing. Do you understand that, Freemason Caleb Crane?"

"Illuminato Caleb Crane," adds Elineo.

You can feel the heat of the fire on your skin. Flakes of ash swirl around like gray snow. The flames are only a couple of houses away.

The three malingerers are recording the moment with their phones.

Kelsey Symmons holds up her hands, and shouts, "No, Elineo! No!"

It is only a slight movement, but the security guard reaches into her jacket pocket, pulls out a taser, aims it Elineo. It's only a partial hit. The probe on one of the wires glances off Elineo's left arm, but he goes down on one knee, howling.

Then he abruptly stops yelling and makes a concentrated effort to catch his breath.

For a moment, no one moves. The only sound is the whipping wind and the crackling of the fire as it consumes the dry fuel that's been awaiting its arrival for months. Then the wind shifts, blowing the smoke straight into your face.

Things snap back into motion. Álvaro de Campos reaches down to help his partner, and Elineo is up, limping off with surprising speed.

"We'll be back," Álvaro de Campos calls over his shoulder, and the two disappear around the corner.

Everyone stands there for a moment, presumably feeling, as you do, a sense of both great excitement and disappointment. It was all over so soon.

You turn to the guard and ask, "Should somebody be chasing them?

"I wouldn't think so," she replies.

"Well, anyway, thank you."

She shrugs. "Just doing what you paid me to do."

# 66

Then you hear your daughter shouting, "Jackson! Jackson!" and her dog is running out of the back door, down the steps into the backyard, and toward the fire. Right behind him is Victoria, but Jackson has already disappeared into splotchy darkness unlit by flames.

Victoria starts down the stairs, but you grab her hand. "Wait a second," you say. "That's way too dangerous."

"I know, I know, I know, but I have to get my dog."

"I understand, sweetheart, but you stay here. I'll get him." And then you are moving down the stairs yourself, into the heat.

"Dad!" Victoria shouts. "Dad, wait!"

You turn at the bottom of the stairs and call up: "He got lost once. I'm not going to let it happen again."

# INSTAGRAM

**poorghostlifer92**

**10,271 likes**

**poorghostlifer92** I am about a mile away, roads blocked by SBFD, but you can see the flames up by the place where PG's plane crashed. Massive amounts of fire trucks rolling up the hill toward Rancho de las Pumas. Not sure what caused it but someone told me the fire is God taking his revenge. Keep thinking of the PG song "Burbank on Fire" even though this is Santa Barbara. #poorghostfire #palominofire #newyearseve #poorghostcrash #poorghost4ever #poorghost

# SANTA BARBARA CHRONICLE

## New Year's Eve Fire Rages in Noleta

**Sat Jan 01, 2022 | 1:45 AM**

Santa Barbara County firefighters are attacking a fast-moving brushfire that exploded Friday evening in the hills above the Rancho de las Pumas neighborhood in unincorporated Santa Barbara. As of 1:45 a.m. Saturday morning, the fire had burned at least 40 acres and was actively consuming multiple structures. Approximately 40–50 buildings are under threat, and the fire is currently at zero percent containment.

Mandatory evacuations are under way north of Cathedral Oaks Road between Fairview Avenue and Patterson Avenue. Strong 30 mph winds are blowing the blaze south.

Multiple strike teams have been deployed. The incident began around 11:10 p.m. at the north end of Camino Palomino and has been designated the Palomino Fire.

A Red Cross evacuation shelter is set up at the Goleta Valley Community Center.

Check back for updates on this breaking story.

**Sat, Jan 1, 2:37 AM**

I was at a party in Bel Air, and it got kind of crazy. But I'm in an Uber going home right now, and I just saw the SB fire on the news. You're not there, are you?

Kelsey????

I was there. Jesus. Terrifying.

What happened? Are you okay?

I'm fine, just scared. Those two insane guys showed up after lighting the hill on fire. Caleb disappeared, went off toward the fire chasing his daughter's dog.

God! Is he okay?

I have no earthly idea.

## Firefighters Make Progress in Palomino Blaze

**Sat Jan 01, 2022 | 6:15 AM**

County Fire spokesperson Jane Bancheiri said that approximately 120 fire-fighters are on the scene, where they are actively defending structures. She confirmed that at least 10 structures have been damaged or destroyed in the 1400 block of Camino Palomino.

While most residents have been successfully evacuated, several are missing, including the owner of a home where a large New Year's Eve party was being held.

"On the positive side," Bancheiri noted that winds diminished somewhat overnight, allowing firefighters to make progress tackling the blaze, which has burned at least 70 acres and is currently 30 percent contained.

# NEXTDOOR

## RANCHO DE LAS PUMAS • 1 JAN

**Elizabeth Hamilton**
**Palomino Fire.** Neighbors, are you all right? There is a Facebook group for the Palomino Fire. Please mark yourself "Safe" if you are safe. Also check in with family and friends to let them know you are okay. Now is the time to take care of each other. We can assign blame later on.

**Maria Moss**
I heard it started at Poor Ghost NYE party. Did anyone else hear that?

**Seth Krueger**
Their music was so loud, it felt like it was in my living room, and I live two canyons away.

**Angie Nguyen**
A friend of mine was at the party, he said it was like a devil worship thing, where they were celebrating PG, and the "fans" set a big bonfire to worship their god, and the guy Caleb Crane he supposedly was the ringleader of it all.

**Pat Lewis**
My house burned down. I swear to god if I see that guy I will kill him.

## Palomino Fire Near Containment

### Sun Jan 02, 2022 | 8:30 AM

The Santa Ana winds that helped spread a New Year's Eve blaze died down yesterday, enabling firefighters to make significant progress in containing the Palomino Fire in the Noleta area of Santa Barbara County.

Firefighters who had come from Ventura and Los Angeles counties to help the Santa Barbara County Fire Department were returning home, with local firefighters now in mop-up operations.

12 houses and 8 outbuildings were destroyed in the fire. One person, Caleb Crane, is still missing.

When asked about reports that the fire was started by Elineo Amis, who is being sought in connection with the murder of his daughter, Esther, County Fire spokesperson Jane Bancheiri had no comment.

As of 8:30 this morning, the fire was 95 percent contained.

# POOR GHOST: AN ORAL HISTORY

## 2017–2021

### *Fear of Everything* (2020)
### US Billboard Peak Position: 1

**JERRY DIMGARTEN:** I was having a drink with Bob Christgau in a bar in the West Village. He was getting a little outspoken in his cups, as is his habit, and I remember him saying, "Poor Ghost is like a bad penny. They just won't go away." I thought *Bad Penny* might be a good title for their next album, and I emailed Stuart that idea in January of 2020, but I never heard back from him.

**ED WINGFIELD:** They'd been talking about a new album for a couple of years. Stuart said he had a set of songs he'd written on the theme of growing old, which didn't exactly sound like chartbusters to me, but I always want to hear them first. Anyway, we finally had everyone scheduled to come to the studio on March 20, 2020. Perfect timing for the pandemic.

**SHANE REED:** After Covid hit in March, we had to cancel plans for studio time. At first, I was a little skeptical of the whole thing. I didn't know anyone who had died. I didn't know anyone who *knew* anyone who had died. I thought people were overreacting, and I didn't see why we couldn't at least work together in the studio. I mean, it had been five years since our last album, and we needed to get something out there or face being totally irrelevant.

**STUART FISHER:** So here comes Covid, and for a couple of months I was just kind of stunned, like everybody else. I holed up in my house, waiting to see what was going to happen. Would society break down? Would America become an autocracy? Were we all going to die? All these possibilities seemed quite real.

**GREGG MORGAN:** The pandemic: not a great time to be in a band.

**STUART FISHER:** It had been five years since *A Revelation in Burbank*, and the songs I was going to bring in before Covid were mostly about aging. The aging rock star, I know—such a cliché. But Kerry and I had been playing two of them whenever we got together, and those two turned out to be fairly relevant for a world turning upside down.

**KERRY CRUZ:** Stuart had a couple of songs that he and I had been working on for a year or so. They just needed guitar and drums. Weirdly, the songs could conceivably have been about Covid, though they weren't. There's "Crazy About Nothing," with the line "You don't know what's hidden inside you," and "Impossible to Breathe," which is really just a love song.

**STUART FISHER:** Initially, I was too flummoxed by the pandemic to do anything but stare at the news. But then you started seeing all these musicians doing shows from their homes via Zoom, and we had that old song from *Ugly Word* called "Live in the Living Room." I recorded a version on acoustic guitar, in my living room, and posted it on YouTube, and it got a good response.

That kind of jump-started me, and in June I started writing again, and then it all came out. There was "Five Bags of Rice" and "Empty Shelves" and "Scorpion in My Tea" and "Essential Worker" and "Is Harry Potter Real?" and "Sheltering in Pasadena." It was my way of dealing with the stress—making up those songs.

**ED WINGFIELD:** You started seeing these musical events—classical and jazz mostly, but still—where the musicians would have their headphones on and they'd be in their little Zoom boxes playing their parts, and it looked kind of dumb, but also kind of cool.

That reminded everyone of how easy it had been for some time to record individual tracks from remote locations, then mix them together in a master track. We'd never done it, because Stuart liked the camaraderie and collaboration of the whole band being in the studio, but these were different times, and it didn't take much to convince the band to give it a try.

**KERRY CRUZ:** Working separately on our parts turned out to be a kind of a gift. Stuart would record rhythm guitar and voice parts, then he'd send the file to Shane, who would add drums, then on to me for bass and possibly keys, and Gregg for a second rhythm and lead. Then it would come back to Stuart, he'd tinker with the song, and send it back to me for the little something extra I could add.

Suddenly we had all this time, so I went online and bought a cimbalom, which is like a big dulcimer that you play by striking the strings with two sticks covered in cotton. I took lessons online, too, from a guy in Hungary, who was a really good teacher. I ended up using cimbalom on three of the songs.

Pretty soon, all we really needed was an engineer and a producer.

**GREGG MORGAN:** Everyone would have a listen, and if they wanted to add a part, well, their suggestion was just an internet connection away from being on the song. So, ultimately, even though *Fear of Everything* is kind of stripped down on certain songs, you always also get this layered sound.

**JENNY KHONG:** I hadn't heard from Poor Ghost since their last album, which was like five years before. After I worked with them, I started my own company. We focus on resurrecting the lives of older bands through social media.

Then the pandemic hit, and suddenly I lost a lot of work, naturally—nobody was touring. But then Ed gets in touch with me, and even if I hadn't had some free time in my schedule, I obviously had a soft spot in my heart for PG. They're like your favorite crazy uncle who kind of understood you when you were a kid.

They told me what they were doing, making a Covid album in quarantine during Covid, and I thought, *Yeah, that is something the content-starved arts media is really going to go crazy for.* And they did.

**ED WINGFIELD:** We needed a really good, imaginative producer, someone who thinks outside the box, so I worked every connection I had, and we got Timbaland. It felt like a miracle, practically. I mean, let's face it: Poor Ghost is one of the whitest bands around.

**TIMBALAND:** I produce hip-hop and soul records, and these guys, I did not really know their stuff. But Ed Wingfield flashed some serious Benjamins, so I said, *Okay. You've got me for one week.* Also, he was a friend of Jimmy Iovine, whom I do respect.

**SHANE REED:** We had to have everything ready to go before we sent the files to him. Timbaland was a busy guy, and we were not his first priority, he made that very clear.

**TIMBALAND:** I had a lot going on at the time: Megan Thee Stallion, Bruno Martini, Missy Elliott, Ludacris. Lots of very successful artists. So why work with these guys? Money, as I said, but also the challenge of taking on a new sound. You get pigeonholed in this business, and I wanted to show I could do something different.

The biggest barrier for me, personally, was getting into their music. I'm not saying I couldn't appreciate what they were doing, on an intellectual level. But it took me a while to *feel* it, if you know what I mean.

**JENNY KHONG:** When I heard Timbaland was producing, I literally almost shit my pants. No lie, that made *everything* on my end so much easier.

**TIMBALAND:** You bring something to me, I'm going to give it, you know, some *bounce*. When I heard a song that didn't feel right—like it wasn't *Covidy* enough—I was like, *Un uh*, no. You can keep that one for yourselves.

**SHANE REED:** Stuart was a little butt-hurt about Timbaland rejecting some of his non-Covid songs, but the guy's a pro, so maybe get over it? Of course I didn't say that to Stuart's face.

**KERRY CRUZ:** Timbaland deserves a lot of credit for making *Fear of Everything* a number-one record, but don't forget he was working with Poor Ghost material. And we gave him some instruments that were new to him, but that he dug. The cimbalom, for instance, has got a very Eastern European sound, which is what you hear in the introduction to "Empty

Shelves." I like to think that little riff I play was at least part of the reason for the song's success.

**STUART FISHER:** "Empty Shelves" really resonated with people. A lot of the songs did, obviously. And while the sound is mostly too "big" and commercial for my taste, there's no denying that the album was popular.

**SHANE REED:** I couldn't believe it when *Fear of Everything* hit number one. I was floored.

**GREGG MORGAN:** When things are very stressful, like in a pandemic, people want the reassurance of something familiar. And in music, what's more familiar than Poor Ghost?

**JERRY DIMGARTEN:** *Fear of Everything* charted at Number One on the nineteenth of September, after Taylor Swift's six-week run at the top with *Folklore.* I think the band would acknowledge that she'd sort of softened lis-teners up for another thoughtful acoustic album that still had some punch to it. And it didn't hurt that Taylor herself gave a shout-out to eighty-five million Swifties when *Fear of Everything* was released.

While there are some great melodies, especially on "Five Bags of Rice" and "Essential Worker," for me, as always, what's most memorable about the album are the lyrics. I love the opening of "Scorpion in My Tea": "It fell from the ceiling / between lumps two and three." And then there are those questions that end "Is Harry Potter Real?": "Do I still have a nose with which I can smell? / Can I still feel the fragments from a bombshell?" It's an album you could listen to again and again in the quiet of your pandemic safe space.

**ED WINGFIELD:** One number-one record in every decade from the 1980s to the 2020s. We hold the record, for the moment, at least—until U2 puts out their next album. But it's something special, no doubt about it. And I was their manager through a lot of that time, so, yeah, I do give myself a pat on the back.

**GREGG MORGAN:** Lately, we've been recording a new album made up of that second group of songs, the earlier ones that didn't fit the Covid theme and that Timbaland didn't think had commercial appeal. Hopefully he was wrong.

**KERRY CRUZ:** We hired an engineer, Pierre Couté, a French guy, very tech-savvy, but we're going to produce the new album ourselves. We're still recording remotely, each of us adding to Stuart's basic tracks. Putting on some harmonies, the guitar and bass and keyboard parts. I've been experimenting with some new instruments, and Shane has been doing some kick-ass stuff with percussion. One song may even have some horns, if we can figure that out.

**STUART FISHER:** The album is tentatively titled *Old*. It should drop by the end of 2021, or early '22. With Covid looking like it may go down somewhat, we're planning to rehearse in August, then in September do a small concert, hard-core fans only, in Santa Barbara, where we've always had great crowds.

**GREGG MORGAN:** Sometimes it's hard for me to wrap my head around the fact that Shane and Stuart and I have been playing together for like three-quarters of our lives. I think it was Pete Townshend who said a rock band is like nothing else in the world. You meet some people when you're basically just kids, and you're stuck with them for the rest of your life.

**KERRY CRUZ:** Everything has to come to an end sometime. Hopefully, that's not where we are, but I don't think it's dishonorable to retire when you've run out of things to say. That day may come. Who knows, it may already have passed.

**SHANE REED:** When I look backward, I'm proud of all we've accomplished, though maybe there are some things I would change about the financial structure of the band. When I look forward, I think that if we can work things out, which of course we will, maybe we'll just die of old age up there on stage, jamming until our hearts give out.

**STUART FISHER:** Music isn't everything. We need to heal the world, and we need to do everything we can to make that happen. I think everybody in the band realizes what's ahead of us as a people and a planet in the next thirty years, and I think we're all on board to fight the good fight. Whatever form that fight may take.

**ED WINGFIELD:** They may never have another Billboard Album of the Year again, but that doesn't mean they can't sneak into the number one spot for a week every few years. Their fan base is loyal, and it's three generations deep. I see them continuing for the foreseeable.

That said, it's worth remembering that a band, any band, is a delicate balance of camaraderie and competition. It doesn't take much to tip it into oblivion.

ROLLING STONE

## Poor Ghost's *Old* Is a Fitting, if Flawed, Final Album

★★★★☆

### By **JERRY DIMGARTEN**

Poor Ghost was in the final stages of recording *Old* when a plane crash killed lead singer and rhythm guitarist Stuart Fisher, lead guitarist Gregg Morgan, and drummer Shane Reed. While they died before their time, the album presents us with a singer, and a band, who are already struggling mightily with the prospect of rocking into old age. The lone surviving member, bassist Kerry Cruz, has said the album was "90% done" when tragedy struck, but *Old* appears to have been rushed out, sadly, to capitalize on the horrific manner of the band's demise. There is a roughness around the edges that would have benefited from extra time in the studio and a more experienced producer than Pierre Couté. Nevertheless, it's appropriate that a group that took so many risks—not all of them successful—should leave us with a fascinating album that falls just short of its potential.

Where PG's Covid-themed, Timbaland-produced *Fear of Everything* embraced the suckiness of Planet Earth, circa 2020, the quickly recorded *Old* is more defiant. "The Death of a Confederate Soldier," a tribute to Heather Heyer, the young woman run over by a racist maniac during the Charlottesville unrest of 2017, describes the pulling down of a Confederate statue "like a child landing a bad belly flop." Fisher continues: "Your skull collapses into your neck / But I don't give a fuck." In the title cut, he sings angrily to someone, perhaps himself, "You are old, sold, borrowed and controlled / You're fled, pled, I'm surprised that you're not dead." It's hard to tell if the mix is intentionally muddy—you can barely hear Cruz's organ laboring away in the background—but the propulsive energy recalls their first album, *Alas, Poor Ghost!* with its snarling, fuck-if-I-care aesthetic. One lovely exception is the acoustic ballad "Throne," which concludes on a mournful note: "Tender is the cloudless morning / As someone carves your headstone / Listen to the marble chipping / As you fall off of your throne."

From *September Pears* to *Between Religion and Hygiene* to *A Revelation in Burbank*, PG has been renowned for their eclecticism, and it's frequently on display in *Old*. "Dance You Monster to My Soft Song"—in classic Fisher fashion, the title refers to an obscure work by the Swiss artist Paul Klee—enters the world of the painting through Cruz's delicate playing of the virginals (an instrument last heard on *The Unbearable*'s "Uphill, Both Ways") and lyrics like "The music rolls from the keys, quiet yet cacophonous / Candles burn atop a rickety spinet: Dude, you're one of us." Similarly odd yet satisfying is "The Death of LBJ," scored for dobro, accordion—is there any instrument Cruz can't play?—and a wealth of percussion instruments, including agogo bells, ganza, rebolo, and gong, which Shane Reed strikes for all he's worth. The song closes with the couplet "O you who believe help always arrives on command / Know that he died with the receiver still in his hand."

Unfortunately, eclecticism can also grate, as on the gimmicky "A Brief History of Jacques Lacan." And despite Couté's best efforts, the album still sounds unfinished. The spare instrumentation on "Ornament Maker" prevents it from becoming the guitar and synthesizer anthem its lyrics "Free from age, free at last!" suggest it wants to be. And "Posturepedic" might have been recorded during the Stones's bleariest *Exile on Main Street* session. Fisher's delivery is even bleaker than the song's subject, a "Salvation Army mattress with the coils poking through."

And yet, unless there is some hidden trove of songs from this far-from-prolific band, *Old* may be the last we hear from Poor Ghost. As such, the album represents an apt culmination of a lifetime's worth of ambitious, tuneful, and sometimes messy experiments in popular music.

## SANTA BARBARA CHRONICLE

### Suspects Sought in Connection with Palomino Fire

**Wed Jan 05, 2022 | 11:15 AM**

The 102-acre fire that erupted on New Year's Eve in the Rancho de las Pumas neighborhood was deliberately set, according to the Santa Barbara County Fire Department.

Multiple cellphone videos show Elineo Amis and Ricardo Reis, aka Álvaro de Campos, threatening Caleb Crane, who was hosting a New Year's Eve party, and who remains missing after his house was destroyed by the blaze. In the videos obtained by the sheriff's department, Amis and Reis imply that they started the fire or may know who did.

Anyone with information about the origins of the fire or the whereabouts of Amis, Reis, or Crane is asked to call the Santa Barbara County Sheriff's tip line or leave a tip online at www.sbsheriff.org/home/anonymous-tip.

# Shocking Revelations About Poor Ghost Plane Crash

## *Shane Reed's Girlfriend Tina Caeiro Tells All*

### January 06, 2021

Tina Caeiro, the 35-year-old girlfriend of the late Poor Ghost drummer Shane Reed, may have finally solved the months-long mystery about how and why the band's plane crashed in Santa Barbara on September 21, 2021.

In an exclusive interview with *People*, Caeiro recounted a conversation she had with Reed several days before the band's plane left Los Angeles International Airport for Santa Barbara. According to Caeiro, Reed, who was heavily in debt, was incensed by lead singer and songwriter Stuart Fisher's announcement, in a private conference with other band members on September 12, that, beginning on October 1, 2021, all royalties from the group's music, past and future, would be donated to charities.

The band's manager, Ed Wingfield, confirmed that while Fisher had always voluntarily divided all earnings from their albums, he was not contractually obligated to do so. "In fact, if you look at the contract itself, you'll see that the royalties for unit sales were actually folded into the songwriting credits, so the other three members of the band weren't *legally* entitled to much of anything. However, through the arrangement they had, Kerry, Gregg, and Shane were compensated far more handsomely than they would have been otherwise. It was a weird setup, and I always told them they needed to formalize the agreement, but Stuart said it would upset the 'group vibe' they had going, and, for obvious financial reasons, no one pushed him on it."

According to Caeiro, Reed began fixating on the idea of having Fisher sign a new contract during the flight from Los Angeles to Santa Barbara, the first time the group members had flown together since before the start of the Covid pandemic.

Caeiro says that as Reed continued drinking that night, he gradually developed a plan. Reed knew that bassist Cruz was afraid of flying and would heavily self-medicate before any trip, so he would likely be unconscious. Reed told Caeiro he would slip Rohypnol into whatever guitarist Morgan was drinking, and that once the other two members of the band were incapacitated, he would force Fisher to sign a contract to formalize the four-way split Fisher was planning to end.

"Shane had this little pistol. I don't know where he got it, but he'd had it since I've known him. He called it his 'Baby Browning.' He said it was perfect protection against anyone who broke into his house. All I can tell you is that it was small, and that he was planning to use it to 'persuade' Stuart to do what he wanted."

Caeiro asked Reed what he would do if Fisher refused, but Reed said that would not happen, that Fisher was a coward. When Caeiro persisted, Reed said he didn't care if they all died, that he'd just shoot the pilot and let the plane crash, that his life would be over anyway if he was broke.

Caeiro says she told Reed that it was wrong to take Fisher's life, and even more senseless to take the lives of Gregg Morgan and Kerry Cruz. "Shane said, 'F— them. They should have been there for me. If we'd stood together, we could have changed Stuart's mind.' When I asked him about the poor pilot, he said, 'F— the poor pilot.'"

Asked why Reed didn't simply sue Fisher, Caeiro replied, "He wanted to, but he took the contracts to a couple of lawyers, and they told him it was pretty airtight, the way Stuart had arranged things. Basically, that he was screwed."

Caeiro said Reed passed out later that night, and when she asked him about his scheme the next morning, he told her he'd been drunk, and couldn't remember saying anything. When she reminded him of the conversation, he said it was "just drink talk," and that he'd never actually follow through on such a plan. "That made sense to me," Caeiro said. "Shane was always full of hot air."

Caeiro said that she hadn't contacted the authorities immediately after the crash because she was afraid. "My friend, she told me the government would send me off to a black site and no one would ever see me again. I was terrified. I mean, I thought Shane was just ranting, but then the plane went down. I've felt so guilty all this time, you have no idea. That's why I finally decided to come forward, and I hope that when everyone sees this interview, they'll know something bad happened to me if I all of a sudden disappear."

After her interview with *People*, Tina Caeiro had scheduled an interview with the National Transportation Safety Board and the FBI to make her statement official.

*People* contacted bassist Kerry Cruz, the only survivor of the crash, and played him a recording of Caeiro's interview. Cruz had no comment.

# SANTA BARBARA CHRONICLE

## Two Dead Believed to Be Elineo Amis and Ricardo Reis

**Fri Jan 14, 2022 | 8:30 AM**

The remains of two bodies found in the Mission Creek channel alongside the northbound 101 freeway are believed to be those of Elineo Amis and Ricardo Reis, aka Álvaro de Campos, the two men suspected of igniting the Palomino Fire.

Though no cause of death was officially provided, authorities have suggested that the positioning of the bodies suggests a murder-suicide.

According to witnesses, Amis and Reis appeared at a New Year's Eve party hosted by Caleb Crane where they made threats against the host and insinuated that they had started the blaze because Crane was in some way responsible for the crash on September 21, 2021, of a Cessna Citation that was transporting members of the band Poor Ghost from Los Angeles to a concert in Santa Barbara.

Santa Barbara County Sheriff Bill Brown said, "There is absolutely no evidence that Mr. Crane was in any way involved with the tragic plane crash involving the band Poor Ghost. Reis and Amis both had a history of mental illness, but it is unclear why they were obsessed with Mr. Crane, other than the fact that he had the misfortune to own the property on which the plane crashed."

In addition to arson, Amis was wanted for the murder of his daughter, Esther. A QAnon adherent, Amis allegedly threw his daughter off the More Mesa cliffs because he believed the girl had "serpent DNA."

Reis, too, was wanted in connection with an earlier crime. He was accused of a Halloween assault on Crane, who has been missing since the Palomino Fire.

# REUTERS

## NTSB and FBI Confirm "Possibility" of Tina Caeiro's Account of Poor Ghost Plane Crash

### January 17, 2021

The National Transportation Safety Board and the Federal Bureau of Investigation held a joint news conference on the steps of the Santa Barbara County Courthouse this morning. Representing the two agencies were Senior Agent Carol Ann Bogan of the FBI and Air Safety Investigator Lowell Padgett of the NTSB.

According to Bogan and Padgett, the "known facts" are as follows:

> On Tuesday, September 21, 2021, a 1998 Cessna Citation 560X owned by Enigma Airlines and piloted by Jeffrey Dunne, 36, departed Los Angeles International Airport at 3:01 p.m. The airplane was bound for Santa Barbara Municipal Airport and was due to arrive at 3:55 p.m. The passengers were the four members of the rock band Poor Ghost: Stuart Fisher, 59, Gregg Morgan, 58, Shane Reed, 59, and Kerry Cruz, 58.

> At 3:38, pilot Dunne disconnected the cockpit voice recorder, apparently by flipping a breaker on the control panel. The last voice to speak was Dunne's. "What?" he asked an unknown interlocutor. After a pause of three seconds, he said, "Okay, sure."

> At 3:47, the plane veered from its flight plan and began heading in a north-northwesterly direction.

> At 3:57 p.m., the plane began a steep descent from 2500 feet mean sea level.

At 3:59 p.m., the plane crashed into a hillside northwest of Santa Barbara, approximately four miles from the Santa Barbara airport. The majority of the plane was found in a suburban backyard, with the tail assembly located in an adjacent avocado orchard.

"That's what we know for sure," Bogan stated. "The rest is inference based largely on our conversation with Mr. Reed's girlfriend, Tina Caeiro, and the band's manager, Edward Wingfield."

"First of all, there has been some speculation that the crash was due to maladaptive stress response on the part of Mr. Dunne," Padgett stated. "We believe that is untrue. Mr. Dunne was known to be a steady pilot, and—despite rumors to the contrary—was not a member of an extremist group. We have no reason to believe he would have deliberately crashed his aircraft."

"In addition," Padgett continued, "there were no weather-related issues. The aircraft's owner, Enigma Airlines, has a stellar safety record, and there is no sign of system or structural failure prior to impact. So, we're looking for something else."

According to Bogan and Padgett, one "plausible" account of what happened in the aircraft is that Shane Reed had decided to go through with a version of the plan he had outlined to Ms. Caeiro on the night of September 18. In that scenario, Reed boarded the aircraft with a small Browning pistol, a dose of Rohypnol, and an updated recording contract.

"We have confirmed, from Mr. Wingfield and a number of other sources, that Mr. Cruz was known to have a strong fear of flying. Mr. Cruz stated that prior to boarding, he swallowed two milligrams of Klonopin and fell asleep soon after entering the aircraft. He says that he doesn't even remember taking off." Padgett confirmed that Klonopin had been detected in Cruz's blood during tests taken following the crash.

Agent Bogan stated that if Reed followed the plan he described to Caeiro, he would have then found a way to dose Morgan's beverage. "Mr. Wingfield has told us that Mr. Morgan loved his beer." Bogan acknowledged that Morgan's blood had not been tested for so-called "date rape drugs" post-mortem. "That's an error on our end," Padgett said, "though it might not have been detectable by that time anyway. In addition, Mr. Morgan's body was very badly burned in the crash."

With Cruz and Morgan unconscious, Reed would have had the opportunity to propose the new contract to Fisher, who presumably refused to sign it.

"Frankly," Bogan said, "it's hardly a brilliant plan, but if Mr. Reed was as desperate as Ms. Caeiro says he was, then it is within the realm of possibility."

Padgett remarked, "I don't know why Mr. Fisher didn't just sign the document if he felt his life, and the lives of the other people on the plane, were in danger. He could have easily had it overturned. The signing was obviously under duress."

"Of course," Padgett continued, "there very well may have been no contract involved at all. Mr. Reed may have intended to shoot the pilot and bring down the plane all along."

"Our thinking at this point," said Bogan, "is that you have an angry and irrational man with a loaded gun in an enclosed space. Based on conversations with Ms. Caeiro and Mr. Wingfield, we believe the most likely scenario is that Mr. Reed shot Mr. Dunne, then pushed the throttle into the full forward position, which essentially resulted in suicide-by-air-crash."

"The fact that we don't have any hard evidence for this theory does not rule it out," Bogan continued. "The plane began a sharp descent approximately a mile and a half from the crash site. That means if shots were fired, the bullet or bullets would be very far from where we were searching."

Bogan stated that, years earlier, Wingfield had once seen Reed playing with a small pistol, which he thought at the time was a toy. An FBI search of

Reed's home did not recover any weapons. "If he had a gun, it appears to be missing," she said.

Padgett noted that Dunne's body was "mangled" by the crash. "The coroner did look for signs of bullet entry wounds," Padgett said, "but, unfortunately, with the state Mr. Dunne was in, he could easily have been shot several times, and there's a good chance the coroner would have missed it. The cockpit, too, was badly damaged. A bullet hole might simply have become part of a much larger hole on impact."

"If Mr. Reed actually had a revised recording contract with him, it's no surprise that it could have been consumed by fire after impact," continued Padgett. "But the whereabouts of the gun is the big mystery. It could have been ejected from the plane on impact, but the NTSB did a wide and thorough search of the area around the crash site, and no gun was ever found. It is a huge piece of missing evidence."

"The X factor is that there were a number of people on site immediately after the crash," Bogan said, "and one of them may have absconded with the weapon. If so, we need that person to get in touch with the FBI immediately. This remains an active and ongoing investigation, and destroying or interfering with evidence is a federal crime with serious consequences."

"We may never know for sure what happened during that fateful afternoon," Padgett concluded. "What we do know is that the world has lost four individuals whose lives were ended far too soon."

# SANTA BARBARA CHRONICLE

## Authorities Identify Palomino Fire Body as Missing Man

**Tue Jan 18, 2022 | 5:30 PM**

Authorities have identified the charred body of a man found buried in the hills above Noleta as Caleb Crane, who went missing on New Year's Eve while chasing his dog in the Palomino Fire. The body was buried in a drainage ditch that had apparently been covered over with dirt by a bulldozer during the latter stages of the Santa Barbara County Fire Department's fight against the blaze.

After several unsuccessful searches of the area, two scent-detecting dogs from the nonprofit Canis Miracula Foundation were employed to identify human remains. "Canine olfaction science really made a difference here," said Sheriff's spokesperson Claudia Hartmann.

According to Hartmann, the cause of death is under investigation and could take several weeks to determine, but the coroner's initial findings suggest that Crane died of first-degree burns and/or smoke inhalation.

Crane's dog was found on New Year's Day, in the Rancho de las Pumas neighborhood, unharmed.

# THE
# AFTERLIFE
# OF
# POOR GHOST

# EPILOGUE

"Crane's dog" is wrong. Jackson belonged to Victoria, though he loved you, there's no doubt of that, despite his inadvertent role in your death.

\*   \*   \*

So many unknowns. Why did you follow Jackson into a fire when you must have realized you'd never catch up with him? Why in the world did you dispose of the gun, which divers have yet to find? And what really happened on that plane high above Santa Barbara on a September afternoon? Was there some karmic reason for it to plunge into your backyard, and your life, or was it just blind chance?

\*   \*   \*

Whatever the teleology, let's drop the pretense of the second person point of view. "You" can no longer speak for yourself, because you are dead. In fact, you have been dead since before the first words of this book were written.

\*   \*   \*

You are nothing but a fiction, "fragments," to quote Eliot, who is quoting Thomas Kyd's *The Spanish Tragedy*, "I have shored against my ruins." I say "my ruins," but they are yours more than mine.

\*   \*   \*

To say you are "a fiction" is another inconsistency. A lie. You were a human being who breathed and suffered, and sometimes joyed.

*   *   *

Your house is nothing but concrete and twisted rebar and a chimney's tall, sad silhouette, and ash, like your body, sown into the wind.

*   *   *

Nevertheless. "You" are the creation of a reporter who would not give up on her story, no matter how unlikely its divagations. Your voice is here. And something like your truth. The facts were all witnessed by me, or reported by you, or by someone you trusted. Your daughter's voice echoes across the pages.

*   *   *

Yet we must call this a work of fiction if we are to include the oral history that binds the book together. That is the unwavering stipulation of the owner of this oral history, Kerry Cruz.

*   *   *

And so the two stories are entwined, like the strands of a rope made from different fibers—entirely separate in origin until they are woven together into a stronger form.

*   *   *

Caleb Crane, poor ghost: yours is the story of Poor Ghost now, and their story is your own.

# ACKNOWLEDGMENTS

I would never have been able to write this book had I not played in so many bands over the years. Some were serious, and some were not very serious at all, but every experience gave me that much more insight into the musicians of Poor Ghost. I'm especially grateful to drummer Eric Prothero, the other half of Falstaff Riley, for his patience, encouragement, and willingness to go along with just about anything I come up with.

When I wasn't borrowing Poor Ghost lyrics from Falstaff Riley songs, I was often stealing lines from my own poems, and I thank my fellow poets—from the late David Case to my friends here in Santa Barbara—for their close reading of my work.

I am incredibly grateful to all the folks at Turner who brought this book to life, especially Ryan Smernoff, who acquired the rights, and Amanda Chiu Krohn, who shepherded the book from manuscript to what you hold in your hands. Thanks also to William Ruoto for his cover and interior design, Claire Ong for her production expertise, and Makala Marsee and Kendal Cliburn for marketing this book.

Above all, thanks to my wife, Sandy, for her unceasing love and support. There is no music without her.

# ABOUT THE AUTHOR

**DAVID STARKEY** served as Santa Barbara's 2009–2011 Poet Laureate, and he is founding director of the Creative Writing Program at Santa Barbara City College, co-editor of the California Review of Books, and the publisher and co-editor of Gunpowder Press. Over the past thirty-five years, he has published eleven full-length collections of poetry with small presses—most recently *Cutting It Loose, Dance, You Monster, to My Soft Song* and *What Just Happened: 210 Haiku Against the Trump Presidency*—and more than 500 poems in literary journals such as American Scholar, Georgia Review, Prairie Schooner, and Southern Review. His textbook, *Creative Writing: Four Genres in Brief* (Bedford/St. Martin's), is in its fourth edition. With drummer Eric Prothero, he records and performs as Falstaff Riley. You can learn more about David and his work at davidstarkey.net.

Printed in the USA
CPSIA information can be obtained
at www.ICGtesting.com
JSHW021941040324
58568JS00005B/5

9 781684 429738